Grown-up Education
(Anal Sex)

Amy requests that Eric show her some things. He learns.

Scarlett Collins

"I bet he wants your butt, as well. Men consistently think ladies need that, and they won't ever do."

I watched different women in the gathering laugh or look down. That was Jennifer talking, and she was prodding Jackie about her boyfriend, whom Jackie depicted as "pretty gutsy in bed."

"What do you think, Eric?" Amy's eyes tested mine as I snapped over to her.

"I believe I'm savvy enough to avoid this discussion," I answered, two or three chuckles from the women.

"Well, that is the pleasant, protected, exhausting answer," Amy scolded. "You will not mention to us your opinion?"

"Alright, I'll take the snare. Like anything sexual, I think it relies upon the lady. Some could never do it, some set up with it for their accomplices, and some truly enjoy it."

"Furthermore, I guess you have the enchantment contact to cause them to enjoy it?" Jennifer's mockery trickled out.

"I said nothing regarding me. Hell, you can find out about this if you need it. They've overviewed a ton of ladies about this, similar to all the other things."

"So what might be said about you?" Amy once more, her eyes shining.

"When did this become a conversation of my sexual coexistence?"

"You have a gathering of ladies here, discussing sex with you, and you're withdrawing? Hi? Is there any red blood in there?"

"Indeed!" I proclaimed—Amy had got me. "I realize they can enjoy it from individual experience. I don't kiss and tell, so I'm not going to uncover who; however, I realize that at any rate, one lady can have incredibly ground-breaking, soul-slamming climaxes that way."

"Furthermore, you're so secure with that? Also, that she needed it?" Jennifer once more.

"At the point when she places a container of lube in your lap and snares her finger at you while she sashays to the room, I believe it's protected to say she needs it. Concerning the climax part, it's more the compulsory side that I got on. Quakes fit. She wasn't in charge of herself."

"What's more, you didn't wed her forever?" Amy gave me a dramatic look of skepticism.
"Funny," I said. "Sex should be the lone part of a relationship. We were incredible in the sack. However, there were different issues. It didn't work out over the long haul."

"A person concedes that there's something else entirely to a relationship than sex?" Jackie joked. "I didn't realize that occurred." different women snickered while I feigned exacerbation.

I investigated at Amy. "So I've spilled a piece, Lady. I'm not going to keep up a single direction discussion."

"All good," she said, snickering. "I'll simply say that I haven't done it, yet I attempt to keep a receptive outlook on things sexual."

"Hold up. Perhaps we have another brave soul in the sack!" Karen noticed. Amy just stuck her tongue out.

"Discussing connections, you and Lisa have been part for a while at this point, right?" Jennifer asked me, changing the subject. "Why you're not snared with some new darling?"

"I attempt to maintain a strategic distance from the bounce back thing. That generally prompts lament. Why do you need to connect? Most likely enough time has passed for me." I needed to get a thorn in at Jennifer.

"In your fantasies, stud," she said, feigning exacerbation while different women chuckled.

They proceeded to a conversation of sweethearts and possibilities, with a lot of snickers and heckles. I participated in the good times.

After another half hour or thereabouts, Jackie peered down. "Resemble's it's the ideal opportunity for me to go. Had the opportunity to prepare for around evening time."

"I'll wager, with your brave sweetheart," Jennifer remarked. "Please, young ladies. We should allow Amy and Eric to tidy up. Incidentally, Eric, that is extremely decent of you to assist Amy with this little evening party."

"I'm trusting you spread this story around with the women. I can begin with a decent standing and coast for some time in my standard apathetic, selfish way."

That got a couple of more giggles and prods as everybody got their things and bid farewell. The majority of different people had left an hour or so back. Amy had worked effectively welcoming a co-ed combination, and the gathering had worked out in a good way. She was correct—an evening party got much more people to come since they could also make evening arrangements.

"Prepared to assist with the dishes? Incidentally, thanks such a great amount for co-facilitating," Amy said.

"Whenever, Amy. We should do it." Amy had been an old buddy of my better half Lisa, and we proceeded with the fellowship with one another after Lisa left. We both felt the misfortune when Lisa moved away; however, the open position had been ideal for her. Lisa and I both realized that we needed more going for her to remain or for me to move with her. Lisa had disclosed to me that I should follow Amy. However, it felt somewhat bizarre to hit upon a companion of my ex. Amy and I lived in a similar condominium building, so we saw each other a great deal.

"Soul-slamming climaxes, huh?"

I saw how near one another we were at the sink. The dishes turned somewhat harder to hold. "Good gracious. Not my sexual coexistence once more," I answered, grabbing for a remark.

"Hello, possibly I'm attempting to help," she said. "I have a companion who's referenced that she needed to attempt butt-centric sex sometime in the future. Would it be a good idea for me to snare you two up?"

I shook my head. "I realize it sounds insane that I'm not seizing the opportunity to get some young lady's can, yet you need to see how I work. I possibly have a good time in the sack if the young lady is making some extraordinary memories herself."

"Who says she will not have a good time?"

"It's not as straightforward as pushing inside and having her faint with joy. That might be what pornography motion pictures show, yet it doesn't work that route, in actuality. While she may suffer it and come to enjoy it in the long run, odds are it will simply be a dreadful encounter. As far as I might be concerned, butt-centric sex comes after a great deal of trust and history have developed. The two accomplices should be alright with numerous different types of sex together, and the woman must have figured out how to unwind and get delighted from that piece of her body. At long last, she's sharing an exceptionally close-to-home, private piece of herself, so she needs to confide in her accomplice. If each one of those fixings meets up, it very well may be

9

astonishing, and she has a decent possibility of cherishing it. Then again, it's simply not something to verify in a connect."

"Sounds like an extremely adult viewpoint, Eric. Or, on the other hand, would you say you are simply searching for a bundle bargain—you know—ensured sex for some time?"

I chuckled. "I think you got me there. I'm a bundle bargain sort of fellow. Presently, if she's keen on that sort of thing, perhaps we should talk. I'm not against it, and you, by and large, have incredible companions. I'm not a major condom fellow, so ensure you get some information about getting tried, so she can rest her brain about that part of things. It's tied in with unwinding and having a good time."

"Sounds right. I'll investigate it," Amy said. "You'll be a fortunate man on the off chance that she says yes."
"Most likely. Presently, if you continue talking this way, I must get a cover on."

Amy snickered her profound, rich giggle. She delighted in prodding and messing around with individuals. "Alright, I'll let you free for some time. We should get the seats and everything off the deck."

We did that, talking about different things. Amy didn't indicate that we had been examining close subjects only a couple of minutes prior. She moved effortlessly through her home, her light hair washing between her shoulders. Ordinarily, I had seen her blend of tight body and bends, taking all things together with the correct spots. With Lisa in the image,

I had been more discreet; however, now I was delighted to have a companion so natural on the eyes. I fell quiet while I enjoyed her.

"What are you thinking?" Busted. Amy consistently appeared to get on my opinion, and she cherished calling me out. For somebody who had to stand as an extraordinary companion and all-around decent individual, Amy caused me to remain alert.

"I figure it may fall into the class of an excessive amount of data. What are you thinking?" I said, attempting to reverse the situation.

Amy gave me a long look with her penetrating blue eyes. "I think it falls into a similar classification," she said. "We should overlay up these decorative liners."

We got the last one collapsed. I put it on top of the others. Neither of us had said a thing.

"Eric."

My eyes snapped back to her. She remained there, delightful. "Indeed?"

"I didn't give you the full story previously, with my companion. Indeed, we have talked about her advantage in secondary passage sex. However, I wasn't requesting her when I conversed with you."
Unexpectedly, an unsteady inclination flowed through me. "Uh, you weren't?" I asked weakly.

She grinned, gazing directly at me. "No, Eric. Your story sounded very great, and I was truly looking for myself. In case you're intrigued, told me."

Time halted. I'm certain I looked staggered. At that point, my cerebrum got back in stuff. My heart was pounding.

"I'd love to!" I exclaimed. I was all the while attempting to fathom what was happening, yet some piece of me knew to reply with energy. "That is to say, at whatever point you would need to."

Amy chuckled. "I'll take that for an indeed, senseless kid. So how could we begin?"

"With an embrace and a kiss," I murmured, moving near her. I took her in my arms. "Goodness, Amy, you've left me dumbfounded."

"You don't need to say anything," she murmured, getting my lips with hers.

When our lips associated, something clicked inside, and I understood the amount Amy had pulled in me from the start. I needed to be more than companions, significantly more. I could feel similar waves falling off of her. Our kiss warmed up. At last, we isolated, both somewhat winded.

"Amy, you kiss incredibly."

"Much obliged to you. I figured you were a decent smoocher, as well, and I was correct," she said. "I think we'll work out together. Presently, I like your thought regarding testing, regardless of whether it eases back us down for some time. On the off chance that we hustle today, we may in any case have time."

"Lead on, Lady," I said. "Do you know a spot?"

"I think I've seen one. However, I will check on the web. Simply a sec." Amy pulled out her telephone, concentrating. Following a moment or somewhere in the vicinity, she settled on a decision.

"We have an hour before shutting. We should go—I'll drive."

My psyche was as yet in a spin while we drove down there. A ton had occurred since I woke up today.

"Eric, much obliged for doing this," Amy nonchalantly commented as she drove.
"Amy, I don't think you need to express gratitude toward me."

"Any person is fortunate just to be with me, huh?"

"Something to that effect."

Amy chuckled. "Things being what they are, you may be keen on supper? Some portion of that 'becoming acquainted with one another' thing you were discussing?"

"I'd love to, Amy."

"Great. How about we plan on it. Possibly we can stroll down along the waterway and afterward search for something."

"Smart thought. We can stroll up a craving."

We found the facility and stopped. As Amy strolled in, I saw a portion of the inconspicuous looks she was getting. The two people looked at her, and I saw the esteem in their appearances. She had a young lady nearby look of shirt, skirt, and shoes. However, they fit her bends perfectly. They took a gander at me, as well, and I got their weak grins as they understood what we were doing together at the center.

We completed and rolled over to the stream. I am accepting her hand as we began strolling. She crushed back, a grin all over.

"Happy the testing part is finished," Amy said a couple of moments later. "Be that as it may, Eric, I enjoy it. You're an incredible person. It will be a taxing week."

"In case we're imaginative, we could chip away at drawing a little nearer without getting excessively close."

"What are you thinking?" she asked, going to me.

"How about we perceive how the night works out," I answered, "and afterward, we'll examine it."

"A little secret for me to consider?"

"Precisely."

Amy gave me another of her looks, shaking her head and grinning to herself. We strolled on, simply partaking in being together. I was strolling on a cloud.

"Recall when we'd bicycle with Lisa?" Amy said as she saw a few bicycles pass by.

"Better believe it, I miss that. You intrigued?"

"I'm. I attempt to remain fit as a fiddle, and it's enjoyable to do things together. I run with my companions. However, I enjoy trekking, climbing, and different things, as well."

"How about we plan on it," I said.
"What about tomorrow?"

"Amazing."

Amy pressed my hand once more. "So what sort of food do you like?"

"As you referenced in another specific situation, I attempt to remain receptive." That got a grunt from Amy.

"Like to behave recklessly, huh?" she tested.

"Can't resist."

Amy chuckled once more. "I surmise I can't fault you. I like to play myself."

"Presently, to address your inquiry, I like anything arranged well. So on the off chance that you have a top pick, how about we do it."

"I'm the equivalent. For what reason don't we walk around, check the menus, and see what gets our attention?"

"Awesome. I'm having a great time."

"Me, as well, Eric." Amy crushed my hand once more.

We found a fish place tucked around a corner with a decent open-air territory. I had been previously and truly preferred it. We kicked back with a jug of Chardonnay, discussing a wide range of things. I had consistently loved conversing with Amy. She consolidated her mind and humor with an energetic, curious mentality.

"Pardon me, Eric. I'd prefer to clean up before the food comes."

"Obviously." I got up and held her seat.

"Such a nobleman. Much obliged to you."

Amy left her telephone and handbag on the table, so I didn't go with her. I took the risk to look at her can while she walked away from the table. It was all that I recollected—adjusted and tight. She unexpectedly turned her head, found me looking, and grinned to herself before vanishing around the bend.

It was my chance to grin, thinking how Amy kept a fiendish side painstakingly enveloped by her new, young lady nearby outside.

I got tidied up myself, and afterward, we enjoyed an incredible feast of fish, wine, some plate of mixed greens, and hard bread. We both arranged to some degree light, not having any desire to back ourselves off.

"Fabulous supper, Amy. A debt of gratitude is for inquiring."

"My pleasure," she answered. "Will we head back?"

"I believe that is an extraordinary thought," I replied as my rooster began to expand.

We strolled inseparably back to Amy's vehicle and afterward drove back to our structure, proceeding to discuss a wide range of things. As we were drawing near, Amy went to me.

"I don't know precisely what you have at the top of the priority list, Eric, yet on the off chance that it includes us being together, maybe you'd prefer to get your toothbrush and go through the evening?"

"Extraordinary thought. I'd that way," I answered. I never enjoyed having intercourse and afterward resting alone. Instantly of understanding, it unexpectedly hit me that Amy knew a great deal about me. Lisa had preferred how I went through the evening, and I'm certain she referenced it to Amy. I thought about what else she had referenced. I investigated at Amy as she appeared to consider the street. It seemed like she understood my opinion.

Amy stopped and accepting my hand as we strolled to my place together. Amy had a little grin all over as she put a spotlight on me once more. She had figured out how to welcome herself in without any planning from me.

"Pleasant attempt, yet I have my place respectable. Couldn't say whether anybody would stop by subsequently."

Amy looked into it, all blameless. I snickered and received only the barest trace of a grin consequently. She followed me into my place, claiming to remain nearby as she had the opportunity to look at my drawers and cupboards. I snatched a bunch of morning garments and a couple of toiletries. When I went to the end table to get a jug of back rub oil, she momentarily caused a stir. However, she never let out the slightest peep.

"I think I have everything," I said as I moved to the entryway.

Amy grasped my hand once more. "Sure?"

"I have you, and that is the primary concern," I answered.

"You express such the prettiest things," she said as she fluttered her eyelashes. "We should go."

We strolled over to her place, and she let us in. Locking the entryway behind her, she reclined against it as though to say I have you all to myself now.

"Why not put your things in the other room," she coordinated. "At that point, we can discuss what you have as a top priority."

"Made you wonder?"

"Room's around the bend, or don't you recollect?"

I snickered and proceeded onward. I heard Amy's sink running, so I accepted the open the door to brush my teeth too. At the point when I left, she got me in her arms. In the brief moment, before we embraced close, I thought I got somewhat more definition in her nipples.

"Indeed—pondering," she said just, gazing toward me.

"Alright. Indeed, we can kiss and hold one another. That felt great previously. However, the way that we can't contact each other in specific spots doesn't mean we can't have a climax eventually, does it?"

I watched her take that in. Her eyes got wide. "You are a devilish young man, aren't you?" she murmured.

"Certainly. You'll need to concede that we will know each other significantly better a short time later."

"I'll say. I haven't played with myself for a lot of individuals."

I can't help thinking about the number of—Amy's unquestionably my sort, I pondered internally. "After we kiss for some time, I was figuring we could move to your bed, and I would give you a back rub. At the point when the times correct, you can contact yourself."

"While you will watch everything."

"Indeed. It will be absolutely hot," I answered.

"You think?" Amy shot back. "I get this. You're encouraging me to share my insider facts. Pretty sharp."

I gestured. "Anything to help a companion."

"Right," Amy droned. "Much obliged for being so thoughtful."

"You are so welcome," I replied. "I may not keep going long when you give back."

"So I will watch, as well?"

"Amy, we will do everything together. Some portion of building trust is that you will become more acquainted with my body also."

"Every last bit of it?"

"Every last bit of it."

"I can live with that. Indeed, I like it a ton. Alright, I'll oblige your little arrangement." Her eyes streaked. "You're a fortunate person, Eric. Simply recollect that."

I pulled her nearby. "I will not fail to remember." I got her lips once more.

We stood close and shared the endowment of kissing. At the point when we slowly inhaled, she grasped my hand and drove me to the couch, kicking her shoes off and pulling me down alongside her. Her hands meandered along my legs and chest, so I moved mine somewhat further. I prodded her for quite a while before I at last squeezed a bosom. She was almost driving her chest into my hands.

"Ohhhhhhh. At last. You are a bother," she murmured.

I laughed against her lips as I tenderly played with her chest. I enjoyed what I felt under her shirt—I speculated a decent, full B-cup. Precisely what might fit the remainder of her athletic form? Her nipples stuck out and brushed against my hands as her breath got hot.

"We should attempt that rub," she said, somewhat anxious.

"Great," I replied.

Amy got up and grasped my hand once more. She drove me into the other room, gotten the back rub oil, and afterward drove me into her room. She went aside from the bed, and I caused her to divert it down from the opposite side.

"A towel to lie on might help," I proposed.

"Smart thought." Amy vanished into her washroom and came out with a shower towel. We organized it on the bed, and afterward, she moved as far as possible.

"Come here," she murmured, crooking a finger at me. We joined for another seething kiss, our hands meandering here and there one another's backs. As she warmed up once more, Amy moved her fingers to my front and began unfastening my shirt. She slid it off me and afterward raised her arms, welcoming me to pull her top off. I slid it tenderly over her head and afterward paused to rest.

"Amazing, you are lovely," I murmured. Her bosoms stood firm, delegated with hard nipples simply asking to be sucked.

Amy grinned. "Simply hang tight for when I can truly get you to myself. You are so lost, young man."

I grinned back. "I can hardly wait."

"Presently, would you say you are simply going to remain there with your tongue hanging out, or would you say you will get my skirt off as well?"

"As you wish, madam." I discovered her zipper and painstakingly worked it down, sliding her skirt down her legs and off. Remaining back up, I took in her figure, wearing just a sheer pair of pink undies.

"Your turn," she said, fixing my belt and sliding the zipper cautiously around my stressing chicken. "Somewhat energized, huh?"

"You could say that," I answered to a delicate laugh from Amy. She got my shorts off, stood, and found me and down. She gradually shut the distance between us.

"You look as great as I envisioned," she murmured, sliding into my arms. "Furthermore, I've been envisioning this for quite a while."
I moaned as she squeezed her nipples into my chest. We formed our bodies together as we kissed; my rose fighters squeezed profoundly into her intersection.

Amy hesitantly pulled back, sucking my lip before isolating. "I could do that the entire evening; however, how about we get on the bed."

I drove her over to the bed, holding her hand as she orchestrated herself on the towel. She wound somewhat and pulled my hand to the fix of her underwear. I slid my fingers under the material and gradually worked them down, helped by Amy shaking side to side. I got them off her feet and afterward pushed ahead once more.

"You are staggering, Amy," I said, and she was. Her hips erupted out into a bent, tight ass that asked to be played with. Amy glanced great in a swimsuit, and it was not difficult to perceive any reason why.

I felt her hand discover my leg and travel up, gently pulling on the midriff band of my fighters. She was a talented bother, and I got the message, sliding to the side to deliver my extending erection. Dropping my fighters over the side, I hungover to the end table and got the back rub oil. I began with a light covering on my hands. Recalling knead meetings of my own, I daintily contacted between her shoulder bones to focus her and afterward slid my full hands onto her back.

The touch was electric, with what felt like flashes flying between our skins. Amy murmured profoundly as I gently worked around her shoulders. I gradually expanded the pressing factor, feeling her muscles unwind under my fingers.

"You have wizardry hands," she mumbled, settling completely into the bed.

"Enjoy," I replied. My hands worked gradually down, going over Amy's lower back. I massaged further into her muscles, gradually loosening up them.

"Ummmm, that feels better," Amy murmured.

I proceeded, at that point moved my hands to her calves each in turn—not breaking the association. I took one hand and added some more oil. Her firm muscles undulated under my touch, while a persistent stream of moans revealed to me that she was cherishing this. I held my hands back from meandering excessively high, be that as it may, to assemble the strain.

My position staggered when I thought I saw a slight pounding movement in Amy's hips. I wasn't certain since I was manipulating her legs. However, her movements turned out to be clearer with time. At that point, the aroma of her excitement hit me. It wouldn't be well before Amy needed to reach down. My hands proceeded on her calves— I planned to make her make the following stride.

Amy attracted a long breath and afterward murmured profoundly. Her correct hand pulled away from her head and gradually meandered down. When it contacted her abdomen, she curved somewhat, and I caused her to draw a leg forward to give her room. As her hand came to under, my hands slid up onto her can.
"Ohhhhhh, God," she murmured. Her rear end pushed up into my hands.

I kept the pressing factor light, drawing out the strain. Baffled, Amy angled her back, pushing her butt upwards. I peered down and was compensated with seeing her swollen pussy materializing, her ravenous fingers sliding between her lips and sparkling with excitement. My rooster solidified to practically difficult levels—this was screwing volcanic.

Since she had admitted her need, I permitted my fingers to manipulate profoundly into the muscles of her can. Amy kept on driving into my hands. She needed to know the show she was giving me. However, it was clear she didn't mind any longer. Her fingers worked all the more immediately between her pussy lips, and a nonstop stream of murmurs and groans gave from her throat.

I slid back a piece on a hunch and lifted a knee to give her legs more opportunity. Promptly, she drew her legs separated, and I moved between them.

"Uhhhh, fuck," she murmured while her butt climbed significantly further into my hands. Amy never cussed—she must be truly turned on. I ground profound into her butt, pressing and manipulating the firm substance while the pucker of her rear-end materialized. Looking lower, I saw the dark red of her internal lips slide around her fingers and the handle of her clitoris pounding between her fingertips.

This young lady is completely lost; I contemplated internally, the sensual energy flowing through me. I prodded around her rear-end yet never went further, even as she kicked and contorted underneath me, attempting to draw my fingers internally.

Her fingers squeezed further and more profound into herself, and I examined her example, learning the mysteries of her pleasure. My eye got a development, and I admired see her other hand drop to her chest. She curved marginally and held onto her nipples, pulling her whole bosom with it. I could not accept how long and hard the nipples reached out as she moved it viciously between her fingertips. I almost blew at sight.

"Uh...uh....uh," Amy snorted with each push. The muscles of her rear end developed increasingly more tense under my hands. Her back is curved and curved.

"I'm going to cum!" she heaved. She climbed her hips off the bed, inflexible with exertion. Her butt and pussy confronted directly at me, hungry for the climax. Her fingers dove profound into her inward lips, playing her clit angrily.

"Goodness, ah, gracious, AHHHHHH!" she howled as she went over the edge. Her butt beat with the compressions and my chicken pulsated with her. Her fingers squeezed profound, gradually moving around her clit to drain all the delight it could give her. Amy surely realized how to make her body react, and I savored everything about it.

My hands kept on stroking her can as she moaned and whimpered her way back to earth. She brought down her hips. However, she kept up the sluggish back rub of her clit and nipples.

"That...was extraordinary," Amy at last said. "Much obliged to you."

"The pleasure is all mine," I answered. "It was extreme for me, as well."

"Enjoy the view?" she said, her body softly shaking with giggling.

"Better believe it, you could say that. My chicken's going to detonate."

"Helpless infant. Would it be advisable for me to help make the torment disappear?"

"I thought you'd never inquire."

Amy extended languorously underneath me. At that point, she raised, a grin playing about her lips as she looked at my extending rooster. Kissing me, she pointed at the bed. "Down," she mouthed.

I chuckled and loosened up underneath her, pulling a leg forward to give my stressing erection some room.

"Pleasant view," Amy commented as she spread oil on her hands.

She contacted between my shoulder bones to focus me; at that point, she followed her fingertips down one or the other side of my back. I moaned automatically as the fire moved from her fingers into my skin. She has wizardry hands; I pondered internally.

With leniency for my seething rooster, Amy avoided the back rub and followed her fingers down to my legs, pressing my muscles between her fingers. The shared unwinding and excitement saturated my skin. She ran near my can yet hung tight for me to take the main action.

I made it. Testing my sanity forward somewhat more, I felt Amy moved in the middle of them to give me room. I came down and shut my fingers around my rooster. I heard Amy's breath get, and a shudder hustled down my spine to know this turned her on.

Roused, I came back to Amy and measured my hand. A progression of oil into my palm disclosed to me that she got the message. I came to advance again and spread the oil around my rooster, savoring the perfection and warmth. Simultaneously, her hands went up to my can, manipulating and following over my skin. A shivering sensation spread through my appendages as I understood how profoundly Amy was associated with me.

I began pushing once more into Amy's hands, and I felt her position herself further back between my legs. She needed the view—I just knew it. So I climbed up my hips and offered it to her. Her hands crushed further, revealing to me she enjoyed it.

The pressure shocked up an indent as I shared so profoundly with Amy. My hand easily siphoned my chicken—climax was hurrying to take me. I held off as long as I could, helping the strain walk the blade edge of joy. Amy's fingers proceeded with their exceptional association.
At long last, I could keep the flood down no more, and I crushed down. Cum flooded up from my balls in explosions of fire as I yelled out my delivery. I shot many more than one rope into the towel beneath me and braved it.

At long last, I returned to earth. I pulled a side of the towel over the wreck underneath me and maneuvered myself down to rest. Amy's hands left my butt; at that point, I moved to one or the other side of me. I felt her weight move, and afterward, a wet pussy contacted the rear of my leg. The pressing factor expanded as she settled straddling it.

"Ohhhhhh, no doubt," she relaxed.

My cockerel mixed. Was this young lady going to bump my leg?

I found my solution as she began granulating her hips. She held her chest area off me, putting all the pressing factors between her legs. She wriggled to and fro, her juices drenching my skin. Her breathing changed to snorts as she worked herself hard. I just lay there, overwhelmed by Amy's crude sexuality.

"This is so acceptable," she heaved, pounding quicker.

"You are unimaginably hot, Amy. Put it all on the line," I answered back.

"Uh, huh."

Shortly, Amy went into overdrive, squashing her mishandled pussy on my leg. I felt the quakes start through her body as she whimpered and groaned above me. At that point, she shouted out her delivery and rode me through a long-distance race climax, her pussy flooding my leg with her embodiment. At the point when her jerks died down, she maneuvered herself down onto my back and murmured happily.

"Goodness, God, that was acceptable," she relaxed.

I laughed. "It sure felt like it down here."

I felt her snicker. "I required that after watching you. I had some genuine repressed cravings."

"Keep them going. How could I get so fortunate to meet a tigress like you?"

"This tigress has been chasing her prey for some time, and it draws out the creature in her."

"We will be incredible together; you realize that, Amy?"

In answer, I got a long kiss on my back.

When we chilled, we moved the towel far removed, and Amy went to spoon together. I put my arm around her, and she murmured and cuddled back against me.

"Much obliged to you for an extraordinary day, Eric. I loved your little arrangement."

"It's been the greatest day ever. Amy, you truly shocked me."

She laughed. "I think I amazed myself."

I floated off, reasoning that everything was direct with the world. I arose to discover her eyes investigating mine.

"Morning, sleepyhead," she said.

"Morning, lovely," I said as I inclined forward to kiss her.

Her face lit up as I pulled back. "Still content with the tigress recollections from the previous evening?" she inquired.
"It is safe to say that you are joking? On the off chance that I'd knew, I would have hauled you into my bed quite a while past."

"I suppose you loved it," she said delicately. "I needed to ensure that I wasn't excessively forward."

I investigated her eyes. "Amy, in case you're stressed that I'll feel undermined or something, set out to settle it. That was the most sizzling thing I've at any point experienced. I've generally longed for a lady who's ablaze, and the previous evening, that fantasy became a reality."

"Much obliged to you," she relaxed. "Much obliged to you for the opportunity to give up." Then she kissed me, and we both clutched it. It warmed up, the two of us sucking each other's lips. My cockerel solidified into her leg.

"Gracious, God, I can hardly wait until I can get every one of you," she groaned.

I replied by sliding my hands around until I squeezed a bosom. At that point, Amy murmured let out an unsteady breath as my fingers shut over her solidifying nipples. She kissed me wildly, similar to she was unable to get enough. We interweaved together, warming up to bubbling.

"On the off chance that I turn over, do you want to discover a spot to rub that beautiful rooster of yours?" Amy talked onto my lips.

" I want to do that," I inhaled back.

"Great." Amy pulled away and afterward moved face down on the bed. I watched her hand slide under her hips, and afterward, she turned her flushed face to me.

"I need to feel your skin on mine," she murmured.

I raised and took a gander at the sight beneath me. Amy's butt undulated to the tune of her fingers looking for her folds. I slid my chicken between her firm cheeks and settled down over her.

"Gracious, no doubt," I said. "You feel awesome."

"You have no clue," she replied. Her hips moved into an attractive granulate that sent shudders down my chicken. We pushed together, and—a veteran now—I watched Amy start her excursion to another climax.

Following a couple of moments, her breath got worn out, and her hips dove into her holding-up fingers. Her butt crushed and drained my cockerel, and my energy ran directly behind hers.

At the point when she came, I felt the shivers race through her body. Energized by hers, my climax dashed toward me. I covered my chicken profound between her cheeks and jerked over her, shooting into her back. At the point when the post-quake tremors died down, I delicately moseyed down and kissed along her neck.

"Ummmm, what an approach to awaken," Amy said. "Need to get a shower and afterward have a little breakfast before I released you?"

"Sounds awesome," I replied.

Amy got the water warm, moved under the shower, and allured me inside. "I'll attempt to stay under control," she said.

"No doubt, I would prefer not to need to give you a punishing," I replied.

"Haven't had enough of my rear end yet?" she prodded.

"Haven't begun," I replied.
Amy giggled. "You know, I sort of outfoxed myself yesterday. I needed to prod and get you worked up about my companion, yet then I understood that I had done too great a task. I truly needed you for myself, so I needed to move quickly."

"I'm happy you did. It's difficult to accept that we were simply 'old buddies' a couple of hours back. Astounding how a couple of words make a huge difference."

Amy gazed toward me. "They do, don't they?" She lifted to kiss me delicately, at that point, drove me away. "We should get this shower over before I assault you once more."

I giggled and snatched the cleanser to begin her back. She kept up a surge of energetic remarks as I went to chip away at her, blending praises like "You have the wizardry hands" with warnings like "Cautious where those fingers are going."

I got her completed, and afterward, she went to chip away at me. With seriously playing and sprinkling, we at long last completed.

"At the point when you get your hands on this body, you gotta pay," Amy said in the kitchen. "You will clean this natural product for breakfast while I get a few eggs moving."

We kept up an exuberant discussion while we ate. Amy and I had been companions for some time, and we both truly enjoyed each other's conversation. We completed, and I encouraged her tidy up.

"Weren't we doing this equivalent thing yesterday?" I said as I worked with her in the kitchen.

"Possibly, it appeared to be identical, yet it sure didn't feel the equivalent," Amy replied.

" I didn't realize I planned to get that sweet ass of yours," I droned, leaping far removed for Amy's snapping towel.

"Exceptionally amusing," she said. "Be that as it may, you will pay for it."

"Goodness, I'm certain I will; however, it will be soon justified, despite any trouble," I prodded.

"Indeed, your first installment is Friday," she said, all efficient. "You're expected here at 5 pm, and you should be prepared to put out the entire evening. Simply appear, and I'll deal with the rest."

"Indeed, Ma'am," I answered, my cockerel mixing once more.

"Alright, I surmise I can release you for the present."

"Don't we have an activity date sometime in the afternoon?" I asked, recalling our walk the day preceding.

Amy got a major grin. "We do, isn't that right? Much obliged for recollecting. What might you want to do?"

"What about bicycling? We could leave from here around 2 if that works for you."

"Awesome."

I connected my arms to her. She floated into my hug. "Amy, that was an incredible night," I murmured into her ear.

"Much obliged to you for imparting it to me," she murmured back. She came up and kissed me once more. "Presently go before I hop you once more."

I chuckled. "My standing would endure if individuals realized I was leaving a young lady who needed to hop my bones."

"Particularly if they realized it was me," she added.

"See you at 2. Bye." I hesitantly left her entryway.

I completed a couple of things and met Amy for the ride. She glanced great in her outfit and kept up a decent speed. We completed, and I dropped her off at her entryway and got comfortable for the night.

"Hi?" she explained my call that night.

"What's that thing about what amount of time it requires for a kid to call after the primary date? I needed to tell you that I'm intrigued."

"Pleasant," she replied. "You keep this up, and you may simply luck out."

"That is the arrangement," I replied. "Presently, what about a decent, virtuous date on Tuesday or Wednesday? Could I take you to supper?"

"That would be exquisite," she answered. "How about we do Wednesday."

I considered several additional occasions paving the way to Wednesday. We talked and snickered like we generally did, and I anticipated seeing her once more. At long last, Wednesday night showed up.

"So you said this was a 'virtuous' date, huh?" Amy asked as we were leaving.

"No doubt. I'm asking why I did."

"I like it—simply having the opportunity to invest some energy with you." Amy pressed my hand. "Additionally, it constructs the pressure for Friday. I can hardly wait to get my hands on you."

"I'm beginning to stress."

"Goodness, I'll get you through—never dread! I have a ton of stunts at my disposal."

"So I simply need to lie there?" I deadpanned.

"No, senseless kid. You simply need to take cues from me."

"Goodness, I get it. If I do as you say, we'll both be more joyful."

Amy feigned exacerbation. "Well, obviously, senseless. I figured you'd realize that at this point."

"I'm a genuine lethargic student on that kind of thing."

"That is the thing that I feared. I'll simply need to continue to deal with you, presently will not I?"

"You do that." We both giggled.

We shared an incredible feast of food and discussion. Amy shimmered all through—it resembled she could feel my fascination, which gave her the certainty to be significantly more herself.

"I made some great memories around evening time," she said as we returned to her entryway.

"I did as well. You're loads of amusing to be near, Amy."

"Indeed, even external the room?"

"And still. Albeit the room doesn't do any harm," I added.
"That is the place where I'm at my best, that is without a doubt," Amy snickered. She inclined in and kissed me abruptly, at that point, opened her entryway, and ventured inside. "Friday," she murmured and shut

the entryway behind her. I grinned to myself—Amy preferred her secret, and I needed to concede that she was attracting me.

The week was delayed, yet Friday, at last, showed up. The center called with the outcomes, and I understood that Amy and I planned to get significantly more cozy in the weeks ahead.

I got a few blossoms and thumped on her entryway expeditiously at five. It promptly opened, and I took in Amy, remaining in a robe.

"How beautiful," she shouted, taking them and breathing in profoundly. "We should get these in a jar, will we?"

I followed her in after she bolted the entryway. She found a jar and organized the blossoms inside it, setting it on the table. "This will look extraordinary for supper around evening time," she said. "Much obliged to you. It's exceptionally insightful."

At that point, she went to me, her demeanor hungry. The robe sneaked off her shoulders and pooled on the floor.

"You've done your best, Eric. This," she said, spreading her arms to offer her bare body, "is all yours. Also, you," she added, moving nearer, "are generally mine."

I took her in my arms for a profound kiss. My hands meandered the smooth skin of her back. Her breath blew hot in my mouth.

"Try not to prod me this evening," she murmured. "I've been standing by the entire week. Take me."

In answer, I squashed her to my chest. She whimpered in my mouth, and afterward, she groaned when my hands pressed her butt, working the firm substance. At that point, I spun her around and pulled her back to me, squeezing her bosoms while my lips looked for hers once more.

"Ohhhh, yes," she supported.

My fingers discovered her nipples, effectively erect and needing. I pulled and rolled the hard focuses, feeling Amy curve her chest into my hands. Her can drove into my hips, looking for my hard cockerel.

"I need your skin close to mine," Amy relaxed. She pulled away and went after my shirt, pulling it over my head. She stooped to pull my shoes and socks off, at that point, fixed my belt, and dropped my jeans. My fighters stuck with the power of my erection, and Amy facilitated the belt over my length. I murmured as I sprang free, and my fighters joined the remainder of my garments.

Amy brought my rooster into her hands and gave the head a profound kiss. "Coming fascination," she mumbled before ascending to kiss me once more. "Presently, were right? Goodness, yes." She pivoted and pulled my hands over her firm bosoms, arranging her butt to settle my rooster in the break.

"This feels so right, to hold you like this," I murmured in her ear.

"You have a place here—holding me," she relaxed.

I worked her bosoms over, contorting her nipples harder as she warmed up and groaned in my ear. Her butt moved around my rooster, pounding wonderful joy into the base. I let a hand meander down, hearing her consent in her relaxing.

"Goodness, God," she whimpered when my hand found the delicate hill over her pussy.

"How about we get to the bed," I directed.
"Ummmm, well," she answered, grasping my hand and driving me back. I discovered her bed turned down, with a few candles copying. I kissed her and guided her back onto the bed; at that point, she opened her legs and settled in the middle of them. Her pussy opened to my look, hot with excitement. I brought down my lips and kissed around it, at that point focused in, noticing Amy's desire not to prod.

"Goodness!" she shouted when I connected. I began lower, yet Amy pushed her hips down, driving her hooded clit under my tongue. Trying to understand, I zeroed in on the hood, hearing Amy whip and groan around me. As I felt her clit arise, I pulled the hood back and lashed the little pearl too and fro.

"Indeed!" Amy hollered. "Try not to stop!"

Amy angled her back, and I admired see her bosoms fix and hurl into the air. I leveled my tongue and let her slam against it as she drove herself to climax.

Amy got my shoulders and moaned as the fits surpassed her. Her pussy beat against my tongue, and I let her brave a long climax. At last, she loosed into the bed and tossed her arm over her eyes.

"Goodness. My. God. That was unfathomable."

"Happy you enjoyed it."

"Enjoyed it? I adored it," she answered. "Furthermore, there's something different I'll adore. Rests. I need you inside me."

I loosened up on the bed and admired see Amy position herself over me, biting her lip in focus. She set my chicken at her passageway and investigated my eyes as she gradually sank. I heaved as I felt the tight, fluid warmth of her passage. She grinned at my response, proceeding with her drop until she reached as far down as possible with a look of fulfillment.
"You feel astounding," I advised her.

"You have no clue," she reacted, inclining down to kiss me. Our tongues interlaced, telling each other our appreciation. At that point, Amy raised, setting her hands on my chest and beginning a sluggish shaking movement. I let my hands travel up her arms and move to her chest.

Amy murmured her endorsement as I squeezed her bosoms, feeling their firm weight while she inclined toward my hands.

I gazed upward at Amy, seeing trust, joy, and something more profound emanate back at me. I wanted to react, not knowing precisely what I conveyed; however, seeing it was something to be thankful for from the little grin that played at the edges of her mouth.

Amy shook somewhat quicker, and afterward, I felt one of her hands slide down between us to play at her clit. My chicken was shocked to realize that—by and by—Amy was unafraid to get what she needed in bed. I winked at her, and she grinned more extensively.

I attempted to fix this second in my mind and value all that was going on. I had a delightful lady on the back of my hips who was glad to be there. Her pussy slid around my rooster, driving a surge of red hot joy that streamed all through my body. I could see the joy course through her body too, and I could feel the pressure in her nipples as they moved under my fingers.

I loose however much I could to permit Amy to get up to speed with me. Be that as it may, her grin turned underhanded as she got a move on my chicken, curving her back to pound profoundly into me. I felt the indications of a single direction outing to climax, so I surrendered to the sensations. Amy's look changed to fulfillment as she saw that I was lost.

My skin shivered, my muscles strained, and I clasped down to draw out the ascension. At long last, the pressing factor was excessively, and I crunched up, crushing my eyes tight as my cockerel pulsated in sweet misery. Amy hammered down, adding significantly more strain to the base of my pole.

"Gracious, God," I groaned, and afterward, I snorted with each impact of cum into Amy's grasping pussy. I failed to remember everything as I discharged her.

After a drawn-out period, I opened my eyes. Amy's eyes decidedly moved back at me—she was enormously satisfied with herself. She was additionally truly turned on, and I felt her hips fire up again, and her fingers occupied themselves on her clit. I moved her nipples between my fingers, and she panted in delight.

"Yessss," she inhaled as I expanded the pressing factor. I tried to understand, pulling and contorting the hard stubs to Amy's movements above me. This time, I had the chance to watch her move to climax. Amy's eyes lost center, and her fingers sped to a haze on her clit. A become flushed spread down her chest, and her muscles strained. She dug in, held her breath, and afterward detonated.

"Ahhhhhh!" she howled, and she jolted and trembled through an incredible climax. Her face reshaped in fixation as she attempted to manage the powers spinning inside her. I watched—intrigued. This young lady reacts to sex like nobody I've at any point known.

Amy gradually recaptured control of herself.

"Golly," she said when she opened her eyes. "That was great."

"I figure you could tell how great it was for me," I commented back to her.

She grinned. "I sort of got on that. Happy I could do that to you."

"That is no joke." I pulled her down, and we communicated our gratitude to one another with our lips and tongues. I adored inclination Amy so close, and it was difficult to give up. We kissed, and grinned, and chuckled, and kissed some more.

"Prepared, Eric?" Amy, at last, said, peering down at me.

"I can't remain here until the end of time?"

Amy ignored me and gradually lifted herself off me. I jerked as my delicate chicken pulled liberated from her pussy; at that point, she extended her legs, and we imploded together.

"I believed that we could clean up and afterward recover our solidarity with supper and some discussion. I'm not exactly through with you yet," Amy said to me.

"Sounds awesome—all of it," I answered. "This date is going extraordinary up until now."

"No doubt, getting laid first is ideal for you men. I'm astonished you're remaining for its remainder."

"Indeed, you said I'm getting laid once more, so I figure I can act intrigued by whatever you're discussing for some time in any event."

"You better work hard acting intrigued, buster."

"Watch me." We both giggled.

Amy drove me to the washroom, and we giggled and prodded our way through a shower. We got some garments on and proceeded onward to the kitchen.

"Something smells incredible," I said.

"I suppose you didn't see previously."

"Not with a beautiful, stripped lady before me. No, I can't say I did."

"Happy I can stand out enough to be noticed, at any rate now and again," she droned. "Presently, would you see to the wine?"

Amy and I went through an enthusiastic night around her table, snickering and examining all ways of things. I had consistently enjoyed her conversation. However, something added a flavor tonight. We were more than companions, presently. Eventually, we got up to tidy up the table and set things aside. We moved to her love seat to complete the wine.

"What?" Amy asked when she saw me taking a gander at her. Our discussion had stopped.

"I'm making some incredible memories, Amy. You're loads of amusing to be near."

"I wager you say that to all the young ladies."

"All things considered, I do. Yet, this time I would not joke about this."

Amy smiled, at that point, glanced back at me. "It is safe to say that you think I'm's opinion?"

"I believe that we're excessively far from your bed."

"Precisely," she said, getting up and grasping my hand. "Come here," she said, pulling me back into the room. "For what reason don't we prepare for bed? I incline that we'll be nodding off after we destroy each other this time."

"Good thought."

I prepared and afterward held up alongside her bed, maneuvering her into my arms. We stayed standing, allowing our hands to meander as we got each other energized.

Amy pulled back briefly and gazed toward me. "Might you want to attempt somewhat 69 and afterward perhaps wrap up by driving into me from behind?"

"Uh, I'd love to," I croaked, my rooster driving into her leg.

Amy laughed and pulled me down to the bed. She winked at me as she put a pad under my head, licking her lips. I watched her athletic body wrap across mine, and afterward, I murmured when I felt her delicate lips circle the tip of my chicken. I kicked occupied and off kissing around her pussy, previously tasting the musk of her excitement.

Amy's ability in giving head coordinated all the other things about her in the room. I could tell that she enjoyed it, and she got on each prompt that my body gave her. While keeping the joy streaming, she did something amazing, prodding and building the strain. I did likewise back to her, not releasing anything for a long time.

"You're an evil man," she said, pulling back. "I'll require you inside me to get any alleviation."

"That is the arrangement," I said, laughing.

Amy jumped up and stooped down on the bed. "Come and get it."

I hopped up and arranged myself behind her. We both moaned when my chicken discovered her passage, and we pushed profoundly into one another.

We pulled back and pushed once more.

"Harder!" Amy instructed, glancing back at me. I put my hands on her hips and beginning maneuvering her into me, getting a snort of endorsement. Her hand wound back between her legs, and she dropped her head down again to zero in on the sensations flooding through her body.

Having depleted me a couple of hours sooner, I had the option to try not to blow it as I peered down at the inconceivable lady pushing once more into me. Amy extended before me, her tight back crookedly prompting erupting hips and an ideal ass. I felt its firm forms with each stroke and the contact undulated outward from my crotch, adding to the delight transmitting from my rooster.
"Gracious, no doubt!" Amy energized as we found a cadence and bobbed against one another.

"Amy, you feel inconceivable!" I replied, at that point lost myself in the vast delight of Amy's pussy.

Amy whipped her hair over her back, and I saw that her face was flushed with excitement. Her fingertips stimulated my balls as she worked her clit hard. Amy groaned with each push, and her enthusiasm pulled mine alongside it.

From profound inside, I felt the sparkle of climax flare into a fire. Simultaneously, I felt Amy's avaricious fingers speed into a free for. Her groans expanded in pitch.

"I'm close, Eric. Harder!" Amy smashed into me, and I hammered back accordingly, resolved to give this young lady what she needed.

A few crashes later, Amy delved her fingers profounded into herself and held them, simply beating once more into me.

"I'm coming!" she moaned and writhed around my chicken. I watched the ligaments of her shoulders stick out while a profound flush surrounded her neck. My enthusiasm took off to watch her cry and whip through her climax.

Abruptly, I was heaved over the edge, hanging in space, while a cold radiance shot out through my appendages.

"Ahhhh!" I howled as my climax surged up to guarantee me. I fell into sweet alleviation, shooting my delivery into Amy's grasping pussy while my body jerked behind her. She pushed back hard into me and held there, amping up the joy moving from my cockerel.

We remained combined for quite a while, at times shaking through a spike in the phosphorescence. I let my hands float over Amy's legs, back, and ass, feeling the smooth skin as she murmured underneath me.

At last, she talked. "Goodness. That was fabulous."

"It was the equivalent for me, Amy. You're stunning."

"Much obliged to you, Eric. I truly required that."

"I was glad to help. Tell me whenever."

"Continuously prepared to take care of a young lady?"

I chuckled. "You have me there."

"Great. I have a ton of requirements. You'll be occupied. Presently, you prepared for me to relinquish you?"

"Not actually, however it should happen at some point."

"Helpless child. Here goes."

I whimpered as my cockerel slipped free, hearing a laugh consequently. We both loosened up on our backs, moaning in unwinding. I moved to my side and hungover Amy.

"That was an incredible night, Amy. I'm happy I remained for everything."

"So the supper and discussion were a little cost to pay for the extraordinary sex?"

"No, they were an exorbitant cost. However, the sex was justified, despite any trouble."

Amy feigned exacerbation. "Whatever, darling kid."

I inclined in to kiss her, pulling back an evolving tone. "Truly, I would check myself fortunate just to eat with you, Amy."

Her eyes mollified. "Much enjoyed, Eric." She kissed me once more, moderate and delicate. "I'll dream well around evening time."

"Me, as well. Goodbye."

Amy turned, and I spooned behind her, floating off with considerations of how fortunate I truly was.

Morning came, and I got up to find Amy's shining eyes investigating mine.

"Morning, darling kid. I trust you didn't think you were accomplished for the evening."

"With horny, destitute ladies, I'm rarely done," I replied, attracting her for a kiss.

I chose to zero in on her pleasure toward the beginning of today, warming her up and afterward reprimanding her pussy until she shouted out in climax. At that point, Amy pulled me up on top of her, and she bolted her lower legs over me as we tenderly shook together, our tongues profoundly twined. I came powerfully, groaning into Amy's mouth. We kissed our way back to earth.

"What an approach to awaken," I advertised.

.

"Very great, Eric. My commendations. You have a sorcery tongue."

"Proves to be useful here and there."

"Keeping penniless women fulfilled?"
"Precisely."

"All things considered, it worked. Incidentally, I'm dazzled." Amy's hand-wound around to my butt. "You went through a whole night with me and never went for my can. Much the same as you said in your little discourse regarding the matter."

"You had any uncertainty?" I giggled. "Furthermore, I realize I will arrive in any case. What's the hurry?"

"Pretty sure about yourself, right?"

"That is the reason I endeavored to have a sorcery tongue," I answered. "Had the opportunity to keep you fulfilled so I can get what I need."

"Furthermore, what, ask to tell, is that?"

"One moment. I don't spill every one of my mysteries so without any problem."

"Ooooh, I do love a test," Amy whipped back. "We'll perceive how long you last."

I just winked in answer.

Amy and I got tidied up and made breakfast together. We cleared out, with plans to get together again for supper. After an extraordinary supper, we were strolling up from the vehicle. Amy put her hand in mine.

"Might you want to go through the night once more?"

"Love to," I answered.

"I think you'll enjoy what I have arranged," she said, winking. I figured I would. I was beginning to value Amy's room way. She needed to lead, here and there, she needed to be driven, and regularly she would react to whatever waves were coming from me.

Amy let me into her place and accompanied me to her visitor restroom. "You'll discover a toothbrush and a couple of different things there," she said.

"A little arrangement ahead of time?" I prodded.

"Never harms," she said softly. "Gracious, and dress for tonight is exceptionally easygoing. I'll meet you alongside the bed?"

"Sounds awesome," I answered.

I prepared, draped my garments in her visitor storeroom, and moved to her room. I thought about what she had as a primary concern. My cockerel figured it was something acceptable because it extended out, good to go.

I sucked in my breath as Amy's body materialized. Her eyes seethed up at me through brought down foreheads. Her nipples extended out on her firm bosoms. Her legs nimbly brought her over to me.

"Happy to see you're energized for me," she said, gently circling my cockerel in her grasp.

"How should I not be?" I answered, attracting her for a kiss.

We kissed long and hard, our breath warming up. Amy pulled me down on the bed and tossed me a pad, snickering as she rode me. I utilized the pad to prop up my head to arrive at Amy's pussy, effectively wet with want. I felt her lips kiss my cockerel as I took the main pass with my tongue. After a piece, I let my hands meander and touch her rear end.

"Uh, huh!" Amy empowered. She came to under my legs and did likewise, as though to say I'll do it maybe.

I grew somewhat more striking, ultimately measuring my fingers over her valley, however not inside. Amy's murmurs empowered me, and she wound under my hand, attempting to get my fingers further. Amy had lifted my knees to improve access, and her fingers kept on imitating mine.

At last, I let a finger momentarily haul across her rosebud. Amy shocked in fervor, groaning around my rooster and pushing her can into my hands. She was certainly OK with this. After a second, I felt her finger contact me in a similar spot. I meandered some more, at that point, let another finger drag, getting another groan. This continued for some time, with Amy getting increasingly more animated. She flew off my rooster to inhale and afterward utilized a hand to hang on. I gave her leniency and slid my fingers straightforwardly over her rear end, touching the harsher skin.

"Yessss," Amy murmured. I lapped at the dampness moving from her pussy, as I felt her fingertips hold up at my indirect access. Amy moved, and her clit crushed into my tongue. Her breath blew teased my chicken while her body strained and shuddered.

"Goodness, God, don't stop!" Amy shouted. I took her to the highest point, and she bounced off with a cry of delivery. Her body shook all over me in a beast climax. I felt her rear end beat to the constrictions hustling through her pussy; everyone joined by a moan of alleviation. I celebrated in Amy's all-encompassing ride and kept my fingers possessively on her rear end while she returned to earth.

"What occurred?" she said in a precarious voice. "I came truly hard."

"How about we talk later. I need to be inside you now."

"Smart thought," Amy snickered. She flipped around and sank onto my post. "This what you need?"

"Definitely," I groaned back.

Amy began pounding her hips once again me, a grin all over. "Come for me, infant."

I did precisely that, giving her ride me access to an incredible climax. Amy had prepared me with her response to my fingers on her rear end, and I came long and hard, allowing Amy to watch me squirm and groan under her. At the point when I returned, I investigated her eyes.

"Turned on a piece, were you?" she asked, her eyes moving.

"You could say that. I just had this hottie come hard everywhere all over."

Amy reddened. "I'm nearly humiliated by how much that turned me on."

"Indeed, we're drawing nearer to 'soul smashing an area."

Amy chuckled, her body setting little stuns along with my cockerel. "I couldn't say whether I can deal with it anymore. Goodness."

"I believe there's a smidgen of the no-no and releasing yourself. Yet, a great deal of it is only that it feels great."

Amy squatted down to kiss me. "Great. A debt of gratitude is for that."

"Any time."

Amy feigned exacerbation. "Duh. You'll gladly get your hands on my butt any time?"

"Precisely. You have one evaluation A, top-notch ass."

"Whatever else, grade-A?" Here eyes streaked a test.
"Everything, Amy. Everything."

"That is the correct answer, Eric," she said delicately. She inclined down to kiss me once more.

We got up to clean up and snuggle together for the evening. The following morning, we chuckled our way through a shower, had a fast breakfast together, and afterward, I returned to my place to prepare for work.

Tuesday night, we were eating together.

"In this way, we're both welcome to the large party Saturday," Amy noticed.

"Furthermore, you're considering how we ought to present ourselves?"

"Something to that effect," she said, her easygoing words at chances with the bursting force of her eyes.

"Maybe we ought to present ourselves as beau and sweetheart," I proposed. "It would give a cover to us being together to such an extent. Individuals will begin to see our bundle bargain."

"That may bode well, Eric. Figure you can fill the role?"

"It will be an appearance for me, Amy. Don't worry about it."

"You express such the prettiest things," she answered, coming around to sit in my lap. She remained there some time, and afterward, we shared her bed.

Saturday showed up, and I drove Amy over to the gathering. I am accepting her hand as I encouraged her out of the entryway.
"Such the respectable man," Amy said, plainly satisfied that I was openly showing friendship. I didn't deliver her hand as we stepped to the entryway, and I kept a firm hold as we strolled into the home. You could nearly feel the responses and recalculations as everybody took in our new relationship, transmitted more powerfully than any assertion. Amy emphatically radiated, making some incredible memories with a particularly striking animal adjacent to me.

Jennifer gave us a long look, positioning an eye at every one of us. "Alrighty then. I can't say I'm amazed. Eric's wild ways interesting to you, Amy?"

"He's a finished fallen angel in the kitchen!" Amy spouted dramatically. "I'm adapting to such an extent!"

"I...see," Jennifer deadpanned. "All things considered, make certain to tell me the high focuses."

I even snickered at that one. Jennifer winked, and afterward, her face got agreeable.

"I believe it's extraordinary. I like you both, so I'm cheerful. You even figure out how to go through with your companions, so it's all acceptable."

We got comparative ribbing from every other person. Individuals were glad for us and made statements like "finally" or "happy that is no joke." We remained together for some time and afterward circled independently as the night extended. Sooner or later, I advanced back to Amy.

"Searching for a decent time, infant?"

"Definitely. Would you be able to help me discover one?" she shot back to snicker from her circle.
"I understand that armies of failing to meet expectations folks have made you tainted, yet I can fix you from that," I replied.
"Oooooh. I like the test in that," she said, sliding an arm around my abdomen. "I'm sooo tainted," she added, feigning exacerbation to her companions. There were a lot of snickers.

"I'll simply stand by until I needn't bother with words any longer," I said, to more snickers from the gathering.

"Women," Amy said, murmuring. "I have another person to assess. I better kick him off. Goodbye."

We left to a melody of heckles. "Back off of him!" "Evaluation hard." "You've given so many F's. Cut him some breathing room!" I halted and pulled Amy close on out the entryway, nailing her with a profound kiss before everybody. She put her hands around my neck and nailed me back. We left in a burst of applauding and cheers.

"So you unquestionably weren't humiliated to concede being my beau," Amy saw as we strolled to the vehicle.

"Chicks burrow the public warmth thing. Little cost to get under their skirts," I replied, gazing directly ahead.

Amy grunted. "Riiiight. Yet, it's working."

I investigated and winked. Amy crushed my hand.

We got to her place, and Amy pulled me inside.

"You're doing quite a few things, Eric," she said, shaping her body to mine.

"I need this sweetheart/sweetheart thing to work," I replied, kissing her.

Amy almost assaulted me by then, getting me rock hard with the waves falling off her body. She pulled back and looked at me without flinching.

"I truly need it to work," she relaxed.

We made extreme, sentimental love that evening. Some kind of limit had been crossed, and we both felt it. Our lips never left each other after she pulled me on top of her, and I felt her climax as my own. We dozed tangled together, secure in our relationship.

"Wake up, sleepyhead," Amy said the following morning. "We're going running, and we need to get out before it gets excessively hot."

"Wouldn't we be able to simply have intercourse and tally the exercise that way?" I answered lazily.

"No motivation to settle on a decision, Eric," Amy said sensibly. "We can do both. You will long for my rear end on the run."

"That run is sounding better constantly. What are you sitting tight for?"

"Whatever, darling kid." Amy tossed a pad at me.

We got moving and taken off the entryway. Amy glanced great in her running outfit, and I tried "following" her at whatever point we expected to run a single record. I heard a laugh each time.

As we were chilling off toward the end, Amy investigated.

"Along these lines, we certainly need a shower and maybe some morning meal. Something else?"

"No doubt," I answered. "Presumably, you need to recuperate in the wake of attempting to stay aware of me. What about a loosening up back rub after breakfast?"

"Recuperate your can," Amy shot back. "Be that as it may, the back rub sounds decent. I'll take it."

"Great. Perhaps it tends to be somewhat cozier than last time."

"It should be," she answered, eyes moving. "Presently, how about we get that shower."

We tidied up, and Amy arranged an extraordinary breakfast.

"Phenomenal, Amy," I commended. "Will we clear the dishes and get the back rub moving?"

"No," Amy replied, getting up. "Give up directly to the great part."

"I like your style," I chuckled, grasping her hand.

I got Amy chosen a towel and spread the oil over her back.

"No doubt, Eric, that feels incredible," she mumbled in a casual, simple voice. "Exceptionally decent after an exercise."

"Continue to unwind, Amy."

She sank further into lethargy as I worked over her back. I kept the pressing factor firm this time, keen on extricating her muscles from the run before bringing back the strain. Amy took cues from me, remaining loose as I worked down her legs. I pressed the enthusiastic muscles between my fingers, valuing the exertion she put resources into her body.

At last, I moved to her butt, yet again kept the pressing factor firm—not having any desire to energize her excessively fast.

"Ummmm," she murmured while I felt her muscles respecting my hands. I kept this up for some time; at that point, I continuously decreased the pressing factor. She murmured at the change, gently pushing her rear end up into my hands.

As my touch helped a stroke, Amy's body warmed up, wriggling and pushing underneath me. I felt her legs isolated, and the primary whiff of hot pussy arrived at my noses. I let the pressure work until I could feel the dissatisfaction in her body. That is the point at which I at long last let a finger brush around her rear-end.

"Yessss," she murmured, climbing her rear end up to welcome me further. I reacted, prodding around the delicate spot until she was gasping under me. Yielding, I brushed over her pucker.

"Gracious, God," she groaned. I gazed upward to see her eyes firmly shut, nullifying all the other things to focus on how my hands were doing her.

My fingers invested increasingly more energy over her most private spot, until where they won't ever leave. Amy's body undulated to the sensations, joined by a constant flow of moans and murmurs.

My other hand tested under her hip, and she promptly really tried to understand, moving up barely enough for me to slide under her. She let out a guttural groan as my fingers discovered her aroused and smooth pussy.

My rooster swayed when she spread her legs and climbed her hips off the bed, adjusted on her chest and knees. I was an ass man, and Amy had her body in the most sexual position conceivable—gave up to wring the greatest conceivable joy out of my hands.

After sawing through her pussy for some time, I slid my fingers up to crush and caress her unmistakeable clit. Amy went wild, pushing and gasping her way extremely close to a dangerous climax.

At long last, her body went inflexible, shuddering in my grasp. I cinched down on her clit, and her climax detonated, undulating through her pussy and ass as she wailed into the sheets. After a since quite a while ago arrangement of post-quake tremors, I tenderly slid my hand away from her desolated clit when she chose the bed. Nonetheless, I kept my different fingers possessively on her butt, and she once in a while wriggled into them. Sooner or later, she let out a long murmur.

"Nice, Eric," she mumbled. "That was mind-boggling; it has a sense of security and warm."

"Your body reacts so well," I reacted in appreciation. "I could play with you throughout the day."

"My body could become acclimated to that!" she reacted. "At any rate, I realize that you're getting a charge out of this as well."

"You have no clue, Amy," I reacted, peering down at my hand stroking her executioner ass. "This is awesome."

Amy conversed with me a short time longer, relating how my hands had made her cum hard. She didn't appear to be humiliated about my hand staying on her butt. She proceeded to tenderly shake under my fingers, plainly appreciating the play.

"On par with this feels, I'd prefer to give back in kind," Amy, in the long run, said. "Why not rests, Eric?"

"Happily," I replied.

"Face up this time," she coordinated. "I have an arrangement."
"Oh goodness," I reacted, getting a chuckle as I loosened up adjacent to her.

"I don't think you need to stress, Eric," Amy said as she settled close to me. "Aren't my arrangements in every case great?"

"Advising me that I should just allow you to assume responsibility?"

"Isn't it in every case better that way?" Amy said, inclining down to kiss me.

"It's difficult to contend when I'm sleeping with a delightful lady," I said as she inclined away once more.

"Particularly when she's going to go down on you," she added. I moaned as her lips shut over my shaft.

Amy gave an exceptional penis massage, sucking and prodding my rooster until I was squirming under her. Her hand stroked my balls and afterward headed out between my thighs to urge me to open up. I did, and Amy slid further, rubbing my perineum.

"Yessss," I murmured to support her. Sooner or later, her hand voyaged further, running ever nearer to my indirect access.

"Ahhhhh," I moaned as Amy discovered it. She worked to and fro between my rear end and prostate, driving me into a free for.

"I'm going to cum!" I said in an unsteady voice, attempting to caution Amy. She reacted by sinking significantly further around me.

I tried to understand and just dropped into the occasion—Amy's awesome lips sliding along my shaft alongside her hands unquestionably examining along with my butt. A cold warmth prickled outward from my crotch, and I kept the conduits down to the extent that this would be possible, going inflexible with the exertion.

Amy sucked hard, building the pressing factor until it was relentless. I detonated into her mouth, moaning sounds torn from my throat as I shuddered underneath her. My climax moved on in a long, fulfilling set of impacts, depleting the repressed energy conceived from feeling Amy's body cum underneath me.

Amy rode with me the whole time. At long last, I loose once again into the bed, and she delicately dialed her lips down my cockerel and her fingers from

"You are astonishing; you realize that?"

Amy's face lit up. "Obviously, yet it's ideal for getting with you," she said as she inclined toward kiss me.

We at last isolated sometime after that, and I completed a couple of errands. Amy was certainly making it harder to stay aware of the ordinary pieces of life—we just fit together so well that the time flew.

Next Friday, Amy met me at the entryway exposed once more. I sure loved this present young lady's style. We kissed and caressed each other right inside the entryway, and she maneuvered me into her room. I saw a jug of lube on her end table, and my cockerel was shocked at the greeting. As Amy got my garments off, I turned her around and pulled her against me.

Amy moaned as my rooster slid up between her cheeks, and she shifted her head back to secure her lips on mine. My hands discovered her bosoms, the nipples hardened and needing. Amy's skin sizzled against mine.

"Damn, young lady, no doubt about it," I said as we paused to rest between kisses.

"Goodness, no doubt," Amy inhaled, crushing her butt much harder into my bar.

We twined together for quite a while, neither in a rush to break our bond. At last, Amy began gradually advancing toward the bed, pulling me alongside her. At the point when she arrived along the edge, she pulled away and masterminded herself face-down on the bed, her arms padding her head. She connected and got a handle on the lube, giving it back to me.

"I believe it's an ideal opportunity to get somewhat more private," she expressed in a guttural voice.

"One 'broadened closeness' coming up!" I said.

Amy's body shook with her chuckling. "For what reason am I enduring you once more?" she pondered out loud.

"Since it feels so great," I answered, manipulating my hands into the cheeks of her can.

"Gracious, better believe it, truth be told," she murmured. "It feels great."

At that point, Amy worked up, so I immediately circumnavigated around to her butt, getting a lot of support.

I stroked around the puckered bud until Amy was wriggling underneath me, her butt driving into the air. I went after the lube with my other hand.

"Thought you'd never arrive," Amy mumbled when she heard the snap of the cover.

"Everything in due time," I answered without any problem. "We'll take this at your speed, so center around the joy." I grasped my hand from her rear end, watching her pucker pound into the air, and afterward followed a surge of lube over my pointer.

"Ohhhh," Amy moaned as my smooth finger discovered her rear-end once more. She pushed restlessly. However, I disputed, not having any desire to surge this. I orbited around, squeezing further. Amy moved and pushed her lower arms forward, preparing herself to crash into my hand with more power.

"Feeling better?" I asked her.

"Indeed, Eric. I need more," she coordinated as her body squirmed on the bed.

"Alright, Lady," I replied. I pulled my finger away to sprinkle somewhat more lube, at that point supplanted it, and delicately pushed. Amy moaned in fulfillment. My finger slid into her pucker, and Amy wound her canto and fro, attempting to get more inside herself. I watched my finger sink past the main knuckle; at that point, I gradually hauled it back, simply allowing the tip to stay inside her.

"Noooooooooo," Amy moaned in disappointment, turning her body considerably harder.

Where did this young lady come from? I contemplated internally. I pushed my finger further this time, feeling the hot dividers of Amy's rectum. I let my finger follow them, getting a groan of endorsement. Amy sorted out my example and didn't say anything negative as I pulled back out once more.

With each stroke, my finger covered itself further into her profundities. At last, I reached as far down as possible.

"Ohhhhhhh, that feels better," Amy gasped, driving herself back to smooth my different fingers over her cheeks. As I pulled back somewhat, she shook forward; at that point, she met my next internal stroke with a solid drive into my hand.

We got into a mood, and my chicken solidified to a bar of steel to see Amy drive herself into my hand with such surrender. Her body contorted and kicked under me, and her butt gripped around my finger.

I came to under Amy with my other hand to discover her clit.
"Goodness, God, yes!" she shouted as my fingers discovered her folds. Her substance ran openly from the heater of her pussy. I outlined her unmistakable clit and began lashing it without leniency. Amy went wild, her body wringing all of the delights it could.

When Amy began snorting with each push, I admired see her face squeezed into the sleeping cushion. My finger kept on siphoning all through her butt, and I felt the strain work in her body. The snorts filled in pitch, and afterward, she pushed back hard. I slammed my finger profound into her and felt her inward muscles start to pulsate.

Amy moaned into the sleeping cushion as her can and pussy detonated in my grasp. I excited to her sphincter beating fiercely around my finger, coordinated by compressions in her pussy. There isn't anything more wonderful than a lady in the climax, and I had the chance to watch an incredible one as Amy's body jerked and shivered through incalculable fits.

When Amy began to descend, I gradually pulled out my fingers from her pussy and let her choose the bed. At that point, I tenderly backed my finger out of her can, getting a whine as her sphincter shut behind it. Amy turned her head and took a gander at me.

"Amazing," she said, "that was extreme. Possibly soul-slamming," she added modestly.

"It looked pretty damn great from here," I said. "You were delightful."

Amy becomes flushed. "Delightful, huh? I get it bodes well since you're an ass man."

"Adequately genuine. Be that as it may, I believe I'm discovering somebody who's as attached to her rear end as I am."

Amy reddened considerably more profound this time. "It's sort of humiliating the amount I loved that."

"You can generally act naturally with me," I reacted tenderly.
"Trust me, I wouldn't be this route with any other individual," she stressed.

"That is the reason I'm a fortunate person."

"No doubt," she shot back.

"Presently, would it help to adjust the score on the off chance that you did likewise to me?"

Amy grinned. "Definitely. That could."

"I'll be directed back." I got up and washed my hands in the sink, at that point, snatched a towel, and strolled once more into the room. Amy was her old self, sitting on the bed with the lube in her grasp and an eager look all over.

She guided me down and continued to work my rear end over with excellent strokes. At the point when the time had come, she copied my movements to slip her finger profoundly into my can, and afterward, I curved underneath her similarly as she had done. I ascended to give her another hand room. However, she wasn't prepared at this point. After she had tormented me enough, she, at last, lubed her other hand and slid it around my rooster, siphoning me to an unstable climax. After braving the result, I settled down on the bed, and she perfectly pulled the towel from under me. She removed consideration, facilitating her finger from my butt.

"That was quite hot, Eric. I could feel everything pulsating inside you."

"Better believe it; I believe it's a significant piece of lady's sexual training."

"I see. Furthermore, what else is significant?" she asked archly.

"Everything in its legitimate time," I said.

"What rudeness, addressing an adoration goddess like me about instruction. Nonetheless, I'll let you pull it off since you're so acceptable in bed. Be that as it may, you better keep it up."

"Trust me, Amy, I expect to."

"Great. Presently, I think I'll tidy up a piece, and afterward, we can sort out how to manage the remainder of the night."

That was quite simple—great food, discussion, and wine, and afterward, another round of incredible sex. We woke up the following morning and went for a climb, chuckling and bantering the entire time. We had consistently been acceptable at exchanging insidious insults, and we returned to Amy's place feeling energetic, chuckling at the residue and sweat on our skin.

Amy spun out of my hands when she shut the entryway and went to confront me. Her eyes moved.

"I'm feeling somewhat underhanded and devilish," she said. "Got any thoughts?"

My cockerel yanked upward as an image framed in my psyche.

"Definitely. I think you'll like it."

"Goodness, goody, I can hardly wait," she said. "Am I stripped?"

"I figure I uncovered might be a superior word."

Her face took on a more out-of-control look. "At that point, I'm beginning at this point." She reaches down to pull her shirt over her head. I stripped alongside her, and soon we stood confronting one another.

"Go get an extra sheet and bring it into your front room," I said. Amy curved an eyebrow, at that point gestured and cushioned off. I went into her room to snatch the lube and met her close to the sliding glass ways to her overhang. I pulled the drapes aside, allowing light to fill the room. Amy gulped.

"Presently, I don't figure anybody can truly see in here. However, you never know without a doubt, isn't that right?"

She shook her head, at that point, gasped as I dropped the lube on the floor to help her spread the sheet.

"Indeed, Amy, I will play with your butt. You will be down on the ground, wriggling around my thumb covered somewhere down in your indirect access while my different fingers play with your pussy. My other hand will cinch your nipples, and I'll be watching everything, and I mean the world."

Amy pulled the sheet tight with me and afterward came over, pulverizing herself against my body.

"Gracious, God, I need that," she said.

I bolted my lips to hers, at that point, slid my hands around her back, going all over her spine. My fingers discovered her could, and she groaned her endorsement. I possessively measured the firm tissue while Amy hauled her nipples across my chest. I pushed a leg forward, and she promptly rode it, bumping with need. At the point when I felt the wetness of her excitement, I came up and pushed her shoulders down. Amy didn't should be told—she sank to her knees and afterward to her lower arms. Her rear end stuck enticingly into the air, and I touched the delicate skin, feeling the dull current stream between us. I let my eyes wander over her body, seeing the pucker of her sphincter, the swollen pink of her pussy and her clitoral hood, and afterward glancing over to see her nipples distending from firm bosoms. I wrapped up by considering her face, seeing the lost demeanor of somebody in profound excitement.

My fingers went ever nearer to her butt, and Amy moaned when I brushed my thumb across it. My other hand discovered her bosom, and I rolled the fat nipples between my fingers. Amy curved her chest down into my hand, and I expanded the pressing factor, setting off a groan of endorsement while she drove her rear end into my other hand.

My thumb presently drifted over her sphincter, scouring and pushing the somewhat unpleasant tissue while Amy kicked underneath me. I let my fingers float down over her cut, and they discovered her swollen and wet—time to move this along.

Amy opened her eyes as my fingers left her body, and a little grin played about her mouth as I sprinkled lube along with my thumb. At the point when I supplanted it on her rear end, she squirmed her hips to attempt to get me inside her. I took it extremely lethargic, feeling her external ring open to me. My thumb facilitated inside a piece and stopped at her inward ring. I moved to and fro, prodding the ring to open, while my other hand changed her nipples once more. I gazed toward her face, and my rooster was shocked at the suggestion of seeing her eyes investigate mine as I opened her can.

I investigated, seeing a combination of weakness, enthusiasm, expectation, and delight flutter across her highlights. I felt her push and her inward ring loose, allowing my thumb to slide into her. I gradually worked to and fro while Amy curved her rear end into my hand. In any case, she looked profoundly at me, looking for a window into my considerations. Her eyes enlarged in shock at something in mine, and afterward, she shut them and covered her face into the sheet, murmuring joyfully to herself.

My thumb had worked into the flare of the subsequent knuckle, and I let my different fingers spread across her rear end, giving her another sensation. She continued shaking and pushing once again into me, driving my thumb to the root. I looked as it slid in further, her rear end extending to oblige the meaty base.

"Yessss," she murmured when she felt my hand press profoundly into her can—my thumb was covered as far as possible in her gut. I followed her movements, coaxing mostly out as she shook forward and afterward driving profoundly home when she pushed back. She gave a little snort each time I reached as far down as possible, plainly lost in the sensations. I watched her experience that her back curving and turning underneath me; at that point, I got her nipples once more, crushing hard.

"Uhhhhhh," she groaned, driving her bosom into my hand. Her longing took off higher as I worked her body over, and I could feel her pressure fabricate. I watched her nipples stretch as I pulled and bent.

"Gracious God, good God, gracious God," she wailed into the sheet, wracked by her dim need with no unmistakable route for discharge. At the point when I felt she was unable to take it any longer, I moved my fingers to her shuddering cut.

"Ohhhhhhhhh, God," she breathed out, her alleviation obvious at discovering some exit from her sweet misery.

Her pussy ran openly, juices streaming down her legs. I gloried in how hot this young lady had become and slid further behind her to improve see.

My fingers rubbed the external lips, pulling away as she curved her back and pushed, attempting to get them on her clit. At long last, I yielded, sliding around the hard pearl, standing pleased from its hood. I kept the pressing factor delicate from the outset. However, Amy had different thoughts, curving her hips to pound her clit against my fingers. Her groans got more limited and higher in pitch, and I realized she was near a huge climax. I cinched down on her clit, squeezing it between my fingers, and she screamed into the sheet. A couple of more bucks of her hips and her body went inflexible.

From profound inside her, I felt the explosion start. Amy shouted as her pussy and ass grasped around my fingers, and her whole mid-region shook with its power. I even felt the waves contact her expanded bosom, her nipples beating in my fingers. Amy's body pulsated for a long spell, and she whimpered and moaned through it, her eyes firmly shut.

In the long run, her climax worked out, and her wracking cries died down. I gradually backed my thumb out of her can. However, I kept it possessively at her passage. She moaned with satisfaction.

"On the off chance that you need my can, it's yours," she said delicately. My cockerel shuddered with the consent in those words.

"Not exactly the time," I answered, "yet trust me, we'll arrive. My rooster is almost blasting after watching you experience that. You alright with me beating into you from behind? I will not keep going long."

"If it's not too much trouble, snatch my hips and take your pleasure, Eric," she reacted.

I arranged behind her and situated my iron pole at her passageway. She slugged back, spearing herself. I snorted with the vibe of her tight sheath grasping my cockerel, and I grabbed hold of her hips and drove myself into her, again and again. Amy remained directly with me, pushing back each time until she can be smoothed. Before long, I could feel the pressing factor fabricate, and I kept down as long as possible. At the point when it became too a lot, I pulled her back firmly against me, crushing her hill against the underside of my cockerel. My cum flooded past in white-hot planes, shooting somewhere down into the profundities of her pussy. I snorted with each impact, appreciating my delivery from the pressure of watching Amy's sensual showcase. When the flames subsided, I backed out and fell on the sheet, pulling Amy down with me. We kissed profoundly; at that point, she settled her head on my chest. We rapidly feel snoozing.

Awakening after a reviving rest, I felt like 1,000,000 bucks. I could feel Amy's heart thumping against me, and the world felt right.

Amy blended, and afterward, she delicately lifted her head to investigate my open eyes. Hers were clear and substance.

"That was...exactly what I required," she said. "You had me totally, yet I could feel the amount you gave it a second thought. Much obliged to you."

"Amy, the thing I like about you best is the point at which you give me a sincere much obliged for accomplishing something that I was biting the dust to do in any case. You are so welcome."

Amy grinned. "On the off chance that I'd knew what a cruel darling you were, I'd have grabbed you from Lisa and never let you go. How could I get so fortunate?"

"I ask myself that consistently."

Amy's eyes hooked on to mine and dove deep once more. She found what she needed, for I saw a grin turn up the sides of her lips.

"You truly do," she pondered. We investigated each other's eyes for some time longer. At long last, I broke her look and pulled her lips to dig for another kiss.

"Prepared to get a shower?" I inquired. "We're each sort of grimy."

Amy giggled. "No doubt. Help me up?"

We made it into the shower and exchanged washing obligations. As Amy was soaping my rear, her hands meandered until she held my balls. She brought her lips near my ear.

"So I need to ask, how could you be ready to hold back from taking my rear end when I offered it to you?"

I snickered. "I would have come in two strokes if I had done that."

Amy snickered back. "I hadn't thought about that."

"Truly, however, there's a period and spot for that. As you're most likely sorting out, a major piece of butt-centric sex needs it. At the point when you're unpleasantly baffled, and you need it so terrible that you'll effectively get it, that is the correct time. You realize it will not do any harm, and you realize it will fix what afflicts you. We'll arrive, and we'll investigate each other's eyes again as you sink and fill your rear end with my chicken. Trust me; I need this however much you do."

"I'm getting horny tuning into you. I can hardly wait," Amy said energetically. I felt her grin behind me. "It would appear that another person can hardly wait all things considered."

We wound up having intercourse in the shower, Amy squeezing me against the divider and taking me inside her. I wondered about her sensuality—weak one moment and persistent the following.

That night, we went to supper with our companion's group and hung out at Jackie's home. We returned to Amy's late and headed to sleep; I longed for Amy the entire evening. The following morning, I woke up to locate her, taking a gander at me.

"Curious what you might be thinking, sleepyhead."

"You truly need to know?"

Her eyes enlarged. "Particularly now."

I murmured. "Amy, do you know how suggestive that was yesterday? That is to say; I realize we're chipping away at butt-centric sex together. In any case, you are past volcanic. At the point when you viewed at me yesterday as I was playing with your can that was about the most sizzling thing, I've at any point seen. You tap into some dim current that is wild and untamed, yet defenseless and cozy. On the off chance that you revealed to me that you were a sorceress, I'd trust you."

Amy took a gander at me for quite a while; at that point, I grinned. "Be that as it may, Eric, I am a sorceress."

"I trust you. You have an enchantment blend of young lady nearby newness, smarts, and something underhanded. At that point, you wrap everything inside a bundle that is very simple on the eyes. I think about the thing I'm attempting to say is that I'm completely devoted to you, and I'm an exceptionally fortunate person."

Amy's eyes held mine. I let her test. At long last, she grinned again and talked delicately, her words standing out from the burst in her eyes. "In case you're attempting to get into my jeans today, that is no joke."

I burst out snickering. "I neglected to add the comical inclination."

"Isn't that what they say about an arranged meeting?"

"Better believe it. So why not screw me senseless, Miss Blind Date?"

She feigned exacerbation. "I generally succumb to the sentimental ones," she said to herself. At that point, she bounced on top of me instantly of power, sticking me to the bed and assuming responsibility. I didn't do anything aside from reacting as she warmed me up and continued to screw the heck out of me. I strongly suggest it.

We recuperated with her leftover on top of me, her tousled hair falling across my chest.

"Don't hesitate to reveal to me how fortunate you are whenever, Eric."

"Gee, I think I've found a spell over you."

"Goodness, better believe it, and I'm defenseless against it." I could feel her grin on my skin.

****

Tuesday night discovered us chatting on the telephone.
"Thursday will be an unpleasant day," she advised me. "We have an audit with a significant customer, who is requesting. We've been getting ready for two or three weeks; however, we hope to be obliterated. I'll be a worried zombie when I return home."

"I have a thought that will cause you to disregard senseless things like what your customer thinks. Intrigued?"

"Allow me to figure. It includes me exposed?"

"Shockingly, it does."

"Well, obviously, I'm intrigued!"

"At the point when you return home, call me. At that point, jump in the shower and clean your insidious pieces great. I'll give myself access with this convenient key you gave me," I taught.

"Thursday doesn't sound so terrible, all things considered."

"That is the soul! Presently, get your rest, and thump them dead."

After work Thursday, my telephone rang.

"It was fierce. However, we endured OK. Also, it truly assisted with having your little secret to anticipate. I'm jumping in the shower now."

I gave a few minutes and let myself in, going to her room and lighting a few candles that I brought. I opened up a jug of wine and two or three glasses, put a French nation stew on her oven, got the plate of mixed greens in the cooler, at that point stripped down, and folded a towel over my midriff.

Before long, I heard the water stop, and Amy arose a little later, a towel folded over her.

"Goodness my, I like," she said, as she took in the candles and the glass of wine I was giving her.

"Great. Presently plunk down close to me and enlighten me concerning your day."

Amy truly had a hard day. As she completed her glass, I took it from her; at that point, I got behind her on the bed and began rubbing her shoulders and neck as she proceeded with her story. At last, I came around and stood her up.

"Continue to talk," I taught.

I reacted to her; however, I followed kisses across her body at whatever point I wasn't talking. I began at the rear of her neck, plunging between her shoulders. I covered her arms, at that point tenderly facilitated the towel from around her, and proceeded down her back.

"It will be difficult to get done with revealing to you this story," she said after a murmur.

"That is the ticket. Continue onward."

I let my hands bother her nipples as I worked down her back. I kissed momentarily down one cheek of her rear end, at that point, began dealing with the backs of her legs. In front, my hands reflected what my lips were doing toward the rear. I could feel Amy getting diverted. The murmurs came to an ever-increasing extent, and she moved her weight between her legs. I climbed, kissing delicately across both ass cheeks.

"Ahhhh, that feels better. I think you have the essence of the story," she said.

"Is it accurate to say that you are certain? I would prefer not to miss anything."

"All things considered, you're not missing anything up until now," she said, squirming her can in my face.

"Reveal to me somewhat more. What happens the following time you meet this customer?"

I grinned to myself as I tuned in to Amy, attempting to center. My lips circumnavigated consistently nearer to her rosebud. I heard little murmurs blended in with her account, and she offered a lovely short response.

"Sounds like you're loosening up quite well, yet I need no doubt. Why not outfit here on the bed?" I encouraged her up and got her down on the ground. "Here's a pad for your head."

"Such a courteous fellow," she snickered, resting her head and curving her back.

"Presently," I proceeded, "I'm attempting to loosen up you, however knowing you, you may begin getting worked up. If it's not too much trouble, feel good to deal with any little issues you may have in such a manner."

"Try not to stress."

"Amazing." I moved back behind her. "Presently, were right? Gracious, indeed, kissing your magnificent ass."

I began once again, working gradually toward her middle. Amy's breathing got, and the aroma of her excitement contacted me.

"Ohhh, God," she groaned when I first touch her butt with my tongue. Gradually, tortuously, I contacted it all the more frequently, looking as her can began squirming noticeably all around.

At last, I gave her what she needed, lapping profoundly across her pucker. I felt her hand slide between her legs to begin playing with herself. I rotated profound strokes with lighter excursions around her edge.

Amy began driving into my face, and I smoothed my tongue to let her discover the pressing factor she needed. Her hand moved quicker and quicker, and I could hear the wet hints of her pussy getting pulverized.

I felt the natural shiver of her body straining for a major climax. She contorted her can into my tongue, totally offered over to the delight flowing through her body.

Amy's breath came in snorts and pants; at that point, she went inflexible, yelling into the cushion as the seizures undulated through her pussy and ass. My tongue was blessed to receive a fantastic view, and it got each quake.

I remained with her as her climax faded away. At that point, she whipped her head around.

"Inside me. Presently!" Amy told her fingers directing me. Her hands never left her clit as I stroked into her, and she came soon after I shot an extremely fulfilling load inside her.

We got done with returning to earth, and I sat down close to her on the bed.

"Pretty unusual, Eric," she said. "You certainly caused me to overlook my day."

"It was my pleasure. I had loads of fun. I love your can."

"I can tell. I surmise if I at any point advise you to kiss my butt, you'll help thinking about what I mean."

"No, I will not," I said.

Amy chuckled her rich giggle. "No, I suppose you will not." She went to embrace me. "I cherished it. I'm happy my rear end turns you on."

"No doubt. Presently, will we evaluate some supper?"

"I was trusting that I was smelling something lovely. I'll need to concede that I didn't see up to this point."

"Happy to hear it. Please." I drove her up, and we got dressed and cushioned into the kitchen, carrying the jug of wine with us.

Indeed, I enjoyed an extraordinary supper with Amy. As we were waiting in the course of the last glass of wine, she fixed me with her eyes.

"Eric, I need to say the amount. I enjoy how you're doing me. You're taking me to places I didn't know existed, and I'm cherishing what I'm discovering there."

"Amy, I can't reveal to you how much fun I'm having taking you to those spots."

"I can see it in your eyes. In any case, there's something else. You realize I've been an enthusiast of yours for some time. What I didn't comprehend was how much the genuine article outperforms my fantasy."

It's practically difficult to acknowledge an incredible commendation like that. I sat back, staggered. At that point, I acted with my body when the words wouldn't come. I got up and grasped Amy's hand, at that point, pulled her up for a long embrace. At the point when we isolated, I got my tongue once more into gear.
"Amy, that caused me to feel great. I'm a truly fortunate person."

"Your boots you are," she reacted. "Be that as it may, I'm a truly fortunate young lady, as well."

As you would figure, our shared reverence society got us all worked up. We had intercourse again that night, and I staggered out of Amy's bed promptly the following morning to return to my place and start my day.

We went through Friday out with companions, at that point, went to supper Saturday with a couple of something else.

"Care to go through the evening?" Amy asked as I was driving us back.

"Difficult to leave behind that offer," I replied, my dick solidifying in my jeans.

"Would you be keen on allowing me to coordinate our sporting exercises tonight?"

"I could go for that," I replied, my dick getting considerably harder. "What do you have arranged?"

"Uh, uh, intelligent kid. That would demolish the fun, wouldn't it?"

"Alright, Lady, I'll let you keep the secret."

We returned to Amy's place, and she drove me inside.

"Do you confide in me, Eric?" she asked, a grin all over that was directly out of a 2nd-grade jungle gym.

"Indeed, yet responding to an inquiry like that consistently leaves me somewhat stressed."

Amy fluttered her eyelashes. "Stressed over sweet little me?"

"Presently, I'm certainly stressed!" I replied, to a chuckle from Amy. "In any case, I'll trust you."

"Great, you will love it. Presently, could I request that you close your eyes?"

I shut them, my different faculties in a flash increasing. I stressed to hear Amy move, yet could get nothing. At last, I hear the delicate cushioning of feet from me, at that point returning behind me. I hopped when I felt the blindfold slide over my eyes. Amy tied it tenderly, at that point grasped my hand, and drove me down the lobby. We went into a room, yet it didn't feel like her room. Amy's hands came around my front to unfasten my shirt, at that point tenderly simplicity it from my shoulders. My shoes and socks were eliminated; at that point, Amy got my jeans off. It took somewhat more work for her to control the belt of my fighters over my uncontrolled erection. Her game was turning me on.

Amy grasped my hand and guided me to the bed, masterminding me on my back, with my head serenely on a cushion. I felt a stirring aside, and a delicate material was circled over my correct wrist. My chicken stressed much harder as I heard Amy stroll around the bed and circle another band over my left. I stayed still as I heard and felt her do likewise to my lower legs.

"Generally excellent, Eric. You do truly confide in me, and I can't reveal how great it causes me to feel. Why not attempt your bonds? Wouldn't have any desire to ruin the fun if they aren't working right."

I moved my arms and legs, discovering I could move two or three inches.

"Hello!" I cried as Amy's hands stimulated me. I attempted to roll away or do anything. However, it was pointless.

"Presently, I'm fulfilled," she said, yielding. "Sort of enjoyable to have you at my kindness."

"What was I saying about being concerned?"

"I like you somewhat stressed," she said, chuckling.

I detected Amy cushioning around the space to a few objections, and afterward, I felt her trip onto the bed with me and reach forward. Shockingly, I felt her draw the blindfold off. However, I was considerably more stunned to find that I was unable to see anything.
"Indeed, Eric, it's completely dark in here. I needed to perceive how our different faculties were elevated when we were unable to utilize our

eyes. Your faculties will be particularly elevated since you can't utilize your appendages. You've been driving me to some extraordinary places recently, yet I'm the sort of young lady who likes to keep the score even. My chance to take you on an excursion."

"Lead on, Amy," I said. "I'm yours."

"That is the reason I like you," she murmured as I felt her inclining down.

My lips felt the gentlest touch possible. My sensitive spots moved, stressing for additional, as she gently brushed her lips against mine. At that point, I felt her path kisses over my face and neck, an electric buzz snapping off my skin any place she contacted.

"Goodness, God," I moaned.

"You're shuddering," she murmured.

"I can't accept how you're not kidding," I murmured back.

"Trust it," she replied, and afterward, I felt her hands softly brush along my arms. Rushes dashed through my body as Amy followed over my bonds and afterward my hands. She worked her way back to my chest, and afterward, I felt her lean down once more.

"Fuck!" I jolted against my restrictions as her tongue contacted my nipples. I felt Amy laugh as she delicately, excruciatingly, did something amazing over the two of them. I didn't have the foggiest idea the amount a greater amount of this stunning torment I could take.

It was then that I felt her tongue slide down my midsection. I jerked and shivered under her considerations—every last trace of my skin snapped with expectation. My chicken was stressed as it would blast.

At last, Amy worked her way to my crotch. She delicately blew a breath at my cockerel, and I leaped to feel frigid fire dart away from my overly sensitive skin.

"Jesus, Amy!" I panted.

She disregarded me, contacting the tip of my chicken with her tongue. I kicked and squirmed at my restrictions, even though I realized it was miserable. She blew once more, and I shuddered from the chill at the tip of my chicken.

For what appeared to be an unending length of time, Amy prodded me pitilessly. She was all over the place, and she was no place. My superheated cockerel would have smoked on the off chance that it could. Licks, breaths, kisses, and contacts—Amy kept me speculating.

At that point, I felt her moving around on the bed, and I detected that she was hanging over me. A hard stub just touched my lips, and I got the clue, tenderly opening them to investigate Amy's nipples. Without my different faculties, it was a disclosure. The skin was delicate at this point, hard under, with little knocks and surface along the length of her nipples. I additionally felt the little knocks of her nipples and underneath the snugness of her bosom. I could hear Amy's delicate breath as she kept herself still for me, causing me to know her in a new manner. I wondered about how much this lady could communicate with her body.

Amy gave me quite a while to play, and afterward, I felt her nipples pull out while she moved once more, the heaviness of her thighs choosing either side of my face. My noses were overflowed with the aroma of hot pussy, and I paused while she settled down. Like her nipples, her pussy softly brushed my lips, and I delicately investigated the folds of her pussy with all the sensitive spots available to me. I felt her external lips, swollen and hot, shuddering marginally as I contacted along with them. Then, I moved to the inward lips, milder and flushed with warmth and dampness. I, at last, let my tongue investigate, feeling everything once again. Fulfilled, for the time being, I licked with more power, abandoning investigating to pleasuring. Amy's delicate murmurs revealed that I was doing it right, and I felt her prodding my rooster once more.

Inevitably, Amy pulled away and pushed her hips back. I shut my mouth and by and by felt a light touch at my lips. This time, it was her upper pussy, and I investigated how the inward lips united at a little hood. I could feel the strain in Amy's thighs as she kept herself down— almost certainly, she needed to slam her clit down all the rage. I tested around the hood and afterward felt under. Amy heaved despite herself, and I thought I felt the little pearl of her clit. However, it was difficult, no doubt. I kissed and snacked in this spot, and Amy began to squirm above me. At long last, getting my tongue included, I delicately whirled around her hood, quietly letting the strain assemble. Amy cooperated, never pounding herself against me.

Amy's pleasure constructed increasingly elevated, and I could, at last, be certain that her clit was standing glad. I whirled around it with my tongue, tenderly lashing it from all sides.

"Gracious, God," Amy groaned. My cockerel could feel her worn-out relaxing.

Her pussy was a wet heater, dribbling onto my jawline. My nose was overwhelmed with the hot tang of her excitement. Her thighs shuddered with the strain.

Detecting all was good and well, I delicately sucked her clit between my lips.

"Ahhhhh!" she heaved. I tightened my lips and let her drag the little pearl out between them. I opened them once more, and she got the cadence, driving her clit in again as I sucked.

From Amy's ambiguous snorts and wheezes, I could tell that she had lost all origination of anything besides the sensation of her clit hauling through my lips. Her pitch got higher, and I realized that she was preparing for a gigantic climax.

Out of nowhere, she went inflexible, simply holding her pussy above me. I could hear the strain in the quick cries coming from her throat. I sucked in her clit as profound as possible and hung on.

The primary fit dashed through her body, gripping every one of her muscles much harder than they, as of now, were. I heard her cry as the unwinding wave went through; at that point, the following compression came significantly more grounded. Her pussy and clit beat as expected, and my delicate lips caught everything. Endlessly it went, Amy shouting with delight so hot it was almost torment.

As the compressions diminished in force, I tenderly loosened my tension on her clit, realizing it was touchy. Amy was almost wailing above me. I automatically thrashed against my bonds, needing to hold her through the defeat.

As it was, I just tenderly rubbed around her inward lips with my lips and tongue, keeping the positive sentiments rolling while she settled through the glimmer.

At last, I felt her draw a full breath in and afterward breathe out in a long murmur.

"I don't have the foggiest idea what occurred there," she mumbled. "That was so extreme; it was startling."

I just gestured under her, and she hopped, laughing at the contact.

At that point, I hopped when she plunged her lips down over my chicken. She snickered, back in charge. Her hips immediately spun away, and I felt their weight settle down with one leg on each side of mine.

Delicate fingers situated my stressing chicken, and afterward, I felt the head enter her smooth passage. I hung tight for her to sink around me.

She didn't. She delicately shook above me, washing the top of my chicken in the fluid fire. I wriggled under her, attempting to get more inside her. Even though I could not see anything, I could feel her grin transmitting down at me. I realized she was cherishing this—my pleasure relied totally upon her.

At that point, the bitch discovered my nipples with her fingers. Delicately stroking, softly scratching, she sent shocks of flow out through my chest. Combined with the sweet desolation consuming the top of my cockerel, she made them shudder under her.

"Amy!" I croaked wretchedly.

She overlooked me. She was a cruel sorceress, playing my body like some evil spirit instrument. Unexpectedly it hit me with frigid lucidity—Amy was imparting her mystery secrets to me. Something basic and basic moved from her, a dim force that shot into my body.

I offered myself to her and let my body react in kind. Something moved from me back to her, an acknowledgment of her clouded side and the noting yell from mine.

We both heaved at the association. To open yourself to another, and afterward to discover what you've generally longed for; all things considered, that doesn't occur all the time.

Amy pummeled down, immersing my rooster in her blazing passage. One hand went to my mid-region, stimulating me to occupy me from the lovely joy transmitting from my cockerel. I knew where the other hand was going.

Amy shook her hips hard, siphoning my cockerel in fluid velvet. Her fingers played her clit, taking herself alongside me. I whipped and squirmed under her, attempting urgently to move away from her stimulating fingers and attempting frantically to remain with them. I didn't have a clue where torment finished, and joy started any longer. It didn't make any difference.

In that obscured room, my faculties centered down to two things: Amy's touch wherever on my body, and afterward an intuition of energy streaming between us. I plunged in, following that turning, beating channel back to its source in obscurity openings of Amy's being.

A feeling of glow coursed through me. At this point, it was not my chicken; however, my whole body consumed under Amy's light. I rose with it, and afterward, a white-hot wave writhed through me. I hollered out as another took me, a sensation of careless happiness filling my general existence. Through our association, I could feel something comparative flowing through Amy.

At that point, I stopped existing.

Afterward, I knew that floods of happy delight had moved through me and that Amy had shouted out with the equivalent. At that point, there were no words for what occurred or for long it went on.

I, at last, recaptured consciousness of myself, and I felt the post-quake tremors shaking through me and the full weight of Amy's hips laying on mine. At that point, I felt it—the association was still there. Not as hot or splendid as in the past, but rather as yet connecting us—seething and prepared to jump to fire once more.

Different sensations came through to me: Amy's breathing, without rushing as she recuperated. Her hands squeezed profoundly into my chest as she upheld her weight. My chicken secures inside her.

We remained together like this for an all-encompassing time. Neither of us needed to break the spell.

At long last, Amy murmured profoundly.

I chose to talk first. "Amy, I don't have the foggiest idea what occurred. However, I'll never go back again."

"We'll never go back again. It hit me, as well, and it unquestionably hit us."

"Who are you?" I pondered so anyone might hear. "Great, agreeable, and charming, yet also dim, puzzling, and cruel. How could I get so fortunate to meet you?"
"I believe you're meeting the individual you've allowed me to become," she replied. "I've never at any point considered allowing anybody to see that previously."

"I trust I will see it on a lot more occasions," I said. "I'm simply in wonderment. You are a sorceress."

"What's more, I cast my dull spell on you, Eric," she said, her voice intelligible and bursting. I felt our association jump once more.

Amy let that wait; at that point, she inclined down and squashed her lips to mine.

At last, I felt her facilitate her hips up and gradually let go of my rooster. She stopped at the head and eased back significantly more, reducing the stun of her lips cruising by. I jerked. However, I enjoyed her mindfulness.

She moved off the bed, and I felt my restrictions being delivered individually. At that point, she returned and settled next to me. I folded toward her and spooned into her back. She snatched my arm and squeezed it profound to her chest, murmuring cheerily. Without sight, my different faculties were as yet honed. I could feel her heart pulsating, moderate, and fulfilled. I feel snoozing with our association still unblemished.

We woke following a soothing evening, actually tangled together. Faint bits of light spilled through the dim covering that Amy had on the windows.

"Mmmmmmm," she murmured, nestling further into me.

I held her, believing her satisfaction stream across to me.

"I could remain here everlastingly," she said so anyone might hear.

"So could I," I replied. "Do you feel it like I do?"

"Indeed," she said, "However, I need you to mention to me what you feel."

"It resembles I have a channel of profound energy associated with you, Amy. It's delicate at this moment. However, it consumed hot and brilliant while we were having intercourse."

"That is it," she said. "I believe the association our mystery sides made with one another."

"You're correct. It resembles I know your genuine nature, Amy, and they go with mine."

"I've never set out to impart them to anybody previously," Amy said. "I'm so glad I did with you."

"From sorceress to blameless young lady," I pondered. "You are every one of those things."

"Furthermore, do you like it?"

"No, I love it," I said and gave her a long crush.

"I do as well," she inhaled and cuddled back once more.

I settled against her and let my hand meander over her legs and hips. It wasn't sexual this time—we had consumed that with extreme heat for the present. Rather we just existed and let our skin express our association.

Ultimately, my stomach thundered, and Amy laughed.

"I'm happy I didn't do that first," she said, chuckling. "I surmise we'll need to get up and grab a bite."

"How about we do it."

We gradually got up, and Amy drove me to the entryway. Before opening it, she took both of my hands.

"Recall what occurred here," she directed, her voice blasting once more.

"I swear I won't ever fail to remember," I said officially, the words sounding valid between us.

"I discharge you," she got done with, leaving me to consider what she was delivering me from. It sure wasn't the dull spell she cast over me— I could, in any case, feel that. I realized she needed me to ponder.

She pulled the entryway gradually open to allow our eyes to change. Daylight gushed through her place—we had dozed late.

She gave me a robe, taking one for herself. "Allow me to get you some morning meal," she said.

"Those were deliberately positioned," I said. "Had this arranged out?"

She looked into it, a smile all over. "Eric. What occurred—you don't arrange for that."

I giggled, profound and long. "No, I suppose you don't. In any case, some piece of you did."

"Are you so sure it was me?" she asked, her blue eyes blazing.

She spun around and was stepping to the restroom before I could reply. Her inquiry hit me like a thunderclap, tossing my psyche into disorder. What had happened the previous evening? What had she begun, and what had I begun? Could I at any point know? I understood that there was a ton behind those blue eyes of Amy's.

We prepared and had breakfast together, Amy controlling the discussion away from the prior night. We got dressed, and afterward, she showed me out. She looked profoundly at me.

"Invest some energy with your heart, Eric. I will invest some energy with mine." She kissed me and delicately pushed me out the entryway. "Call me."

I staggered back to my place and got dressed for a long bicycle ride. In no way like actual work to clear the head. I pushed out and required around thirty minutes to get into a mood, my muscles heated up, and the energy streaming.

I, at that point, sank into my heart, detecting it siphoning life through me. I opened myself to my emotions about Amy. The original was a mass of dread—the dread that I would lose myself in her and dread that I could be profoundly stung. I investigated my dread, realizing that I needed to respect it to move past it. Amy should mean a ton to me for me to be this stressed; I contemplated internally. I pushed past and investigated further.

The following inclination was dread once more—dread that I was succumbing to Amy explicitly, yet not totally. I felt further into my heart and realized this wasn't correct. I adored being around her for herself.

As I investigated further, it hit me with power. I needed to impart my heart to Amy, and I was unable to live without her. At that point, I was lost, and the lone way was to twofold down and drew nearer to her. Such a lot had happened so quick—however, it felt so right.

I investigated that for some time. Did I feel any uncertainty? Was there some concealed notice signal in my heart?

No, you moron. She's the one for you.

"Much enjoyed," I said so anyone might hear, laughing at myself. "Happy that is settled."

What's more, it was—I could feel that profoundly. I rode with that feeling for some time.

With such minor things settled as who I needed to consume my time on earth with, I could proceed onward to different subjects, similar to what the heck happened the previous evening. Unmistakably, Amy needed to even the score a bit. I had been the lead for most of our relationship, and she needed to reverse the situation and take me on an excursion. She almost let go completely when I was lashing her clit. Interesting how I was the one tied up; however, I had her completely devoted to me.

Powerless to resist me. Perhaps that is what she implied when she suggested that I had begun it the previous evening. Perhaps she was reacting when she cast her spell on me. Whatever she was doing, she did something extraordinary for herself.

Then again, as I looked through my heart, I could feel that she had been working her spell on me for quite a while—in any event since the day of our gathering together—and most likely a whole lot sooner. She had risked a great deal to uncover her inner feelings to me the previous evening. In any case, I could feel the association with her—something I had never imparted to anybody.

I quit thinking and just rode home in an ocean of sentiments and feelings—all great, yet also terrifying in their power.

That night, I called her.

"Ideal to hear your voice," Amy said. "What did you do the entire evening?"

"Precisely what you said. I took a long bicycle ride and invested some energy with my heart."

"Furthermore, did you learn anything?"

"Indeed. A lot, truth be told."

"Anything you'd want to share?" Her voice was light and well disposed of. However, I could detect her listening eagerly.

"It was quite ground-breaking stuff, Amy."

"To make sure you know, I went through the evening with some ground-breaking stuff of my own."

I realized that she needed—no, she required—for me to go first in this little game. Also, a lot was on the line. Twofold down.

"The principal thing I felt, Amy, was a mass of dread. Dread that I was losing myself and that I could be profoundly stung."

Her voice got delicate. "We need to place extraordinary trust in those we care about. It implies a great deal that you're placing that trust in me."

"I do confide in you, Amy. Also, I pushed past that dread. In any case, the following thing was another type of dread. This time, about me. Could I be certain that I wasn't simply succumbing to you explicitly? That is to say, I needed to concede, the sexual part has been wonderful."

Amy's lilting chuckle got through the telephone. "That is putting it mildly, and I enjoy the hidden supplement. What did your heart advise you?"

"Not to stress. I was succumbing to the total bundle for quite a few reasons."

"I...you...thanks." Amy's voice was thick with feeling.

"Something more that I'll discuss around evening time. I inquired as to whether there was some uncertainty, some admonition signal that I should think about."

"What's more,

"Nothing."

"Eric." I could feel the quiver in her voice. The line got genuine calm. "Eric—to make sure you know—my heart is exceptionally cheerful at this moment."

I could feel her keeping down the cries. "Amy, why not offer your heart sometime later? I think we've had a major day, and it's most likely an ideal opportunity for some rest."

"Much obliged, Eric," she murmured. "No...Thanks. Goodbye."

"Goodbye, Amy," I replied and cut the association. She required the opportunity to herself.

The following morning, I had a message on my telephone.

"Would I be able to prepare you supper?"

Simple three-letter answer.

I halted by the flower specialist and showed up at Amy's entryway for certain blossoms. She is a real sense, hauled me through the entryway, and squashed me in a hug. Her words arrived in a surge.

"Eric. You need to know. My heart feels precisely like yours. What you said—it was far beyond what anybody has at any point said to me. Do you realize how upbeat I am?"

"It just felt right."

At that, she burst into cries. My tears followed hers.

"I guaranteed myself that I wouldn't cry," she cried into my shoulder.

"Amy. You can generally act naturally with me." I embraced her tight.

We, in the long run, unraveled, bashfully giggling at one another's red-rimmed eyes. Amy drove me to a seat and served me an incredible supper, her eyes shining each time I got them. It didn't take a lot of knowledge to see that she was coasting on a cloud. I glided with her, scarcely mindful of what we discussed.

When we completed, I expressed gratitude toward her, and afterward, I rose to help her reasonable the plates.

"No," she directed. "I'm serving you around evening time. Your responsibility is to converse with me while I move this set aside."

Amy wrapped tidying up and returned to me, offering me her hand. She lifted me and kissed me, at that point maneuvered me down the lobby, and shooed me into the restroom.

"Meet me in my room in almost no time. Try not to wear excessively," she coordinated. I tidied up, taking as much time as necessary, at that point stripped. I strolled back to Amy's room to think that its lit with a few candles. Amy remained by her bed and coaxed me over.

She slid into my arms. I felt the smooth skin of her back as she kissed me. We shared the joys of one another's lips, and afterward, Amy tenderly pushed me back onto the bed. I lay back while she rode me and drove me through a night of sentimental lovemaking. My primary recollections were of her eyes, looking profoundly into mine as she delicately shook above me, and the grin that played about her face. We never looked away, even as we each jerked in the climax.

We lay together and talked; at that point, Amy began kissing me once more. In the long run, she turned and rode my face, driving us through a 69 meeting that got us both worked up. This time, she lay back and pulled me on her, and we kissed profoundly while we gradually worked to another fantastic peak.

"Much obliged to you for going through the night with me," Amy said as we recuperated. "I delighted in having the opportunity to investigate your eyes the first run-through and afterward feeling your tongue in my mouth the second."

"Any time, Amy," I answered. "I'll do it above, I'll do it beneath, I'll do it behind, and I'll do it genuine sluggish."

"What's more, you'll do it in my home, and you'd likely do it with a mouse," Amy noticed drily. "I would be advised to get these candles out before I need to tune in to substantially more good times TV."

At the point when she got back in bed, I pulled her nearby.

"Amy. Much thanks to you such a huge amount for having me over. You're unique, and it's extraordinary that your heart is falling for a comic."

"I wish I could help myself, yet I can't," Amy said as she cuddled further into my arms.

I tenderly stroked her back until she subsided into rest, and afterward, I followed her.

We gave each other a couple of evenings off after all the feeling that had poured out throughout the most recent few days. Nonetheless, I had welcomed Amy to supper with a gathering of companions Friday.

"Just on the off chance that you consent to return to my place for a nightcap," she had advertised.

"I want to do that," I said.

Jennifer, with her standard instinct, cornered us at the bar before supper.

"Both of you appear as though you're on a cloud. Things should get going truly well between you."

Amy peered down, a become flushed crawling up her cheeks. I could feel my face getting warm.

"Presently, you've disclosed to me everything," Jennifer said. "I'll be forgiving and let you be, Amy. What's more, you, Eric, I believe you're dealing with her?"

Amy and I both snickered—a piece anxiously.

"Goodness, my, both of you are lost. I could pose more inquiries. However, I think I know the appropriate responses." Jennifer's face brides out into a grin. "I can't reveal to you how cheerful I am for you both. Presently, we should guide the discussion to more secure subjects."

"Extraordinary thought," I croaked out. Jennifer winked.

We overcame supper with no more off-kilter minutes. We strolled up from the vehicle with our fingers interlaced.

"Still need that nightcap?" Amy inquired.

"Anything at your place would be extraordinary," I replied.

"Anything?"

"Sweetheart."

Amy feigned exacerbation and got me through her entryway. She bolted it behind her and went to me.

"Would I be able to be your nightcap?"

"I'd love that, Amy."

She snickered and shut the distance between us. Her delicate lips discovered mine, and we failed to remember our chat. Her body smoked in my arms, her breath hot and her lips unyielding.

At long last, Amy pulled back to take a gander at me. She took every one of my hands and attracted them behind her to lay on her butt, which wriggled against them.

"Eric. What did you say about being appallingly horny and baffled? I feel that at this point."

"You mean..?"

"Indeed, you know precisely what I mean."

"How about we go slowly," I said warily.

"Be that as it may, don't be excessively mindful," she said. "I need this."

"Need it terrible?" I prodded.

"You have no clue," she murmured. She shut the distance between our lips and kissed me savagely. My cockerel hardened to steel in my jeans as she ground into me. My hands went here and there, her back as she warmed up. I simply sporadically wandered down to her rear end, prodding her barbarously.

"I ask for from these garments," she relaxed. I encouraged her to strip everything, seeing the hunger in her tight nipples. She caused me to uncover, and afterward, I pulled her back into my arms, proceeding with my delicate stroking of her back.
I could feel the strain working in her body, so before she got excessively disappointed, I spun her around and pulled her back into me.

"God, yes!" she groaned as my chicken found the separation between the cheeks of her rear end. My hands rose to locate her stressing bosoms as she pushed her butt once again into me. Her head lolled back when I palmed her bosoms, shutting my fingers to pull and turn her nipples. I began somewhat delicate. However, I expanded the pressing factor to her whines of consent. Amy pushed her rear end profoundly into my chicken, and I changed her nipples hard.

"Eric, I'm ablaze! Pleasssse," she asked.

"We should get to your bed," I coordinated.

Amy snatched my hand and, in a real sense, hauled me to her bed. She grabbed the covers and tossed them back, imprudent of where they landed. As yet holding my hand, she opened her end table and pulled out a jug of lube, giving it back to me. She let go and afterward loosened up face down on the bed, spreading her legs somewhat and climbing her rear end out of sight. I paused for a minute to savor the sight: a delightful lady, horny too much, spread out before me, standing by eagerly for me to loot her tight ass.

"You are wonderful, Amy," I murmured.

"Get your hands on this wonderful body," she directed.

I burned through no time and moved alongside her. She can be wriggled underneath me, hungry for my touch. At long last, I offered it to her.

"Yessss," she murmured.

My fingers followed over the hurling skin of her rear end, so delicate yet so firm underneath. I helped remember our first night together when she urgently attempted to get my fingers on her indirect access. This time, she didn't need to stress. I let my fingers plunge over her private spot; at that point, I went to kneading the ring of muscle. A ceaseless series of murmurs and murmurs disclosed to me that I was doing the correct things.

When I felt her ring unwind, I went after the lube and flicked open the top. Amy's breath trapped in her throat, and her rear end climbed up eagerly.

I sprinkled some lube on a finger, at that point, but it at her rear end.

"Ummmmmm," she murmured, and I felt her delicately push out, loosening up her sphincter for me. My finger pushed inside, gradually, tenderly, getting access to her most private space. I halted at her subsequent ring and hung tight for it to unwind completely before I pushed in. At that point, I delicately pulled out and gradually pushed in further.

"Ohhhh, God," Amy moaned with her face immovably squeezed into the sleeping cushion. Her butt waved noticeable all around, pushing back when I pushed inside and pulling out when I did likewise. Before long, I had my finger covered to the root, and I gradually took long strokes in her can.

"Yeahhhhh," she empowered. As Amy got energized, she shifted her rear end further up and drove back more diligently, flagging me to push more earnestly myself. Before long, I was sawing my finger in profoundly, squeezing the remainder of my hand solidly against the cheeks of her can.

Amy whimpered and groaned, her hair spread around her covered face. All her consideration was on the finger doing sorcery to her can.

"Prepared for somewhat more?" I murmured.

"Pleasssse," she murmured back.

I gradually pulled out my finger and went along with it to another, sprinkling lube over them both. Amy's rear end bumped noticeable all around, missing the inclination inside her. She groaned when my fingers reconnected with her rear end.

I took this extremely lethargic, allowing Amy to acclimate to the sensation of size. Once more, she can lose, and I felt the opposition blur, and my fingers begin to spread the ring of muscle. They slid forward, at that point, held up at her subsequent ring. It loses, and I tenderly pushed inside. I let the ring open up; at that point, I slid my fingers out a piece, letting her rest. At that point back in, and this time she loses completely, willing me into her body. She pushed with her hips, and my fingers slid to the subsequent knuckle, joined by a robust groan. I halted there and gradually hauled somewhat way out.

"Ahhhhh," she energized on the following push. I went slightly further, at that point, back out. Each time, somewhat further. At last, I arrived at the end.

"So great," she mumbled. Her hips shifted up once more, and she offered me everything. Encouraged, I pushed more diligently and marginally turned with each stroke. Her back angled, and her can rose to meet me. She adored this.

We got into a musicality, and I sawed all the more solidly. I began turning my fingers in general, extending her open, preparing her if she needed to go further with this. I needn't have pondered.

"Eric, I need you inside me. Presently. I'm prepared," Amy coordinated.

"I realize you are," I replied. "I will lean against your headboard, and you will let yourself down on me."

"Awesome."

I slithered up next to her and settled back against the headboard, extending my legs before me. Amy lifted herself from the bed and rode my legs. I gave her the lube, and she sprinkled another measure over my rooster. I shuddered as her hand expertly jacked my chicken while she spread it around.

As yet holding my cockerel, Amy worked her knees forward until she lingered above me. I turned upward into her grin and the wild edges around her eyes. Amy deliberately situated my chicken at her back passage. We both murmured when the head settled at her external ring. Her eyes never left mine as she gradually brought down her hips. Shockingly, I didn't feel a lot of opposition as she opened to get me. I saw a similar inclination in her eyes. When I hit the internal ring, I felt opposition, yet Amy eased back down and let herself change. Unexpectedly, her eyes went wide as her internal ring loose. We both realized that this planned to work.

Amy's inward ring stroked the top of my chicken in hot velvet, sliding open gradually. She halted, rose marginally, and sunk. Her butt opened up somewhat more, and on the following plummet, the head slipped inside. My hands discovered her cheeks and stroked.

"Ohhhhhh," she relaxed. Her eyes grinned down at mine while she kept on working me inside her. I let her see the excitement she made in me. Her rear end was hot, smooth, and tight. Here and there she went.

"We're doing it," she pondered so anyone might hear.

"Definitely. Amy, you're inconceivable," I replied.

"This is so hot." Amy's hands came to the back and spread her cheeks separated. She angled her back and let herself down; I felt her cheeks brush my legs. Inside a couple of more strokes, she rested her full weight, my rooster drove right inside her.

I tore myself away from the staggering circumstance before me: a lovely, horny, hot lady straddling my hips with my rooster covered as far as possible in her rear end. I expected to concentrate elsewhere before my rooster emitted from the sheer sensuality; all things considered, Amy was a great spot to center, so I slid my hands around to her sticking bosoms, measuring and crushing the nipples.
"Yesssss," she murmured, sinking, so my cockerel skewered her rear end. I shifted my head back, and Amy tried to understand, dropping her lips down. She kissed me eagerly, driving her tongue into a sweet duel with mine.

Amy wound above me, her body reacting to the impeccable sentiments flowing all through. Her lips remained stuck to mine, and her breath came hot and hard.

I ensured I recollected which hand had avoided her can, and afterward, I let it trail down her side. I felt the grin all the rage.

"Gracious, no doubt," she groaned into my mouth. My hand gradually worked between her legs.

"Uhhhhhh." Her swollen pussy drove hard into my hand. It was doused with excitement, and I spread my fingers, keeping the pressing factor aberrant. Amy made it troublesome, contorting and driving her hips to drive her clit into me. I orbited around it, thinking hard to keep her baffled and hold me back from blowing my stack.

Amy sped her movements, enjoying long puffs all over my post. I could detect her workday from provisional movements to full-on stroking, secure in the joy transmitting from her butt. I yielded and let my fingers meet on her engorged clit.

"Ahhhh," she murmured in help. I twisted my pointer and let her groove her clit against it. She crushed her pussy into me, her breath coming in short wheezes. I kept on focusing on her clit, contemplating anything besides the goddess on the back of my hips.

"Goodness, God, Eric, I'm going to cum," she declared, pulling away from me.

I at long last permitted myself to think once more at her. Our association jumped to life, and I felt my shaft expand and solidify to unadulterated steel as I took a gander at the unalloyed desire emanating from Amy. I squeezed her clit in my fingers, and by the other hand, did likewise with her nipples, pulling hard. My climax worked down underneath, holding back to bubble over. I pressed back, holding off.

"Goodness, fuck, gracious fuck, gracious fuck," she gasped to her pushes. At that point, her body strained as her climax accumulated power. Her jeans got higher in pitch; at that point, she tossed her head back and shouted out as the principal fit tore through her. I felt her pussy tense; at that point, her breath got, and she shouted as her butt bounced back from my hard dick inside. I heard more indiscernible cries tear from her throat, and afterward, my climax requested its due. I wailed out my delivery as the primary impact flew up through my cockerel, showering profound into her shaking insides. Many shoots proceeded, the joy from her clasping ass almost terrible. My balls just kept on discharging into her.

After I don't have the foggiest idea how long, I felt her body droop against me. I delivered her nipples and diminished the tension on her clit while we both whimpered and jerked through the consequential convulsions. We took as much time as is needed.

At long last, I opened my eyes again to see hers looking profoundly into mine. I could detect the slight grin playing all over.

"Amazing. What occurred?" she pondered.

"That is called soul-smashing."

"Kid did it ever," she said and chuckled. I snickered with her, the two of us jerking with our most delicate spots associated. Amy quieted down and afterward twisted down to kiss me.

"Much obliged, Eric, for being so delicate with me. That was unfathomably acceptable."

"You are so welcome, Amy. I can't consider any place I'd preferably be."

We kissed profoundly, expressing gratitude toward one another with our lips.

"Prepared, Eric?" Amy pulled back and asked, looking again at me.

"Indeed, Amy," I reacted.

As yet associating with her eyes, I felt Amy raise herself from me. She jerked as my head passed her rings and afterward grinned at my whine when her sphincter shut over the withdrawing head. I slid down, and she brought down herself alongside me.

"Ahhhhh. I didn't understand how hardened I was," she conceded, gazing toward the roof.

"I think we were both somewhat enveloped with the occasion," I replied, coming down to delicately knead her thighs.

"Feels better," she relaxed.

I kept on working for my hands over her skin as her eyes shut. Feeling her floating off, I pulled the covers over us; at that point, I laid my head on her shoulder and hung my arm over her. She cuddled into me and moaned, and I permitted sleep to overwhelm me.

My psyche meandered in profound dreams, presumably energized by the ground-breaking lovemaking of the prior night. At last, the mist lifted, and morning's light separated through the window ornaments as I opened my eyes.

I just refreshed and delighted in the harmony, Amy's breathing without rushing next to me. At that point, it got, and she attracted a full breath as her eyes opened. They flickered and went to discover mine.

"Morning, Amy," I said tenderly, grinning at her.

"Morning, Eric." Amy grinned back and inclined in to kiss me. We embraced tight.
"What an evening," she said when she pulled back. "I rested awesome. You should?"

"Strong and profound," I replied. "I didn't wake until a couple of moments back. Everything is direct with the world."

"Allow me to figure. Incredible supper, extraordinary friend, awesome sex, profound rest. Is that your equation for bliss?"

"Basically," I snickered back. "You need to concede: It's difficult to beat."

"All things considered, the sex was incredible. You, at last, took me there, Eric."

"Furthermore, you were mind-boggling, Amy. It took all that I needed to hold back from blowing it the subsequent you brought down yourself onto me."

"I could see it in your eyes," she said, grinning. "In any case, at that point, the tables turned when I came. I've felt nothing that extraordinary."

"You were completely lost," I thought back. "Head tossed back; creature clamors coming from your throat. It was the most blazing thing I've at any point seen."

Amy reddened. "It's a touch of humiliating to concede the amount I preferred that."

I grinned back. "You were open and helpless. I cherished it."

"You're the one person I can open up with," she said.

"Never show signs of change," I replied.

Amy's arms lurked around me and pulled me in a warm embrace, saying everything with her body.

"Prepared for a shower?" Amy asked when we, in the end, unraveled.

"Good thought," I replied. We helped each other up and cushioned into the restroom connected at the hip.

Soaping her back, I posted an inquiry. "Amy, would you say you were OK with me contacting you after my fingers had been in your secondary passage?"

She giggled. "I don't think I even saw, yet indeed, I'm fine. Your hands felt very great on my chest, and I realize you care where you put them. Keep it up."

"Keep it up, huh? So there will be a subsequent time?"

"Goodness, no doubt. There is unquestionably going to be a subsequent time." I burst out chuckling, and Amy went along with me.

"How about we get completed, and I'll prepare you breakfast. I'm insatiable," I said.

"Need to get your solidarity back in the wake of bewitching me?"

"Precisely."

We wrapped up, and I discovered breakfast trimmings in Amy's fridge. "Anticipating organization?" I inquired.

"I calculated that I'd have some horny person over this end of the week and that he would require food following a night with me."

"You're not kidding," I concurred. I got occupied while she sat at a barstool.

"Sort of amusing to have another person cook in my home," she noticed.

"Simply recollect, few out of every odd horny person treats you this well."

"No person has at any point treated me that well, in bed or out."

"No young lady's always treated me that well possibly," I replied, turning upward from our omelets to see her moving eyes. "Off by a long shot."

"Not even Lisa?" she asked wickedly.

She found me napping, yet I immediately recuperated. "Lisa and I were a decent pair. However, there is something in particular about us, Amy, that goes past anything I've known."

"I know precisely what you mean," she chuckled. "Yet, I prefer to prod you."

"No doubt, I don't see that evolving."

"You wouldn't need it to." I turned upward, and she winked. I snickered, realizing she was correct.

We went bicycling, getting down to the stream, and having a nibble for a break. In transit home, we accelerated by a recreation center and enjoyed a reprieve under an overhanging tree. We both set down and turned upward into the leaves.

"Eric, thanks again for the previous evening. It was stunning. It didn't do any harm, and you felt great inside me."

"I'm a fortunate person to get expressed gratitude toward for what we did the previous evening," I explained a laugh from Amy. "In any case, my pleasure. At the point when two individuals set aside the effort to fabricate trust and involvement in butt-centric sex, it tends to be phenomenal. You've figured out how to confide in me, and all the more significantly, you've figured out how to confide in yourself. When I gave what you call my 'little discourse regarding the matter,' that is the thing that I implied. I'm truly happy that you delighted in it."

Amy grasped my hand and pressed hard.

We went through the end of the week generally together, visiting companions and having intercourse. I wondered again at how much fun Amy was to be around. I staggered out of her bed Monday morning and returned to my place to prepare for work.

"Jennifer might want to meet you for a beverage," Amy said sometime after that via telephone.

"Just me?" Like any person, I was playing this mindfully.

"Just you. I revealed to her I'd inquire. I think she has a few things she needs to advise you. Likely about me, or us. She's an old buddy, so I heed her gut feelings. Keen on hearing what she needs to say?"

"You're not worried she will share some profound, dim, mystery or qualm?"

"You've seen her glance at us, Eric. Does she appear as though she has any hesitations?"

"No, she sure doesn't," I conceded. "No doubt, I'd be glad to meet her. Perhaps I can acquire some influence over you, in any case."

"Try not to think you have enough as of now?"

"Never damages to have more, particularly with a sorceress like you."

Amy snickered. "No doubt about it."

So that is the way I wound up holding up Friday night at the place Jennifer proposed. Tasteful, with barely enough commotion to make private discussion conceivable. I didn't stand by well before she showed up, decked out in a sundress. Luckily, I had followed Amy's recommendation and dressed modestly.

"You look shocking, Jennifer," I said. "What would I be able to get you?"

"My, my, a commendation and a courteous offer. Amy's doing great with you. Gin and tonic, bless your heart." Jennifer sunk into the seat I offered, folding her legs and showing a ton of tanned thigh. Her brunette hair fell down her shoulders, outlining a rich face overwhelmed by puncturing green eyes. I painstakingly got my eyes far from her chest. However, I could detect that a trace of cleavage drove the eye down to pleasantly expanding bends. Jennifer grinned at all that entered my thoughts.

"Such a refined man," she murmured. "Feel somewhat shrewd, meeting another lady while your sweetheart is at home?"

"A bit, yes. So I'm glad that the lady's such acceptable organization."

Jennifer giggled. "Eric. You are simply the fiend! You're finishing this piece of the assessment incredibly well. Presently, how is your mom? I recall conversing with her when she visited."

I reacted, realizing that Jennifer was looking for her chance to jump. She took as much time as is needed, and we both visited pretty much all way of things.

"Like another?" I asked when her glass was vacant.

"If it's not too much trouble."

Our beverages came, and she got hers. I did likewise, and similarly, as I was going to taste, she hit me.

"Amy truly prefers you, you know."
I played it as cool as possible, taking a taste and reclining while I purchased time. I'd generally experienced difficulty reacting to that line, beginning back in 2nd grade.

"Presumably not however much I like her," I said, feeling satisfied with an answer that didn't sound weak or self-important.

She grinned. "I'm not entirely certain about that. Yet, I am certain that neither of you realizes how profound it goes. How should you? You have a lifetime to discover."

"A lifetime, huh?"

Jennifer didn't reply. She just took a gander at me.

"At any rate," she went on, "I needed to help you both out. You're both made for one another. Yet, in the long run, something Amy will get under your skin. When that occurs, you will recollect this discussion and the amount you value everything about Amy. What an incredible individual and companion she is. How athletic and excellent she is. How much fun she is. Also, in particular, how underhanded she is. She can be a guiltless young lady, an intelligent competing accomplice, and each man's wet dream—any way she picks. Do you hear what I'm saying?"

"I think you know the response to that, Jennifer."

"Advise me, Eric, so you'll recall. What is it about Amy that you enjoy most?"

"She simply quite loads of amusing to be near. She causes me to remain alert, positively."

"She's your equivalent, Eric. She's your sidekick, presently and until the end of time. There aren't numerous that can make that cut."

"A little commendation for me? I don't think I've at any point heard that from you, Jennifer. I'm complimented."

She grinned, a wide, certified grin from somewhere inside. "I generally give my #1 individuals the most hellfire. On the off chance that you'd attempted your karma with me, Eric, you may be shocked where it would have driven. In any case, I'm cheerful you didn't. Amy is the young lady for you, and you are certainly the kid for her. Ensure you love her. She's shining so brilliant at present; I'll realize when you're not treating her right."

I snickered. "You have a method of simply knowing things, Jennifer."

"What's more, even I fail to understand the situation, some of the time," she moped. Her green eyes fixed on mine. "I need to withdraw a specific assertion I made about what ladies need and don't need."

I felt my cheeks get hot. "I'll give you a pass on whatever it is that is no joke."

Jennifer laughed. "Amy, let me free similarly. It was amusing to make her wriggle—the odds don't come that regularly. You by the same token."

I grinned back at her.

"In some cases, quietly makes the most intelligent answer, does it not?" she said gently.

"In reality."

Jennifer burst out snickering. "This little meeting is significantly more fun than I suspected it would be."

"You have an intriguing origination of the word 'fun,' however at that point do as well, I."

"Thus does Amy," Jennifer added. "Presently, I wouldn't manage my work without separating, in any event, something more that you enjoy about her. Any thoughts?"

"Definitely," I said, investigating Jennifer's eyes. "Amy dives deep—way profound. There's a great deal to investigate, and I like investigating."

"Both your answers were about who Amy is within, and that has a backbone. Certainly, she's perfect. However, there are other dazzling young ladies. Me, for example."

I dunked my head in affirmation.

"However, there's nobody very like her, is there?"

"That is the thing that my heart advises me." Wow, I had said a ton.

Jennifer grinned. "Much obliged for sharing that, Eric. You let your gatekeeper down a piece; however, your heart needed to. I'll save that for an uncommon time with Amy. She'll cherish you even more for advising me."

I bowed my head again. At that point, I turned upward. "Much obliged to you, Jennifer."

Those green eyes fixed on me once more. "Say more."

"Meeting me; having this discussion. It shows you care about Amy—a great deal, and that you care about me. Likewise, I can feel something coming from Amy through you. You're shining all in all too, for your companion."

"Perceptive, Eric. My pleasure. Presently, I'd best be going soon, before this meeting turns out to be more enjoyable than it ought to. You'll recall what we discussed?"

I investigated her eyes. "Indeed. I will recollect."

"Amy said she'd recall too," she added, getting up. I got up with her. She inclined in and kissed me on the cheek. "Fortunate fiend," she murmured before turning around and strolling off. I realized she needed me to ponder who she implied. In any event, I got an opportunity to look at her as she danced out the entryway—she realized she looked great.

"Decent woman," the barkeep advertised.

"Very," I concurred.

I called Amy when I got to the vehicle. She didn't reply.

Afterward, she called.

"We both chuckled when your call came in. We had a wagered on what amount of time it would require."

"Indeed, even I'm savvy enough to assemble my young lady after conference one of her companions for a beverage."

Amy chuckled. "I'm taking you out this evening, Eric. Jennifer gave an exceptionally certain report on her little mission. Said that you were unbelievable—that you did everything right. She needed to stretch out the great parts—a lot to advise me in one day. You should have truly turned on the appeal."

"I'm adulating her if this doesn't work out."

Amy's snicker made me giggle also. "At any rate, Mr. Comic, get here."

Amy offered me an incredible supper, her radiance elevating the great vibes. Driving back, she investigated.

"Jennifer enlightened me concerning how she dressed to execute and how you enjoyed her yet kept your look cautiously on her eyes. She unquestionably saw that you needed to breeze through her little assessment. Might you want to go along with me for another little test this evening? This time, it's about the amount you can take a gander at all of my body."

"I like that test."

"I figured you would."

We spent another extraordinary end of the week together, including some incredible lovemaking. We kept in contact via telephone during the week, intending to meet Friday after work. Sleep time Thursday night, my telephone rang.

"Hi, Amy, what's going on with you?" I replied.

Her voice was low and guttural. "I need something truly downright awful; you're the solitary individual who can offer it to me."

My chicken mixed—this sounded intriguing. "Anything. How might I help?"

"Anything? I'll need to consider that. Yet, I understand what I need at this moment. I'm laying bare on my bed, face down. There are candles all over. I need something from you, seriously, profoundly. Would you be able to come over and help?"

My cockerel was rock hard. "I'll be directly finished."

"Leave your garments by the entryway. Rush."

I rushed, opening and facilitating her entryway open to see delicate candlelight. I stepped in, bolted the entryway behind me, and leaped out of my garments. A path of candles drove back to her room. I followed them to the glimmering light pouring from her open entryway.

"Amy..." my breath trapped in my throat.
"Eric. Much thanks to you such a great amount for coming." She was loosened up on the bed, candles all over, and a container of ointment close to her rear end. My heartbeat jumped in any event 30 pulsates.

"I'm so animated, so horny, so disappointed," she proceeded. "Do you understand what I need?"

I peered down to see her legs marginally spread, her knees drove into the bed, and her rear end pushing into the air. Her hands were under her chest, playing with her nipples.

"I think I have it sorted out," I laughed. "Furthermore, I can assist with your little issue." I loosened up on my side adjacent to her. "Might you want to cuddle once more into me and let me play with you for a piece?"

"Ohhhh, I'd love that," Amy answered, folding once again into me. Her can discovered my rooster, and she wriggled until I was settled safely between her cheeks. She pushed back hard, groaning and crushing. I stretched around to palm a bosom, testing its weight and feeling the hard stub of her nipples sticking out. I accumulated my fingers and pressed the nipples, hauling them out and curving.

"Yeesssss," she murmured, pushing her butt into my cockerel. I felt the slight harshness of her butt haul along the underside. Amy was ablaze, and I let her fabricate the warmth higher. She undulated into me for a few minutes, and her butt kept climbing until the top of my chicken discovered her secondary passage. She murmured and wound, attempting to get me inside her. My precum had slicked everything back there, and Amy stressed to utilize that as oil. I grinned to myself—she needed it terrible. She was exactly where I needed her.

"OK, angel. Back on your belly."

"Ummmmmm." She turned over and spread her legs, climbing her can up. I got the ointment and showered some over a finger, at that point, slid it down to prod her opening. She wriggled under me, battling to get my finger further in her rear end. At last, I kept my finger still to allow her to pierce herself. With a long groan, she lifted her butt, and my finger slid inside without any problem. Amy began shaking her hips, siphoning my finger to and fro. I could feel how loosened up she was as I began winding inside her. On one of her pushes, I pushed too.

"Oh," she murmured when I reached as far down as possible, the remainder of my hand possessively palming her butt. I let her enjoy the vibe of giving over her rear end for some time; at that point, I gradually pulled out to the sound of her whining.

I showered more lube on two fingers now and moved them back to her opening. All the more tenderly this time, I let her wriggle against them and gradually draw them inside. Her external ring-opened effectively; however, I stopped at her inward ring. Amy murmured, and I felt her unwind and push out. My fingers moved internally, and I stopped, retreated somewhat; at that point, let her draw them inside once more. In a couple of cycles, I was covered once more to another moan of fulfillment from Amy.

Once more, I let Amy push into me while I tenderly curved my fingers, loosening up the full circuit of her sphincter. I likewise fixed on Amy, learning about her fervor level and her availability for additional. She was turned on yet additionally profoundly loose, completely partaking in the thing we were doing together. I could discover no tension of what was to come. My eyes revealed to me a similar story. Amy's body squirmed under me; her fingers braced to her nipples.

"You prepared for me inside you?"

"I thought you'd never ask," she reacted from someplace far away. Before I could say much else, she drew her knees forward and lifted herself, climbing her rear end into the air with my fingers covered inside. I saw her draw her arms in and raise her chest too, laying on her elbows with her arms crossed under her, pulling at her hanging nipples. I didn't think it conceivable; however, my rooster solidified further at sight. I let her become acclimated to this new position; at that point, I flipped the top open on the lube and showered another segment onto my rooster with my other hand.

I rearranged forward and rested the top of my rooster adjacent to my fingers, sawing all through her.

"Eric. If it's not too much trouble."

I yielded and gradually pulled out my fingers to another delicate cry from Amy. I got the top of my chicken situated at her passageway and let her set the tone. She moaned and gradually propelled herself back. I felt the head open up her external sphincter; at that point, I felt the pressing factor from the internal ring. Amy stepped back somewhat, at that point pushed back once more. Her inward ring gradually extended, feeling like a delicate wave riding along the top of my chicken. It wasn't such a lot of infiltrating feeling as it was a feeling of her unwinding. Out of nowhere, the pressing factor facilitated.

"Gracious, God," she murmured. We both realized that I was in. Amy stopped to acclimate to the new sensations; at that point, she began shaking her hips gradually, drawing me more profound and afterward pulling back. Her passage was a heater, washing my cockerel in fluid warmth and pressing factor. I watched my rooster logically sink into her until her cheeks contacted my crotch.

"This feels so great," she relaxed.

"This feels fabulous," I replied. Indeed, she felt so fabulous that I drew my concentrate totally onto her, deferring the spring of gushing lava working inside me. I followed my fingers over her legs and back, feeling the sparkles stream between us. Amy crookedly contorted her hips, investigating and drawing out all the sensations inside and around her can. Her groans and whines authenticated the crude delight flowing through her body. I gradually pushed and pulled, letting her control the speed and profundity.

At that point, I saw it—the development of one of her hands back between her legs. She dropped her head down to consistent herself on the bed, and afterward, she moaned as her fingers discovered her elusive folds.

She began moderate, not having any desire to race to climax excessively fast. I could tell: she was mixing the new sensations from her rear end with the recognizable shiver of her pussy lips. I let her investigate.

Before adequately long, her body changed gear, and she moved from the conditional to the sure. He can be pushed back hard, and I met her pushes. She moaned, crushing her hips each time we reached as far down as possible. Her fingers got a move on her pussy, incidentally stimulating my balls. Amy was in the zone, ass brimming with rooster and cherishing it.

Is there anything better than this? A perfect lady turned on to excess, moving on the finish of my cockerel. Even better, she adored me, and if I was straightforward with myself, I cherished her comparably much.

Amy's breath presently came in snorts, coordinated with her shaking into me. We began to skip into one another, and I got her hips to pull her back with power.

"Goodness, screw yes," she moaned. Her fingers gave her pussy an exercise that I could feel in her rear end. Enough messing about. She was pushing for a climax—presently.

"That is it, child," I empowered. "Ride it hard." I crushed down on the ejection, taking steps to blow inside me, trusting I could make it until Amy was prepared.

"Gracious, better believe it. I'm going to cum soon," she gasped. Little pinpricks of work broke out on her skin. She pushed, and bent, and wheezed her way into unadulterated desire. I could feel her muscles tense, and afterward, I knew it: she was past the final turning point.

"I'm cumming!" she shouted and smashed into me. I met her and hung on. Her voice broke up into throaty snorts and groans as she came, hard. Her rear end beat around my bar and afterward bounced back, making her screech in enjoyment. Her climax tore my own from profound inside me, and I yelled as my semen battled and erupted past her grasping sphincter, multiplying the joy.

My memory of the following a few minutes is murky, involved as I was by thoughtless happiness. Nonetheless, I have a dream of Amy tossing her head back, gutting out a climax that was so ground-breaking it was practically difficult. She whimpered and groaned through the withdrawals, really imprudent of what she resembled.

We gradually returned to the real world, jerking with the delayed repercussions as usual. Amy measured her pussy, and I remained somewhere inside her, the two of us drawing out the last leftovers of our association.

"Gracious. My. God." Amy at last shouted.

"Soul-smashing?"

"For sure."

I grinned. "You were genuinely delightful."

Amy laughed. "So you think a young lady shouting out in thoughtless bliss is lovely, huh?"

"Without fail."

We ultimately got unraveled and set down close to one another for a rest.

"Like to share a shower before we rest?" Amy inquired.

"Showering with a lovely young lady? I'm generally up for that."

"Presumably. Presently go kick the water off, entertaining person."

I stood and offered a hand out to her. She grinned and took it, glancing brilliant in her post-orgasmic sparkle. She shooed me into the restroom to kick the water off. While I was changing the splash, I detected her coming in and putting something on the fenced-in shower area's highest point.

At the point when I ventured back to allow the water to warm, she pulled me to her for an embrace and kiss.

"Much obliged to you, Eric. That was fabulous."

"Amy, similar to what I said previously. I don't think you should express gratitude toward me."

She giggled. "Keep up the commendations, Eric. You'll get wherever with them."

She tried things out and pulled me inside. We began soaping each other up, and I could detect something energetic in her blue eyes. At the point when I got to her bosoms, she gasped and groaned.

"Get them truly spotless," she said a little energetically. My rooster blended. This young lady kept on astounding me.

Amy came up and kissed me. "Possibly, if I pivot, your hands will fit them better." With that, she spun around and settled back against me. I took my hands back to her bosoms, and she moved my chicken between the cheeks of her butt.

"No doubt. Ridiculously, clean," she coordinated. At the point when she shifted her head back for a kiss, my rooster solidified. She groaned into my mouth and began granulating her can maneuver into me.

She was hot and needing. Her nipples hardened in my grasp, and I took them in my fingers. Amy murmured her consent, and I began rolling the hard stubs. She can be moved around my chicken, and I accept her groans as clues to press and pull her nipples harder. Amy's tongue consumed in my mouth.

Amy broke our kiss to curve her back, and I felt the slight unpleasantness of her butt haul along the underside of my cockerel.

"I could do it once more—on the off chance that you need to," she said, glancing back at me.

"Is it accurate to say that you are certain?"

"Lube's up on the railing. That disclose to you how sure I am?" she said energetically. If her words didn't persuade me, I had her body crushing all over me for proof of her energy.

For an answer, I dropped my hands onto her can cheek and pulled them separated, crushing my rooster profound into her break.

"Gracious, God," she shouted, smashing her butt back against me. I got my hands back on her bosoms and pressed her nipples hard. Amy was in the mind-set to need it somewhat harsher.
"Yesssss," she murmured. I let her crush against me, topping her energy level.

After a spell, her butt moved, and I realized she was searching out the top of my cockerel. I dropped a hand to control it to her pucker, and she groaned. I reared up to the divider and inclined toward it, letting her direct the pressing factor she needed to apply.

Amy tried to understand, granulating back against me. She bent and squirmed her rear end, attempting to pull me inside with the abundant pre-cum spilling out of my cockerel. The head had just vanished into her inviting external ring. Alright, she truly needs it, I pondered internally. I came up to get the lube, not needing her enthusiasm to push things excessively quickly.

"Ummmmm," Amy murmured when she heard the snap of the container. I thought about releasing her straight with my rooster; however, I saved that for one more day. She may need a little agony later on, yet these first occasions should be loose and simple. I sprinkled some lube over a finger and began a similar delicate extending routine I did previously. Amy made it go quicker this time—she was hot to jog. When she was sawing effectively on two fingers, I got my chicken lubed and put it at her passage.

"Goodness, definitely," she inhaled, and she began pushing once more into me. With me inclining toward the divider, Amy was in finished control. She went much quicker than I would have, and soon my head could feel the velvet touch of her inward ring opening up. Amy kept consistent tension on me, and I slid past.

We panted together, lost in the sensations. Amy worked to and fro, driving me profound into her. At the point when her cheeks contacted my crotch, she moaned in triumph. On the two or three strokes, she had her cheeks straightened against me.

"God, this is acceptable," she shouted, delighting in the capacity to do anything she desired. I could feel increasingly more of her weight pin me back as she pushed further than I could at any point have done. I watched her hand sneak down between her legs, and I got my own hands back on her swollen nipples, coordinating the pressing factor she concerned me.

Amy began contorting her can with each stroke, getting bunches of skin contact before straightening against me. Her fingers worked her pussy with firm strokes that I could feel through my chicken.

Luckily, I had exhausted my balls into her once effectively tonight, so I had the option to unwind about blowing it too early. I reclined and enjoyed seeing Amy's body squirming in delight, her hair hanging in wet strands down her back. This was all her, and she was cherishing working my chicken profound into her guts.

Amy's fingers got a move on, and I felt them move to focus on her clit. I let my body react to hers, and she drew me along the street to the peak. My cockerel pistoned easily in the hot, tight touch of her back passage.

Her heaves expanded in pitch, and her fingers sped to a haze. My climax pooled in my balls, and the pressure transmitted out through my appendages. I peered down, and Amy's body was unbending, simply shaking on her feet to hammer into me.

"Gracious, God, I'm cumming once more!" she cried, and afterward, I felt the fits tear through her can. Amy lost it, shaking and snorting roughly through another unbelievable climax. Her peak dispatched my own, and I blew another heap profound into her entrails. I had barely sufficient synapses working on getting Amy to hold her back from falling over in the shower.

Much the same as in the past, we both whimpered and jerked our way back to earth.

"Amazing." I didn't have the foggiest idea of what else to say.

"Soul-smashing," she said and laughed. I jerked with my touchy rooster still in her can making her snicker stronger. We both wound up chuckling even though wheezes accentuated my snickers.

"Should I show leniency?" she inquired.

"If it's not too much trouble."

Amy tenderly pulled forward, and I gradually pulled out from her passage. Her sphincter shut over my head, and we both bounced a little as I pulled free. Amy extended back upstanding and turned around. I investigated her eyes and pulled her nearby for a kiss.

"You're unrealistic," I moaned when we pulled back.

Amy's blue eyes moved, and she stuck me to the divider for another long kiss.

In the end, we unraveled and got tidied up, this time with no further extracurricular exercises. We got each other dry, and I kept Amy's give over to the bed. We moved in and spooned together, expressing gratitude toward one another for the night and both falling profoundly sleeping.

The caution pulled us back from our sleep. We bounced in for another speedy shower.

"Last time we were in here, you exploited me," Amy said energetically.

"Uh, right," I replied. "I view at it more as assisting an urgent lady with getting what she painfully required."

"What's more, you did it so well. Possibly I'll require you to do that once more."

"I sure as damnation trust so."

Amy chuckled and smacked my can.

"Thus, advise me, Amy," I proceeded. "What might you have done if I was unable to come over?"

Amy gazed toward me, straight at me. "How about we see, Eric. I call you and offer a night with an ideal piece of ass. Some way or another, I had an inclination that you'd acknowledge. Yet, on the off chance that you hadn't been home, I surmise I would have quite recently fantasized about what might occur and deal with it myself. Understand what I mean?"

I chuckled. "I do. Also, you're correct. You have my number similar to your butt."

"Incidentally," she said, gazing toward me. "It was phenomenal. I'm happy I've done this little project as you would prefer. As you said, when

I'm that horny, I think just about the positive sentiments to come, and I'm completely loose about the thing we're doing."

"I'm happy you cooperated, Amy. You've been stunning."

"So are the climaxes. 'Soul-smashing' is correct. I can't accept how extreme they are."

"Your secondary passage needs to contract during your climax. However, my rooster forestalls that. You can then bounce back outward, extraordinarily expanding the delight. So now you get it."

"I 'got it' okay!" We both giggled and wrapped up, getting each other tidied up. After another seething kiss, I immediately halted my place to get some new garments and will work.

We went through one more end of the week together and wound up Sunday night at Amy's place. She made us supper, and we competed and giggled our way through another dinner.

I whirled the wine in my glass and investigated at Amy. "I believe it's an ideal opportunity to talk about something."

"Indeed?" she replied, her face a smidgen more genuine.

"However much I've delighted in it, I think we've satisfied a restricted meaning of our unique bundle bargain."

A touch of shading colored her cheeks. "I'll need to concur that you are right. However, you said 'slender.' What may a more extensive definition incorporate?"

I reclined. "A more extensive definition would be thorough in a literal sense. It could require some investment—quite a while—to satisfy. It's most likely something we'd need to consider before submitting ourselves."

Amy took a gander at me for quite a while. Her eyes shimmered. "I think you'll see me willing to examine the points of interest of a far-reaching bargain whenever you're prepared." She let that wait noticeably all around. "Meanwhile, I'm glad to expand the first arrangement with extra special care. It's been functioning admirably for me."

At last, we dedicated to an "extensive" arrangement, and I understood that a lifetime was too short to even think about understanding everything about Amy—goddess, mother, companion, sweetheart. She stayed "horny and baffled" all through, and I was glad to mitigate her strains and hold her indirect access fulfilled. She reddened a piece when the children got some information about how Mommy and Daddy met; however, we got by with the tale of us "living in a similar condominium unpredictable and running into one another constantly." Maybe sometime we'll tell the children somewhat a greater amount of reality.

Get up to 10 eBooks Totally FREE?!

If you are a devourer of erotic books and would like to receive up to 10 books immediately and totally **FREE** of charge, all you have to do is register for my list!
See below for more details!

Benefits of registration:

As a member of the list, you will receive the following benefits:

- 2 FREE books upon registration

- After registration, you have the possibility to get 8 additional books totally free of charge.
- The chance to have access in a totally free way - FOREVER AND AT ANY TIME - to ALL THE BOOKS already published and all of those that will be later on!
- The chance to participate in the creation of future books that I will publish!

I always listen to the ideas and requests of my readers and I strive to bring new and intriguing stories for all tastes.

You will have the opportunity to let me know not only what you think of my books, but also to suggest particular ideas such as the topics, settings, or characteristics of the main characters in the stories!

Every month, I will choose a proposal from the list of subscribers and make it into an erotic story.

If your idea is chosen, ONLY IF YOU WANT IT, you can be mentioned as a special thank you in the story!

Go to the link below and register now!

http://bit.ly/Scarlett_Collins

I really hope you enjoyed the book!

As you know, Amazon and the community rely on people like yourself for feedback on products so that others can also be informed about what they are buying. A little of your time and a few brief words goes a long way!

If you feel like giving me a TON of help, please leave me a positive review on Amazon! It really helps and encourages me to write more and more and give it my all!

Inside the Gallery
(Anal Sex)

A more seasoned man meets a young lady, hot sex resulting

Scarlett Collins

1. The Meeting:

We meet, go to the 'Drama,' and then kick the bucket is projected!

~

She stood 5'9", potentially more, on thick heels around 3" high. She had blonde mid-length hair on a charming, open, somewhat Asiatic face. Standing sideways on to me, her perfect figure drew my consideration. She probably had some compassionate sense since she turned and met my eyes, giving me a little half-grin. The full face on, I could see her high cheekbones and eyes with a slight inclination which highlighted a, perhaps, Eastern European or Eurasian birthplace. I guessed she was 20-ish and stood apart among all the wonderful youthful things drifting about the show for me at any rate.

For a longish stay in Australia, I was visiting the display with my sibling who lived in Sydney. He was a companion of one of the photographic artists displaying and had hauled me along for some ethical help. I wouldn't fret, for I had booked in for three evenings at one of the lodgings close to the Opera House that neglected the harbor and scaffold. He was returning to suburbia where he resided, leaving me to investigate.

I'm apprehensive I gazed! She had dismissed currently, visiting with two lady friends, and I set eyes on the most lovely pair of hips and a brilliantly wide and shapely base. I can sincerely say that she blew my mind! Her high-obeyed shoes push her base out provocatively beneath the swell of her streaming hips. I should add that her legs, exposed, I thought, were likewise solid and shapely. She was, without a doubt, a joy, especially for an ardent baseman such as myself. The short, evaded dress she wore emphasized her shape as it dangled from her hips, scarcely coming to past her shapely thighs. Indeed! I gazed, and she got me! It didn't appear to upset her notwithstanding, as, investigating her shoulder, she streaked me another timid half-grin.

Well? Did I think? Maybe? I should concede I would be astonished at the same time, as I had just been depicted as 'recognized,' I may, in any event, have a great time conversing with her. Look - I'm no oil painting, and at what I thought was multiple times her age, I didn't expect she'd be intrigued. I was separated, so single, and allowed to 'play' so - here goes!

She turned around sideways as individuals blended and again - a third time - streaked a half-grin, more certain this time. I grinned back a welcome. She didn't dismiss. However, she reacted with a revolting grin and went to confront me. Seeing her all out wasn't a failure! Little breasted, with stunning ladylike slanting shoulders, she was ridiculously beautiful and, I suspected, maybe a couple of years more established than I had first suspected.

I stood and strolled over. She didn't dismiss however met my eyes with hers as her companions saw me. "Hello," I said, grinning and, unfortunately, overstating my English pronunciation, "some decent pictures?" OK, not the unique line, but rather, it was a display, and it was a presentation of photos.

She grinned back, "Mmm. You're English!?"

I giggled and bowed my head in affirmation. "Indeed," I said, "for my wrongdoings, I am. Also, you are Australian!"

She giggled back, playing the game. "Amusing spot to discover somebody right from England!" So I clarified that I was on vacation visiting my sibling and that he was a companion of one of the exhibitors. I was astonished, truly for she appeared to be truly intrigued. Her eyes didn't appear to leave mine, and I felt an unmistakable 'shock' of fascination as we talked.

I proceeded to clarify that I was remaining in Sydney throughout the end of the week in one of the lodgings sitting above Circular Quay. I guess that that disclosed to her I was really rich. Forget about it, I was!

I figured out how to prise her away from her companions to acquaint her with my sibling. I could see from the old delinquent's face that he completely appreciated her excellence. He encouraged me out by hauling us both further away from her two companions to meet his picture taker buddy then they floated off together, letting us be.

Indeed, faint heart never screwed a pig, as we used to say at home in this way, "Look, I realize we have just barely met; however would you do me the honor of permitting me to get you supper?" She wavered, not astonishing truly as we had just barely met yet, I guess, my sibling and realizing an exhibitor worked in support of myself. I floated on tossing alert to the breezes. "I can guarantee you of shining mind and repartee and lovely discussion. What's more, you can pick the absolute best eatery." She giggled.

"Mmm . . . Alright," she said after a slight faltering, and modestly I thought. Maybe she wasn't unreasonably capable. At that point, she grinned, "When does the shimmering mind start?"

I chuckled accordingly, "Well played!" I said at that point, "will we go now?" I needed to get moving in a hurry - I didn't need this exquisite young lady to adjust her perspective.

She grinned once more, "Mmm, OK. When I know your name!"

"There!" I said happily, "Your magnificence so overpowers me that I'm failing to remember the basic kindnesses. My name is Mike Watson. Reasonable," I giggled, "presently reveal to me yours!"

Another grin, "Gina, Gina Ventakova."

"Is that Russian?"

"Mmm, path back, however."

"It suits you." It did!

"I should tell my companions," she said, "we should be going out together!"

"I'm complimented," I grinned. She grinned back, again bashfully, I thought.

"I don't ordinarily yield so effectively," she said with an anxious chuckle at that point, "yet . . ."

"I know," I chuckled, "I advised you - it's the shining mind! Will we discover your companions? You can present me - and make them desirous," I added with a major grin.

She chuckled again, and we cleared our path through the jam-packed room where I was put on an act'. I could see two sets of eyebrows raise as Gina revealed to them I was taking her out to supper, and afterward, one said suddenly, "Hell Gina, you've just barely met him!"

Gina streaked me a humiliated grin and shrugged her shoulders. "I like him," she said.

"Be that as it may, . . .!"

I chuckled, "Women - please. Gina will be completely protected with me! I can offer my visa as a guarantee on the off chance that you wish!"

"Try not to be dumb, Megan," said Gina, "both of you go on."

"However, Jake's anticipating us all!"

"He'll need to 'unexpected me at that point, will not he!" Gina reacted abruptly. She took my arm, "I know simply the spot for supper! 'Bye, both of you!" She drove me out of the exhibition into the road.

"Who's Jake?" I asked delicately. I would not like to be the reason for a wrecked relationship nor get her on the bounce back.

"He's Megan's life partner," she said. "Bleeding torment!"

"Alright," I said, calmed, "where to?"

"Anyplace?"

"Obviously. It's your night." She caused a commotion. I said, "- in any case, any place you pick will be hugely improved by your quality!"

She becomes flushed and chuckled anxiously, "Toady. Would we be able to go to Aria?" she asked rapidly.

Well, I realized that Aria was a pricey café close to the Opera House however chose to play oblivious. "Aria?"

"Mmm, I've for the longest time been itching to go there."

"At that point, you will!" I flagged down a taxi, and off we went. The night was a joy. Gina's character was both complex and credulous simultaneously. I turned on all the 'polite' ascribes dealing with her like a princess. The eatery was enchanting, and the food brilliant. Before the finish of the supper, I had discovered about her. She was just about 22 and at Sydney University considering Art. I accumulated that she didn't have a current sweetheart; however, her tone and way, especially her dress, made me figure she wasn't unpracticed in-room expressions!

We left the eatery to blend with the Friday night swarms processing around the Quay and the Opera House at last halting for espresso at the Opera bar.

"What time do I need to get you home?" I asked happily.

"Well . . ." she reacted reluctantly, "I was remaining with Megan, so I wasn't normal back around evening time. Any time I assume . . ." Was she indicating something here? I didn't know.

"Well, there's bounty going on here." There was: a lot of individuals processing about in bars and eateries after the drama.

"Mmm. I like it here."

Time to attempt to enchant! Not hard for reclining across from her crossed legs left little to the creative mind. "I like it here as well," I said, grinning, "the view is wonderful!"

She becomes flushed, "Goodness!" and uncrossed her legs.

I snickered, "Sorry," I said, "couldn't avoid it! Truly, however," I added discreetly, "tonight has been a pleasure; made so by your quality!"

She becomes flushed, and she grinned. Maybe she wasn't utilized to such disgusting applause? We visited for a long time as I revealed to her something about England and London. It more likely than not been near noon, and groups were diminishing when I, at last, chose to dive in.'

"Gina," I said delicately, putting my hand on hers, "Gina - might you want to return to my space for a last nightcap before I get you home?" The expression all over plainly showed she understood precisely the thing I was proposing. If she concurred, she wouldn't leave the room until morning, and she knew it! She faltered long enough for me to understand this would be another thing for her. Her eyes had broadened in shock at the outright proposal, and I immediately chose to ease off.

"Gina, love, how about we get you a taxi. I'm heartbroken!" I made to stand.

Her hand halted me. "I haven't chosen," she said unobtrusively, "I probably won't return home!" I took a full breath. Men of my age didn't regularly get to this situation with a delightful 22-year-old understudy—especially one with a figure to pass on for.

I felt that presently was the time. She would or she wouldn't! "There is a sofa!" I chuckled.

"Alright!" she said and stood. My eyes went here and there, her body taking in her lovely hips and base. She looked as I respected her, and I don't think I envisioned her slight dress!

"Sure?"

"Certain," she grinned. "Lead the way!" So we advanced back to my lodging.

~

2. At the Hotel:

In which we have intercourse, talk about butt-centric sex, and make arrangements for the remainder of the end of the week:

~

The 'condo' comprised of a kitchen close to an eating territory: at that point, a parlor prompting an overhang sitting above the Quay and the Harbor Bridge. The different rooms bordered the open washroom with a Jacuzzi and stroll-in shower. I had been dazzled, and Gina was too.

"There," I said as we entered, "you can have the bed; I'll take the lounge chair!"

She chuckled, appearing quiet now as she understood I was giving her an 'out.' "That doesn't appear to be reasonable," she said, "it is your room!"

"Alright," I said, giggling, "I'll take the bed; you take the lounge chair!"

She snickered accordingly then checked out the entryway into the room. "It's an exceptionally large bed!"

I took another full breath. "Espresso?" I asked, not having any desire to push excessively hard. Her reaction was to move close.

"No," she murmured discreetly, "not quite recently!" Her eyes gazed upward into mine and her lips separated. Hands pulled my head downwards, and we kissed. I'd felt a shock previously - presently, it was more grounded.

My hands wandered her back and shoulders as I kissed her while hers held me close. Heart pulsating, I permitted my hands to follow her hips' delicate bend then the strong swell of her base. This acquired a murmur her kiss. We broke, and my lips kissed her neck and shoulders, facilitating aside the lashes of her dress. Moving marginally separated, then we kissed and stroked. Her hands crawled inside my shirt and stroked my chest.

Kisses turned out to be more energetic and tongues laced - she was, in a real sense, blowing my mind! Moving endlessly again, she kept on unfastening my shirt and run her fingers through the hairs on my chest - extremely refreshing.

"Turn round," I murmured. She didn't dispute and transformed, gradually, pushing once more into me. I moved away, my hands slipping to her thighs underneath her short dress. I heard a sharp admission of breath as my hands felt the glow of her skin. I started to lift the dress, hands following the flawless bend of her hips. I felt her undies as my hands proceeded with their excursion, and the dress was lifted higher. Peering down, I could see her meager lilac pants - not exactly a strap and unmistakably inadequate to cover the brilliant reach of her base, vanishing between her disgusting cheeks. At her midsection now and back to warm tissue, my hands proceeded with the excursion.

It appeared to be the dress would fall off this way, so I continued. Gina moaned as I contacted her bra ties. At that point raised her arms upward. The dress slipped over her head effectively and was tossed to the floor. God, she was/is flawless. I remained back, devouring my eyes on a scanty lilac bra and considerably skimpier underwear.

"Wow!!" I oversaw as she turned around to confront me.

"Not reasonable," she mumbled as she took off my shirt at that point, began my jeans. These immediately joined shirt on the floor, and my cockerel, as hard as it had at any point been, was allowed to tent my fighters. She more likely than not felt it - I unquestionably felt her! We were all the while standing, kissing, and stroking. The time had come to move to the bed! Slipping hands around her body, I lifted her and conveyed her into the room. Laying her delicately on the bed, I stood peering down at this lovely young lady.

I grinned, "You're excellent," I murmured delicately, and I lay next to her. She becomes flushed imploringly. Moving ahead on the elbow, I bowed and kissed her lips. "Sure?" I murmured. She gestured in answer.

My hand-measured her smallish bosoms at that point crawled under the bra and prodded her areolas. A delicate moan got away from her lips. "Turn over," I murmured. I needed to fix the bra, yet I needed to see her base this way significantly more. Eyes broadened being referred to. "Bra," I said cheerfully.

She grinned back and drowsily turned face down. I fixed her bra and drew it off over her shoulders; then I bowed up. As in the past, she blew my mind! Her hips, wide and shapely, streamed into her base—a practically wonderful shape. 'Air pocket butts' are decent, yet Gina has the lower part of a goddess - wide with amazing bends. Cheeks firm with a slight up bend as they met her legs. Her underwear, caught between her exquisite cheeks, made the entire scene considerably hotter. The slight wetness as the material measured her pussy showed her excitement. My hands on her hips, I tenderly moseyed her undies down, uncovering her most private spot. As I slipped them off, Gina opened her legs marginally, wriggling crookedly to get settled. The valley between her cheeks was open now, her small star visible - accessible. Her sex is likewise totally visible in this position. She was an outright pleasure.

I more likely than not hushed up for some time, basically taking in the view for Gina, turning somewhat and breaking my dream, said, "What . . .?"

"I'm heartbroken," I said happily, "yet you have the most awesome base! I was simply respecting the view!" She reddened and grinned.

"I haven't done that," she said, meeting my eyes. My psyche faltered! What did she say? Heart beating and, unexpectedly, chicken starting to pulsate considerably more, I caused a stir being referred to.

"Sorry?"

"I haven't done that," she said once more, "you know. I'm certain you do!"

I was starting to turn out to be very energized because, if she implied what I figured she did, she was a 'butt-centric virgin.' So I chose to be cautious. "Gina, love, I don't know what you mean?"

She snickered, seeing through me, I think. "I figure you do, "she said, "look, and she gestured at my chicken, which was standing considerably prouder. Future time clean [or dirty?].

"You mean you've never engaged in sexual relations in your base," I said, holding my breath.

"Mmm. I haven't. Have you?" she asked abruptly, "I wager you have!"

"Well," I addressed gradually, "if you mean have I at any point done that to a lady, at that point yes."

"A ton?" God, this discussion was raising my circulatory strain!

"A considerable amount," I answered genuinely.

"Is it pleasant?"

I giggled, "I delighted in it."

"No! You understand what I mean. I've seen it [that I just needed to explore!]. It appears to be pleasant, however . . .?"

"Well," I said gradually and cautiously, "the vast majority of my accomplices have delighted in it."

"Does it hurt? It doesn't look as though it harms the young ladies in the movies [Wow!?] yet it must? Most likely?"

"Gina, love, you are annihilating me!" She snickered. I giggled in kind.

"Advise me! Does it hurt?"

"Well," I replied with a bold grin, "to be straightforward, I've never had it done to me! I have had toys in there and, if it's done tenderly, it didn't hurt that much."

She moped, "Gracious you! You understand what I mean!"

I giggled, twisted, and kissed her cheek. "Well . . . It appears to be that occasionally it does the first run-through or two, yet most of the ladies I've had there have appreciated it. I realize I have!" As I said this, I ran my finger down her spine, sending a shudder across her body. Not having any desire to talk about it further, she moved onto her side and pulled me close.

"Kiss me," she requested as our lips met. My cockerel, rock hard now after the past conversation, was squeezing into her stomach. I felt her hand reach down inside my fighters and surround it, stroking gradually. "It feels enormous," she inhaled enthusiastically. I grinned.

"Lay back, Gina. Now is the ideal time?" An assertion and an inquiry. She could ease off now [and leave me ridiculous frustrated]; however, I needed to give her a last chance. If I screwed her, I needed her to need it. Her reaction was a major grin and a development on to her back. Her eyes responded to me!

Slipping my fighters off, at last, I facilitated her legs separated, bowed between, and looked down at her excellent youthful body. She was grinning, to some degree anxiously, I thought, and her tongue was flicking out and licking her lips. Hardened chicken in one hand, I leaned forward and took my weight on the other. With unerring exactness, my cockhead discovered her delicate warmth. As she felt the principal pressure, she let out a delicate moan; shock and joy blended. Stopped somewhat inside, I took my weight on all fours, gradually forward inclination her hot wetness.

"Gracious God!" she groaned delicately as my cockerel filled her vagina. She was tight, wicked tight, and inconceivably grand! Energized by our restricted foreplay, she was extremely wet, and I slid inside without any problem. I needed to stop briefly and take a couple of full breaths to quiet down. Recapturing a proportion of control, I started to press further until a large portion of my erection was touched in her smooth snugness. This is near paradise. Her eyes were wide in astonishment, I think, as I halted once more.

"Alright?" I asked, grinning down at her.

"Gracious God, yes! Enormous! It's large," she added energetically.

I grinned, "Too huge?"

"God help us! No! Try not to stop. Please!" Well, I wasn't going to! Alright false. I would have had she said as much - consistently had faith in a lady's entitlement to say no whenever. Presently, she said yes, so I started to move gradually to and fro, pushing a little more profound each time and dragging out her sensation of being filled.

"Gracious God! Gracious, please! I never . . . . Ooooohhhhh!" Her entire body appeared to shiver. Her vagina grasped like a bad habit as I gazed down into the eyes of a young lady in the climax. Wide-peered toward, she came to up and pulled me down, mouth covering mine in an urgent kiss. At long last, I oversaw to pull myself away from her hug and recover my position, weight on my arms. At that point, moving upstanding, I lifted her legs a little and started to screw her directly through her first climax. She appeared to be shocked that I was still hard, and her eyes enlarged further as my rooster slid to and fro inside her. Gradually from the start, then faster, harder, I filled her pussy, thighs slapping against hers.

Her moans developed stronger, and her legs came up around my midsection and held my body. Gazing at her, I could see her climax rising once more. Her pants became stronger as I bowed my head and drew my teeth tenderly along her hard areolas. Her heaves went to, "Gracious god! Indeed! Please . . ."

Seeing this stunning young lady in the pains of climax for the subsequent time brought my own nearby that I could do this for her! I expanded both profundity and speed of push as my body reacted. My balls fixed, and I felt that strained sensation in the base of my spine "Goodness, screw Gina," I groaned as spirit streamed into her.
She probably felt the beats, three or four, I think, for she groaned, "Indeed, yes! Fill me!" I did heaving as my rooster beat inside her heavenly cunt.

As could be, it didn't keep going long! My rooster mollified - not totally, but rather enough to tell me I required rest and time tore-energize. Cialis [I had taken one earlier] is an incredible help; however, rest is required between - particularly at my age - and I especially needed to re-energize. I had not tasted her pussy at this point or her tight rear-end, nor had she my rooster! At that point, there was the possibility of her exquisite arse and the chance of taking that virginity.

I moved from over her as my rooster slipped from the paradise of her cunt and lay next to her, head close by looking down. I grinned as she transformed her head and investigated my eyes. "Alright?" I murmured.

She came up and pulled my lips to hers. "Goodness yes!" she grinned, "gracious yes. It hasn't been similar to that previously." I caused a commotion. She becomes flushed as she wriggled her base easily into the bed. "I've never . . . you know . . . twice like that." I grinned. "It's constantly been finished so rapidly." She laughed. "At times, it didn't occur by any means! Much obliged to you," she murmured.

I kissed her. "I haven't wrapped up!"

She moved her hips and thighs, moving to confront me. Her eyes met mine with a stressed look. "You came inside me!" It wasn't an inquiry - she probably knew. I gestured. "I'm not . . . you know . . . taking anything."

Her importance was clear. "I have had a vasectomy," I grinned, "such a large number of years before the need to recall. So," I giggled, "no infants!" She looked concerned.

"I've never . . . you know, done it without a condom. I didn't, don't, have any desire to find anything!"

Aaaagh, I thought, presently I understand what she is inquiring. I, being modestly indiscriminate, had consistently been cautious about STDs. As a rule, I wore a condom myself, and I needed to admit to the idiocy of not wearing one at this point. I guess that I had been overwhelmed by the circumstance - the chance to screw a particularly young lady made me toss alert to the breezes [a standing prick has neither inner voice nor fear!]. I had additionally concluded that Gina didn't appear to be the sort of resting around. That legitimization may have been both self-fancy and misguided thinking, yet I didn't think so—time to put her psyche very still. I'm something of a passivist!

"I'm cautious, Gina, love. I was a few months back," I grinned and kissed her cheek, "and you are the primary." She grinned favorably.

Presently her hand came to up and pulled my lips to hers. "You said we haven't completed," she laughed coyly.

"No," I snickered back. "We should investigate the shower." Her eyebrows raised, yet she didn't challenge me as I grasped her hand and drove her to the washroom. She entered first. I remained at the entryway. I'm apprehensive I gazed! She was as near flawlessness as I could wish to envision. Her tenderly inclining female shoulders appeared to complement the offensive progression of her hips. She strolled straight, upstanding, and, even in uncovered feet, her arse was both glad and irritable. My chicken started to mix at the remotest chance of taking her there.

"You like my base?" she said abruptly.

Found napping, I immediately saw that she could see every last bit of me in the huge mirror. She probably watched my eyes and noticed my cockerel. Future time clean. "Gina, love, I will not mislead you." I grinned my cut-sided grin. "You are a wonderful young lady," she started to become flushed - it was radiant. "Furthermore, you have the absolute best arse!" Did she stand simply somewhat straighter?

I drew nearer. "I'm apprehensive, Gina, holy messenger, that that piece of a lady is the part that pulls in me most. It's not the most important thing in the world but rather, as far as I might be concerned, it is indisputably the; the what tops off an already good thing cake, I guess you could say."

She turned. "I've never done it, I said."

"I know," I murmured, taking her in my arms, "and, until further notice, we should not specify it. We should shower."

She gave me a bizarre look. Shock, frustration, delight? I didn't know yet she transformed into the shower. I followed. I immediately changed the showerheads, two, and the divider planes, and we both gloried in the progression of heated water. She was the encapsulation of beauty— a water fairy quiet bare with me in the shower. My eyes adored her. She was amazingly dazzling. She appeared to luxuriate in my profound respect and, inevitably, went after the cleanser and wipe gave.

"I've never showered with a man," she said guiltlessly.

"Well," I said, restoring her grin, "time you discovered how much fun it tends to be!" She snickered accordingly as I took the cleanser and wipe.

I started to wash her, running the wipe over her delicate bends: her shoulders, her hips, her thighs, and the great cheeks of her base. Before long, I lost the wipe and utilized my hands, focusing on her tits, catching her enormous areolas between my fingers. She started to groan delicately, then stronger as my hand meandered across her stomach and stroked her mount of Venus. My other hand touched her bare cheeks.

Before long, my hand covered her sex totally, my center finger delicately pushing on her passage and prodding her clit. Her groans expanded as I stepped my hand to and fro, squeezing somewhat harder. My other hand, which had been delicately crushing those exquisite arse cheeks, presently found the valley between. As I stroked her cunt, the center finger of this hand stroked delicately across her rear-end.

"Ooooohhh," she murmured delicately, "oooohhh yesssss!"

I could feel her legs starting to debilitate. "Put your arm around my neck," I murmured. "It'll help." Languidly her arm wound around my neck. Presently two fingers tenderly examined her cunt the delicately squeezed inside. Another finger tenderly prodded the tight star of her rear-end. I immediately found the delicate tissue of her 'G' spot and started to stroke it.

"Goodness FUCK YES!!!" she groaned. "Gracious God!" It didn't take some time before I felt her fluid stream. As it did, I squeezed more diligently on her butt, which appeared to empower an increased climax. Her legs nearly fell now, and I felt her weight against my body, so I delicately sat us both on the seat gave. She laid her head on my shoulder briefly then kissed my neck.

"That was pleasant," she murmured, then chuckled, "I think I like showering with a man!" I snickered. "My turn," she said. Then she took the wipe, pulled me up, and started to wash me. She appeared to appreciate running first the wipe, then her hands over my body. Hell, I'm no Adonis, except it created the impression that she was 'investigating' the male. She appeared especially to like investigating my cockerel and balls, and it wasn't well before I was hard once more. She grasped my cockerel, turned, and sat on the seat, pulling me with her. Bowing her head, she flicked her tongue across the tip of my chicken at that point, sucked the head inside her mouth.

"Goodness, screw Gina!" I oversaw as I felt her warm mouth overwhelm my chicken head and her lips touch the delicate zone just underneath. She gazed toward me, mouth grinning around my cockerel, as she sucked delicately on the head. It was clear she was genuinely knowledgeable about this division! Presently she started to stroke my rooster with one hand while the other supported my balls.

"Poo Gina, love, I can't take a lot of this!" She figured out how to frown around my chicken! "Gracious you darling'," I chuckled, "on the off chance that I was 20, you could, yet I'm not! I need to screw you once more!" Now she grinned up at me and sucked a greater amount of my cockerel inside. I could feel her tongue on the touchy tip - I needed to pull away!

"I need to taste that later!" she said with a steamy grin. It appeared to be the entire circumstance was drawing out the 'monster' in her!

I accept a full breath as I lifted her to her feet and kissed her on the mouth. "I'm yours to order," I giggled. Flushing off, at last, we dried each other with the warm cozy towels and slipped on the white drying robes and shoes the inn gave. She even glanced great in that!

"Would you likc a beverage?" I asked, "I'm quite parched."

"Mmmm, that would be decent," at that point with a steamy grin, "would we say we are done?"

I pulled her to me and kissed her mouth, "Goodness, Gina dear, unquestionably not. I haven't eaten at this point!" She looked confused as I smiled at her and flushed as she understood what I implied.

"Gracious! Gracious, I see!"

I kissed her again as we entered the kitchen region. I made the beverages, and we sat discreetly drinking.

"It was superb," she at long last murmured delicately, eyes meeting mine over the edge of her glass.

Time to gamble. "Gina, love," I said delicately, kissing her cheek, "do you need to be anyplace tomorrow?" I looked at the clock, "today, I mean," I chuckled. It was 2.30!

"No," she said, grinning, "why?"

"What might be said about the remainder of the end of the week?"

"No. I should remain with Megan."

"Stay with me?" I asked, taking a full breath and fixing her with my eyes.

"I don't have any garments," she said happily, "yet on the off chance that I did, I would!" She kissed my lips, "I'm certain there is a LOT more to do!"

"Garments are unquestionably not an issue," I snickered, "I like you stripped!" She giggled back. "Yet, it truly isn't an issue. We can go out in the first part of the day and get you a few."

"Get me a few?"

"Mmmm. It will be enjoyable!"

"Yet, . . ."

I snickered, "'But me no buts, '" I said. "It will be fun, I can guarantee you. We can get some pleasant hot stuff!"

"For you to take off?" she asked teasingly.

"Presently, that would be fun too!"

"Alright," she said happily, "I'll stay." She settled on the choice rapidly.

I hung over and kissed her cheek. "Great."

~

3. Having intercourse with Gina for the Second Time:

In which I investigate Gina with my tongue, we have intercourse once more, and butt-centric sex is talked about and advertised:

~

She held me. "Have intercourse with me once more," she asked delicately, "I need you once more!" I sneaked off the love seat and bowed at her feet. My hands stroked her lower legs at that point calves lastly, slipping the robe aside, her knees.

Moving into her, I murmured, "Open Gina love, open for me!" She looked stunned; however, my grin carried one to her face as she revealed herself and facilitated her legs separated. I drew nearer.

"Slide forward," I said, encouraging her until her base laid on the edge of the lounge chair. At that point, I lifted her feet to the lounge chair. She was open to me now. Her beautiful pussy on her tight butt. She looked perplexed; however, that look vanished as my mouth discovered her cunt and covered her clit.

"Oh my God!" she shouted as I sucked, "good god, don't stop!" I wasn't going to. She tasted great, new, and fruity. I sucked some more, tongue flicking her clit. Gina kept on groaning, her hands finding my head. I licked, sucked, and nibbled delicately, then moved my mouth to her sex, sucking her cunt lips and staying quiet tenderly, my tongue driving profound into her vagina. Gina squirmed as my tongue and mouth pleasured her. "Gracious fuck, yesssssss! Harder. Please!" she cried again and again as I kept on eating her flavorful pussy. I made the most of her for seemingly an age, and afterward, I pushed further and tasted her fluid stream as she shivered.

Turning upward as her climax retreated, I could see her mouth somewhat open, eyes shut. Twisting back, I proceeded my 'attack' on her pussy, sucking her under her lips before my tongue down across her perineum to the tight little star of her rear-end.

"Goodness! Gracious! Goodness!" she cried as I licked her minuscule rosebud. I lapped to and fro across it, pushing a little harder each time, at times getting back to suck her clit. At long last, I focused on the indirect access to delight itself. I rimmed her arsehole, covering it with salivation; at that point, I pushed the tip of my tongue against the tight muscle. Gina moaned and mumbled a repressed, "Indeed, indeed, yes! Do it!" I did! I licked all around the small muscle, my tongue at last pushing past the normal obstruction of her sphincter and slipping inside. She was so close! To be expected for a butt-centric virgin, I assume. I delighted in the impression of my tongue tip held in the bad habit of her sphincter, my nose squeezed to her cunt. I could taste her, cleanser, newness: the substance of her. I sneaked out of her indirect access and kept covering her rear-end without hardly lifting a finger section. A little harder, a little more profound each time, until I was tongue-screwing her arse. It was awesome - particularly as I heard her loud cry of, "Gracious fuck, yes!", felt her rear-end contract appearing to attempt to trap my tongue, and had my face shrouded in her fluid for the subsequent time.

Rapidly standing, I sneaked off my robe and held my cockerel: a chicken stone hard from my ministrations to Gina's cunt and arsehole. She took a gander at me, at that point at my cockerel, and grinned. "Screw me!" she mouthed. Hands around her lower legs, I lifted her advantages and separated, pulling her practically onto her shoulders. Inclining forward, my cockerel discovered her wet vagina and slipped inside. I was hot for her, the waiting taste and smell of her acting like a creature love potion. With little artfulness, I drove inside her filling her profundities with my chicken. I felt my balls slapping her arse as my enthusiasm rose.

Gina was groaning a consistent, "Indeed, indeed, yes! Screw me!" as I crashed to and fro into her. Such energy couldn't keep going for a long time and, as I felt one more shiver across Gina's body, I started to cum inside her. Just a few heartbeats, however, extraordinary. I drove profound, held, and covered her internal parts with my warm moxie. She is more likely than not felt it, for she muttered, "Gracious yes! Cum inside me!"

As we both descended from our highs, I moved Gina back down on the couch and, sitting close to her, embraced her. She turned her head, and we kissed.

"Goodness Mike," she murmured, "that was brilliant. I never felt like that."

"I'm happy," I said happily, "happy I could please you."

"I need to satisfy you," she said delicately.

"You do, stunningly."

"No! I need to do it!"

"Do it?" I rehashed curiously.

"There," she said, "in my arse!" I probably looked astounded. "At the point when you licked . . . Your tongue . . . It was paradise. You made me cum there! I need to . . . Check whether that," grinning, she gestured towards my gradually arousing chicken, "feels as great. In any case, you should be delicate," she added rapidly.

I grinned, "Well Gina, you holy messenger, I couldn't want anything more than to do that; however," she looked concerned, "yet I was somewhat exhausted a few seconds ago and, while the soul is willing, the substance is, shockingly, powerless." Gina looked frustrated.

"You are remaining tomorrow evening," I said happily, "so a lot of time for recuperation!"

"Indeed," she said splendidly, "I need to do it." My chicken, spent after two heavenly cums, hardened somewhat. She took note. "See," she snickered, "he is intrigued!" and she came to down and started to stroke off my delicate rooster.

"Gina, Gina, love! Please!" There was no chance I could deal with another round, and my chicken head was thus, so delicate after my last climax. "Tomorrow," I chuckled, "tomorrow I will do anything you need!"

"Mmm, I like that. Guarantee?"

"I guarantee," I giggled, "wild ponies couldn't stop me!" With that, she let go of my rooster and kissed me.

"I will hold you to that!" she murmured as we embraced one another.

"Bed, I think," I murmured, then added, chuckling, "I need my rest if I stay aware of a youthful filly like you!" Gina snickered in kind and jabbed out her tongue.

"Alright, on the off chance that you have had enough, we should hit the hay," and she got done with a major yawn.

I giggled, "I figure YOU have had sufficient young lady!" I stood and pulled her tenderly to her feet at that point drove her into the room. Gina immediately visited the washroom and was back two or three minutes. The gigantic bed looked extremely welcoming, and she immediately went along with me, and we cuddled under the covers.

Rarely do since I go directly to rest, yet holding this lovely young lady in my arm appeared to settle me totally, and I was headed toward rest in an instant.

~

4. The Morning After:

In which I investigate Gina's arse, and we have intercourse once more:

~

I hadn't set the caution or anything, so light sparkling in the window woke me at some point the following morning. As is ordinary, we had floated separated during the evening, and Gina was still sleeping. I moved onto one elbow and peered down at her. God, she was flawless! Her light hair outlined her face. Her lips were marginally open as she lay practically on her back. If I am not resting alone, I quite often wakeful with a lovely strong erection notwithstanding any past exercise, and toward the beginning of today was the equivalent. It's part want and part 'piss-glad.' It doesn't make any difference truly; it's as yet fun!

I moved the sheet a tad to uncover her energetic bosoms and, bowing my head, ran my tongue over her areola. This inspired a delicate moan from Gina and a development onto her back. I kept on licking the initial one areola than the other as they solidified. Gina wriggled her base into the bed, still evidently sleeping. It was warm in the room, so she didn't appear to see as I pulled the covers directly back, uncovering her exposure. Leaving her stunning bosoms, my tongue made a trip across her stomach to the delicate hair than to her pussy. A pussy somewhat wet as of now! My tongue dove into her wetness and, more likely than not, discovered her clit quickly, for she moaned, shivered, and mumbled, "Goodness yes!!!"

I raised my head and grinned down at her. She was conscious. "Try not to stop," she said cheerfully, "it's pleasant!" I kept dropping down the bed and between her legs. I licked here and there her sex, diving into her vagina before focusing on her clit. Moving my tongue around, I utilized my lips to chomp the swollen joy place. More groans from Gina as I proceeded to joy her. Inevitably, she shivered, and fluid streamed. I utilized my tongue on the finish of her clit directly through her climax, at that point dropped down to lick and suck her pussy lips. I could taste her newness, taste the evening, on her. At that point, to her butt. I lifted, separated her legs at that point examined her tight muscle with my tongue, pushing hard to perceive what occurred.

"Gracious indeed, yes! Do that! I need you to. Please!" I pushed more diligently at the muscle, and she loses, letting my tongue inside. I could feel her grasping firmly and had a minor emergency as I envisioned her sphincter complaining my rooster. I utilized my thumb to prod her clit again as I tongue screwed her tight arsehole. Gina was groaning a delicate reiteration of, "Indeed, indeed, yes," again and again. I appreciated this attack of her most private spot and thought the time had come to test some more, so I supplanted my tongue with my center finger after covering it with salivation and pussy juice.
"Gracious God! What . . . .?"

"My finger," I murmured, grinning. "Advise me to stop on the off chance that it is excessively." I pushed at the tip of my finger inside her. It slipped into her spit greased up arsehole, no sweat.

"Wow!"

"Alright?"

"It feels so enormous," Gina said enthusiastically. "Furthermore, that is just your finger?"

I chuckled delicately as I pushed more inside. "More?"

"I don't have the foggiest idea!"

I halted and pulled my finger back. "Alright, stop now."

"No, no! I need to attempt it. Well," she proceeded with a bashful snicker, "your finger at any rate!"

"Loosen up then, Gina, love," I said as I pushed against the muscle again, and my finger slipped back inside to the primary joint. "Alright?" I asked as I moved it to and fro, delicately screwing her tight arsehole.

"Indeed!" Gina reacted breathlessly, "Yes! I like that. Ooooohhhhh!" I had driven practically the entirety of my center finger into her arse and now started to screw her gradually with the entire length. "Goodness dear! Goodness Fuck! Indeed!" Raising my head, I investigated her eyes. She grinned, "You are a terrible man! Ohhhhhhh!" She was taking my finger somewhere down in her arse and appeared to appreciate it. I twisted my head and, proceeding to finger screw her, touched her clit with my lips.

"Indeed!" Gina cried as another climax washed over her body. Her rear-end grasped my finger firmly as she came, and her fluid streamed. Time for me now. I pulled out my finger from her arse and bowed, held my chicken, and slipped the head into her sopping pussy. My eyes bolted on hers. She grinned and gestured. I pushed forward and filled her with one driver making a noisy pant of delight escape from her lips.

Piss-pleased methods are enduring slightly more, so I started to pound her pussy long and hard. I was hot with the possibility of her tight arse around my cockerel, so I should concede I got down to business. Gina didn't appear to mind, her legs coming up and grasping me around the midriff. I twisted my head and kissed her, our tongues moving together as my cockerel drove all through her willing body. I was differing my speed presently, welcoming her on and controlling my climax. Time to analyze! How long? 10, 15, 20 minutes, I assume.

"Turn over," I said, needing a change at that point, pulling back and bowing, "and stoop." Gina looked uncertain. I grinned, "Actually, no, not that - yet at any rate - simply some assortment," I said, causing a stir.

Gina grinned, turned over, and put her perfect arse noticeable all around. I very like the pup for clear reasons, and I just stroked my cockerel tenderly as I looked at the superb sight before me. Gina knew obviously and thought back behind her with a grin.

"Please then, Mike, do your most noticeably terrible! God help us!" she shouted as she understood what she had recently said - and insinuated.

"I will do nothing like that, Gina love, not until later at any rate," and I moved marginally, planting my cockhead at her pussy.

"MMMMMMM, I like that," she murmured as I drove home. I screwed for a brief period then she turned her head once more. "Contact me!" she said happily, "contact me there!" 'Mmm,' I thought, she enjoys it! I wetted my thumb, gathered some juice from the back of her wet pussy, and stroked it over her rear-end. This brought a delicate moan and a shiver. I pushed more earnestly, not entering her rear-end, however prodding. I was close now, filling her arse with my rooster, causing expanded pressure. I screwed her increasingly hard: one hand on her hip pulling her on, the other with thumb stroking her sphincter.

It didn't take long! "Goodness, yes, Mike! If it's not too much trouble! Please!" Gina's body shivered, and her pussy held my rooster. I felt the typical pressure in my lower back, my balls fixed, and my heap - pretty little tragically - left my body and flew profound into Gina. Only a few heartbeats as her body responded to my expanding and erupting cockerel.

I was spent before long and shook out of sorts, my conditioning rooster slipping from the paradise of her vagina. Gina fell forward on the bed, moaning. As she moved onto her back, I lay on one elbow close to her. I grinned, "Well?"

"Mmm, that was decent," she mumbled and pulled my lips to hers. We kissed then lay holding one another. Inevitably she lifted herself and went to the washroom. I watched her lovely bare figure walk around the room. Her hips were so superb, and her last a fantasy. She halted at the entryway and thought back behind her. "Well? Like what you see?" she grinned teasingly, remaining on one leg and inclining toward the door jamb.

"Goodness, yes!" I giggled, "didn't I simply show that?"

She chuckled back, "Please you - shower. I need you to wash me!"

"Continuously a joy," I said at that point, "I'll request breakfast."

"Mmm, I'm starving!"

~

5. A Short Shopping Interlude:

In which we search for Gina's outfits:

~

With that, I followed her into the shower, and we went through the following 20 minutes soaping and washing one another. Gina appeared to be captivated by the male body and went through an age playing with my spent cockerel and balls. She likewise appeared to like the state of my arse! Presently I am not fit as a fiddle, and I figured how much fun she may have with a truly solid youthful body - didn't specify it, however! Breakfast was conveyed to the room soon after, and we sat on the gallery in the late morning daylight and ate. At that point, the time had come to go out and get some garments for Gina. She was humiliated from the outset. However, I should concede, I delighted in seeing her pick things. We began in her nightdress, which wasn't suitable for shopping, yet immediately bought a few pairs of pants, a top, and some sneakers. She utilized one of the shops changing rooms to get into the more appropriate 'road' garments. She glanced heavenly in the tight pants! I realized I planned to appreciate watching her take them off!

As we hadn't got out until not long before lunch, the vast majority of the evening was spent shopping. I brought her some ordinary garments. However, she had a problem with me spending a lot on her. I realized we would be going to 'luxurious' cafés - I needed to show her off all things considered - so I demanded she has evening garments. I likewise brought her adornments and paid for clothing she picked - not allowing me to see it! Notwithstanding, she had interrogated me concerning what I preferred, so I have foreseen that I would be reasonably intrigued.

All in all, you say, why get her every one of these things? I appreciated shopping with her. I delighted in the looks we got from the staff in the different shops, which attempted to sort out what was happening. We 'was a tease' with one another continually, Gina appearing to appreciate being the focal point of consideration as garments were chosen and taken a stab at. She especially appeared to appreciate displaying them for me - I realize I delighted in it! The lone cloud not too far off happened as we sat having an espresso some path through the evening.

Gina appeared to be somewhat contemplative briefly. "What is it, Gina, love?"

She fixed me with her eyes, "I don't have the foggiest idea," she said, "is it right you should get me every one of these things? I feel . . . I don't have a clue. I'm heartbroken!"

I thought about the thing she was experiencing in her brain. Delicately I said, "You stress that I am getting you?" She appeared near tears abruptly. My hand covered hers, "I'm not 'getting' you or your kindnesses."

"I'm, unfortunately . . . it just seemed like it: particularly the jewelry and studs."

"Hello," I grinned, "did I get you anything yesterday other than supper?"

She investigated my eyes. "No."

"Furthermore, look what occurred," I grinned. "I didn't 'get' you yesterday, and I am not today. These things are because you remained with me, and you don't have any garments - practical as it were. I got you the gems since you are excellent and wonderful ladies ought to have lovely things. Nothing that has happened today is contingent on you remaining around evening time."

"You imply that?"

" I do. If you stay, on the off chance that you go - it's your choice."

She grinned, "I'm, as a rule, senseless. However, I've never been dealt with like this."

I grinned back, "Indeed, appreciate it, Gina love, we have a couple of things to get!"

She giggled, "Indeed, some more clothing!" We polished the espresso and set off again for the shops. Even though we had gotten back to the inn to leave a few things there, we had an extensive heap of bundles when we, at last, got back in the late evening.

~

.

5. Back from Shopping:

In which Gina sucks, I lick, and we have intercourse once more:

~

We got into the room and dropped everything in the parlor. Gina went to me, "Goodness Mike! I don't have a clue what to say: all these flawless things. Much obliged to you!" and she came into my arms. We kissed, and my hand ran over the bends of her hips and arse, pressing delicately. "Mmm," she mumbled into my mouth, "Have intercourse with me!"

I grinned down at her. "My pleasure," I answered as I kissed her neck. At that point started to fix her pullover. Catches delivered, it vanished to a pile on the floor as I kissed down her shoulder and to her exquisite bosoms. "Turn round," I murmured at that point. I needed to feel her arse squeezing into me. I left her bra on. However, I appreciated kissing her exposed shoulders and back as my hands squeezed her bosoms, the fingers holding the two areolas through the brassiere. I could likewise feel her dazzling arse squeezed again my undeniably developing erection. She probably felt it, too, for she started to crush her body once more into me.

I kept on kissing her neck and shoulders as I tenderly crushed her tits and areolas. Gina rested her head back on my shoulder as her arse revolved on my chicken. "You are something different, Gina love," I murmured, "your arse is brilliant!"

"Mmm," she mumbled, "I realize the amount you like it!" I dropped my hands down and started to fix her pants. It didn't take long to see them slipping around her lower legs. She ventured out of them and, away from me at that point, turned. She blew my mind as she remained there wearing plain underwear. Underwear that previously showed a minuscule wet fix.

"Try not to move," she said discreetly, then bowed at my feet. Her hands came to up, and she stroked my erect chicken through my pants. She appeared to appreciate the vibe of its hardness through the material. At that point, she unfastened the fly and, scavenging into my undies, dealt with some trouble, I may add, to get my rooster out. She grinned up, "I've fantasized about doing this," she snickered. "You have all your garments on, and I'm almost stripped."

Presently she stroked my rooster to and fro, holding it hard as she jerked off me. Her hands dug inside again and, with a touch of wriggling on my part, got my balls out too. Her eyes turned upward into mine, and she grinned provocatively before bowing her head and covering my cockerel head with her mouth. Isn't this quite possibly the most magnificent encounters in and out of the room? This lovely blonde 22-year-old butt-centric virgin is practically bare, stooping at my feet, sucking my rooster! I realized I would need to be extremely cautious here because it is not difficult to fill her mouth with cum - and I needed to save that for her arse. Her mouth was hot and wet, her lips delicate as they slid to and fro along with my cockerel. It appeared she had twelve tongues as she washed the head, testing the minuscule opening every so often. One hand delicately touched my balls; the other stroked off the base of my cockerel. Gina didn't 'profound throat,' not that it irritated me, for she was doing a very great job at any rate!

Sometimes she would turn upward at me, normally with my chicken somewhere down in her mouth—another extraordinary inclination and to an extreme.

"Gina, Gina love," I needed to say at last, "you'll need to stop! I can't take substantially more of this!" Her mouth left my chicken, yet her hands remained.

"Don't you like it?" she sulked, causing another emergency.

"Gina, I love it! You could do that for Australia!" I chuckled. She grinned back. "Yet, I will cum - and I need to save that for . . . . ."

"My arse?" she said unobtrusively.

"Indeed," I answered, "for your arse - on the off chance that you need it."

She stood then lay back on the bed. "I need you to have intercourse with me," she said as she gazed toward me. First work - dispose of my garments! Gina had a delicate grin all over as she watched me strip. This was immediately done, and I stooped toward the finish of the bed, peering down at her.

"Your turn," I said cheerfully, 'bra first. She turned over face down - intentionally, I figure, unfastened her bra at that point moved back. "Mmm," I mumbled, "you have beautiful tits!" And she did! Not very large and entirely shaped. Decent, enormous earthy colored areolas on little hillocks. She grinned back up at me. I could see the wet fix between her legs. "Underwear now!" She moved face down again and put her base open to question. I'm almost certain that she understood how she was doing me as she came back and squirmed out of her underwear at that point turned around.

"You are a minx!" I said with a grin at that point, going two or three cushions, lifted her hips, and set them under. Gina had that tranquil, practically possessive, favor her lips. I'm certain she realized I planned to eat her, so she was very glad to lay back and appreciate.

I opened her legs, held them up and separated, and crept between. "Keep your legs down, Gina, love, let me get at your dazzling pussy!" Still grinning, she did as I asked and opened herself totally to me. Her pussy was wet from her fellatio, I expected, and her clit was swollen, so I began there! I sucked and nibbled with first my lips, then my teeth - softly obviously - and, following a couple of moments of this consideration, she came! Fluid spouted. I dropped down to her cunt lips, sucking those and tasting her juice before testing profoundly with my tongue. I sucked and licked pussy and clit until she returned once more, body shivering in the climax. I delighted in hearing her groans, her inspirational statements, and the sensation of her hands holding my head set up - not that she expected to!

After her second climax, I lifted my head and peered down at her. She was shrouded in a delicate gleam of sweat that was so attractive it wasn't correct. I needed to screw her then, yet first, I needed to prod her arsehole a little to check whether she was as yet keen on taking my cockerel there.

I lifted her legs somewhat more so her rear-end accessible to mouth and fingers back down once more. At that point ran my tongue from the base of her spine to the rear of her wet pussy. Gina moaned, and a delicate, "YESssss," got away from her lips. After about six passes, each bringing another delicate "Yesss" from her, I halted and focused on her butt. A delightful star with simply a sad remnant of the sphincter muscle around it. She was right there - to be expected for a butt-centric virgin - even though she appeared to unwind as I rimmed her arsehole. Covering the entire region with spit, I at long last examined straightforwardly at the middle with my tongue, utilizing a screwing movement to attempt to entice her to unwind and give it access. After a bit of cajoling, she did, and, paradise, the tip of my tongue slipped past the muscle.

"OOOOHHHHH Fuck!' she cried as her body shivered. She enjoyed this! I tongue screwed her arsehole a few minutes, getting a charge out of each second, at that point moved and sucked my center finger into my mouth and covered it with salivation. Time to perceive how she truly felt about her arse being entered!

"Going to utilize my finger again, Gina?" I expressed this as an explanation and an inquiry to give her the alternative to cannot.

"Goodness god!" was her lone answer, so I took that for a yes! At the tip of my finger, I utilized it to stroke around the tight rosebud briefly, then pushed it delicately at the focal point of her butt. I detected a strain in her body, not abnormal in the present circumstance. She planned to have something pushed in her arse for just the subsequent time - well, I suspected as much around then.

"Loosen up, Gina loves. Simply unwind on the off chance that you need to feel it." I felt her take a full breath then her entire body lost its strained quality. Her sphincter loses, and my center finger slid into her arsehole to the main joint.

"Wow! That feels soooooo enormous!"

"It's just my finger," I chuckled then added, all the more truly, "would you say you are OK?"

"Indeed! It feels unusual. It doesn't do any harm, simply feels so enormous!" There was just about an unanswered inquiry here - how large could my cockerel feel? I didn't reply, just tenderly moved my finger in and out. I did not expect finger screwing her arse appropriately; this was simply to check whether she could manage a delicate addition once more.

"Ooooooohhhhhhhhhh! Wow!" Gina was breathing profoundly, yet it was still until this moment that she pushed back and took practically the entirety of my finger in her arsehole. "Gracious WOW! That is . . .

fascinating! oooooh! Do that!" I moved my finger to and fro. "Goodness GOD! Tenderly . . . Yesssssssssss!"

Her body spasmed in the climax. Her rectum grasped my finger, and her sphincter held like a bad habit. Gradually I pulled out my finger, moved into her, and put my cockhead at her vagina. Pushing gradually inside, I bowed forward and murmured, "You like my finger in your arse, Gina?" My cockerel was mostly inside before she understood, I think!

"Goodness FUCK, yes. Goodness screws me - please!" This was soooooo troublesome! I filled her immediately at that point, hands grasping her legs for influence as I screwed her hard and profound. Gina appeared to have a practically nonstop climax as I push into her. Groans, delicate 'Yes's,' and yelled 'goodness god's occupied the room as my chicken smashed into her delicate paradise of a cunt. It appeared to be a practically creature enthusiasm that crawled over her. Her eyes were wide, her lips separated, and a delicate sheen of sweat on cheek and lip. She looked sufficient to eat. Me? Well, I needed to consider something besides the thing that that was occurring here. It was everything I could don't to pull out, turn her generally finished, and bugger her. I didn't be that as it may; die the idea for considering it nearly made me cum.

After various shivers, her cunt holding my chicken all through, Gina quieted. I pulled back and sat down adjacent to her. She moved towards me, and I embraced her. We just lay there unobtrusively, close to one another in that magnificent after sex shine - however I had held off cumming - Gina laying her head on my shoulder. I figure we may have napped for a couple of moments.

~

6. A Discussion on Anal Sex:

In which Gina settles on an official conclusion:

~

I became cognizant again of this lovely young lady in my arms, and I turned my head to kiss her cheek. Wakeful now and recuperated, she grinned up at me. It was an underhandedly naughty grin, however, with a slight trace of inquiry in her eyes. I saw before long, for she wriggled from my arms and moved onto her front. Her eyes looked for my response.

In truth, I was dumbfounded. I have waxed expressive about Gina's base's excellence, and now she lay before me once more. Her legs were somewhat separated, and I could see the lump of her delicious pussy - lips were swollen from our previous liaison. Over those sexy lips was the split of her base; she rear-ends - that small star - plainly noticeable.

I took a full breath to attempt to control my pulse - and my longing. In no way, shape or form did In't need to think too long about Gina in this position. I could likewise feel the impact somewhere else in my body for my cockerel, near climax when I screwed her pussy, was currently pretty much as hard as an iron bar - the Cialis was working!

I moved my eyes from the brilliant sight of her base and investigated hers—a delicate grin shaped on her mouth. "Presently?" she asked unobtrusively.

Gina probably speculated the impact of lying face-down like this would have on me since she realized that my specific 'thing' was the female base even though she couldn't in any way, shape, or form, realize that this position was my top pick for butt-centric sex! Not that I would take her that route unexpectedly. Later maybe, on the off chance that she truly delighted in the experience.

I grinned back at her getting her mind-set. "You are a coldblooded lady Gina!" I said.

She unexpectedly got genuine. "You need me?" I caused a commotion, not having any desire to think about how conceivable I may have added a lot to the inquiry. She saw my delay. "My base, my bum? You need me there?"

"Gina! Gina sweetheart," I said gradually, then took a full breath. It would be pointless to lie, for I had revealed to Gina before the amount I couldn't imagine anything better than to have her like this. She knew. "Indeed Gina, definitely, however . . . just if you need to. I could never do it without my accomplice's permission."

"You realize I've never done it," she said discreetly. "I'm baffled, however, "she added with delicate grain, "why a ton of my companions, and a portion of the books we read, criticize it? Like it's uncharacteristic; it harms; it's not agreeable?"

I wasn't certain about where Gina was going with this. Is it safe to say that she was prodding? It appeared to be not normal for her. I chose to play it straight. "I can't offer you positive responses, Gina. Uncharacteristic? Maybe it is from one viewpoint, be that as it may, if two individuals concur? I think not - yet that is only an assessment." I grinned, "Men have been utilizing that backup way to go for a prolonged period."

Gina grinned and gestured. "Concerning the realities that it damages and they hate it? Well, I sincerely figure that is because it wasn't 'done' appropriately the first run through." Gina gestured as though in the arrangement. I stroked her hair. "This is murdering me," I said, snickering.

"I know," she chuckled back, "clarify!"

"Minx! The man must be obliging. You can't simply stick it in' with pussy squeeze and spit!. Lube is fundamental, fundamental. As is a delicacy, care, and tolerance." Now Gina was seeing me wide-looked at. She was so dazzling! "Furthermore, I kept grinning, "the woman must be loose also. A few climaxes - and she should truly need to attempt it since it tends to be awkward, even excruciating, the initial few occasions. Not really; however, it can. That is the reason a lot of lube is required!"

"Yet, ladies don't . . you know . . have . . . what is it you men have? Goodness! A prostate."

"No, I know!" I chuckled. "I was unable to disclose to you why they appreciate it - you would need to ask somebody who does," I said with a grin at that point, "Gina . . . is it true that you are playing with me?"

She grinned up at me and wriggled her base. My rooster grew an inch - a reality that wasn't lost on Gina as she looked down! "Actually no, not actually," she said delicately, "I need . . . I need you to do it!" My heart practically halted. Gina, this perfect young lady, was offering herself. "I need to . . . like you said," she added unobtrusively. "I need to know. To understand what it seems like and I realize you will be . . . I don't have the foggiest idea . . . delicate. I'll become more acquainted with appropriately."

I bowed and kissed her lips. To be allowed the chance to present a delightful youthful butt-centric virgin to the joys of that course! "Sure?" I asked, practically not having any desire to accept my ears.

"Indeed," she grinned, "exceptionally sure! 22 and never been messed up the bum!" She giggled, "Time to change that!" Her mind-set had out of nowhere helped as though the choice had eliminated any uncertainty. "Come here and kiss me!"

My rooster was hard now as she moved back, finished, and pulled me down. We kissed, and her hands started to stroke my erection, developing further by the second as my body acknowledged precisely the thing Gina was inferring. "Gina," I said unobtrusively, "are you . . "

"Sure?" she interfered. "Indeed. Indeed, sure. I've seen it in pornography films." I caused a stir. She grinned, "We young ladies watch them some of the time you know and, all things considered, felt fingers in there. Presently the time," she took a gander at me and grinned brilliantly, "particularly when I have a man who understands what he is doing!" Now she chuckled, "And you will demonstrate my sweethearts and the books wrong!"

"I do?"

"Indeed! On the off chance that I appreciate it and request that you do it once more!"

I giggled, "Gina! You are precious!"

"I surmise so," she snickered back. "Presently," she proceeded with genuinely after a speedy kiss, "what do I need to do?"

"Well," I addressed unobtrusively, "on the off chance that you are not 'readied,' it very well may be muddled and awkward." She caused a commotion at that point, become flushed, and gestured in understanding. "You must be vacant," I proceeded.

"You mean . . . the restroom?"

I gestured, grinning, "Indeed, the emptier, the better! The initial not many occasions it's acceptable on the off chance that you can be unfilled, however."

"I don't get it?"

"You utilize a douche to exhaust your insides." I grinned, "Sorry to be somewhat rough, yet 'prep' is in support of butt-centric sex, Gina. Prep should almost immediately as much as possible. On the off chance that you like it, at that point, less prep is OK when you are accustomed to having your base filled." She becomes flushed yet gestured.

"How would I do that?"

I grinned. "I was somewhat pompous after what you said the previous evening," I replied. "While you were in the changing space for that drawn-out period, I flew nearby to the drug store and got a purification pack."

She gave me a 'good old' look at that point grinned. "Great," she said, "so I will do that?"

I chuckled, "Indeed, if you might want. Or then again, I could do it for you?"

She becomes flushed brilliant red. "Are there guidelines?"

"On the case."

"I'll do it at that point." She came down to my cockerel and tenderly kneaded it. "It would appear that you need it now?"

I took a full breath. "Indeed," I said, "Gina love, your base is flawless and, well, to put it roughly, screwing your arse would be great yet just on the off chance that you are prepared and need it."

"Well," she said happily, "I need it - presently I need to prepare. Keep that," she gestured towards my erection, "prepared for me!" She left and set out toward the restroom, presenting at the entryway and saying, behind her, "Is it in here?" I gestured, and she carried on into the washroom with an influence of hip. The entryway shut, a few minutes after the fact, I could hear the running water.

I laid back on the bed, getting a charge out of what was going on in the restroom and what planned to happen quickly. It's only one out of every odd day that a person my age will do this, so I proposed to relish each experience. Much more critically, I needed Gina to leave, having made the most of her first experience of butt-centric sex. I trusted that I would take her there more than once throughout the following two evenings for, as I have said, again and again, she has a delicious arse that is by all accounts made to fuck!

She came out again after around 15 minutes and stood, bare, in the entryway. "That was . . . fascinating," she said with a major grin. At that point, seeing that my rooster was somewhat collapsed, I sulked and proceeded, 'You don't need my arse?"

I grinned, "Gracious yes, Gina, love, particularly without a doubt. Simply needs a little incitement!'

"Gracious, I can do that," she grinned at that point, intersection to the bed, bowed between my legs. Two hands stroked rooster and balls before her mouth shut on my cockerel. Her sucking and tongue washing before long took me back to original capacity, and she raised her head and grinned down at me. "You two or three climaxes previously . . .?"

I chuckled, "You've just had those," I reacted, causing a stir.

"Well . . . I recently felt that before that enormous thing, there goes into my arse." Wow, she had positively adapted rapidly how to light my fire! "I figure I might want a couple more!"

I snickered once more, "My pleasure," I said, 'jump ready!" She chuckled, and she did. The delicate velvet of her cunt included my erection as she slid her body down onto me. Inclining forward, she started to buck to and fro and here and there. "Your rooster feels so great in me," she murmured, "I can't help thinking about what it will feel like in my arse?" Well, of course, this was a risky area for my psyche to meander into, so I just grinned and pushed up into her, making an effort not to think about her tight arse and rectum around my chicken. Gina shook around for some time, groaning and breathing profoundly, at that point inclined right back and siphoned hard. I felt her cunt grasp my cockerel and had another emergency as her climax crested. Encouraging her on her way, I push up into her over and over.

At long last, she inclined forward and kissed me. "Wow, that was acceptable! You need my arse now," she asked with an underhanded grin as she squirmed her base on my crotch.

I grinned back, "In a moment," I reacted, "dismiss round and face." Gina caused a commotion. "Distinctive position," I clarified, "and I get a great glance at your arse!"

"Goodness." She mouthed and afterward turned. She oversaw without really getting off of my rooster - that was acceptable in itself! "Gracious, yes! I like this," she said, glancing back at me and starting to skip all over on my chicken. "It feels sooooo unique!" At that point, I let her have at it for some time, slipped my finger into her cunt with my cockerel. "What?"

"Simply getting some grease," I said, then hauled my finger back along her butt-centric separated. Like this, her arse was spread wide; she rear-ends accessible. I wasn't going to squander the occasion. I circumnavigated the muscle getting a greater amount of her juice on and off until she was groaning uproariously and pushing both back and down on my chicken. This is a fascinating inclination; chicken bowed forward into her [fantastic for butt-centric as well - as I trusted I might encounter later]. Presently at the tip of my finger was at her butt, directly at the focal point of her star, and, each time she pushed back, it entered a minuscule portion until, at last, she pushed back more earnestly and took half inside. She came right away. Her cunt held my rooster and her butt grasped my finger. It didn't prevent me from screwing her arsehole tenderly directly through her, apparently, drawn-out climax.

She, at last, descended from her high and laid, face down, next to me. There was a delicate grin all over as she said unobtrusively, 'That was incredible. I'm prepared. I need to feel what it's like!" I bowed up and peered down at this delightful young lady who offered her most private spot to me. You can do one of two things in this position. You can bugger her. Take her for your pleasure and appreciate the experience enormously. Chances are you will not at any point do it to her once more! Or then again, you can do as I planned to do, take her delicately, cautiously, and gradually, so she had each chance to appreciate it. Alright - self-centered. On the off chance that she delighted in it, she would need it again - that was the arrangement! I had this evening, throughout the day Sunday, and tomorrow evening with her. I needed to exploit that - what red-blooded man wouldn't?

~

7. Her First Anal Experience:

In which Gina surrenders her butt-centric cherry:

~

While Gina was preparing in the restroom, I had discovered my inventory of oil [it was quite a while since I had been a boy trooper, yet I always remembered the motto!]. I had a container of Astroglide - the best all things considered, and some little, one-shot, cases with a long, slim spout intended to be embedded and crushed. Together these would guarantee she would have the most obvious opportunity to make the most of my cockerel in her arse.

"Open your legs," I murmured in her ear. She did, and I stooped between. Isn't this perhaps the greatest sights that the unstoppable force of life has given us gentlemen [and a few ladies as well!]. Gina's hips were wide, and they spread over the heavenly ascent of her base cheeks, full and round. Between, her cunt was dribbling juice from her climaxes or more than the little, quite small, star of her rear-end called.

I stroked, touched, and kneaded the cheeks of her arse, running my thumbs at the edges of the valley containing her butt. Gina was groaning in delight and empowering me with a ceaseless, "Yes!' Finally, I twisted my head to her base and ran my tongue from the rear of her cunt, up and across her butt. Again and again, delighting in the taste and the impact on her. At that point, halting and rimming her sphincter with my tongue, examining thee tight muscle and, as she loses, pushed past and inside her virgin arsehole.

Grasping her hips, I slipped her into a bowing position - the best I think for the principal experience - and moved her to the edge of the bed. I needed to remain in charge, not skipping on the bed, for this first time. It would have been troublesome enough to hold off my climax as I entered her, and I would not like to be lost by the impact of the delicate bed. I knew from our initial pup that standing I was the perfect stature for my cockerel to slip inside her arse.

"Head down, Gina love," I said unobtrusively, "knees somewhat separated and stuck that exquisite bum out!" Always a marginally extraordinary situation for butt-centric than vag!

"You're horrendous!" at that point, "This way," she grinned, investigating her shoulder. WOW - troublesome than not to get it done. Take her. Didn't, however - and that is significant. I needed to make the most of her arse for some time and, ideally, slip her into her first butt-centric. I started again to touch and stroke her at that point, twisted my head to arse, and licked along the valley between her cheeks. What is magnificent about this is hearing the positive moans, remarks, groans from the woman - and Gina unquestionably appreciated things up until now!

Time to proceed onward, so I went after the lube and wound the tip off the little cylinder. "I will utilize some lube Gina," I murmured, inclining forward, "inside, so unwind."

I could see her body unwind as I placed the little application tube at her butt at that point and pushed it inside. "Oooooooooooh! Feels interesting." Then, "Goodness dear! That is strange!" as I pressed to lube into her rectum. Lube is thus, so significant, particularly the initial not many occasions, so I needed to ensure there was a lot inside her tight back passageway.

"All OK still?" I asked, inclining forward once more.

"Goodness, yes! Don't you dare stop now!" Well, I wasn't going to - except if she advised me to. I facilitated the little utensil tube out and spurted some lube around her butt and afterward some onto my chicken, stroking it along my iron-hard erection. Utilizing my center finger, I started to work the lube around and into her sphincter. "Mmmm, that feels better," she said delicately as I prodded her to rear-end. "Goodness GOD!" that was my finger pushing inside. "That feels enormous - your finger? Gracious indeed, do that. Ooooooohhhhh!" I was sliding my finger in and out. Such a ton simpler than before because of the lube. As Gina became accustomed to this, I added my pointer at first under the center.

"Wow! That is significantly greater!"

"Two fingers!"

"Gracious FUCK!" I was gradually screwing her arse with these two fingers now. The expectation was making my chicken nearly burst with want to be in there yet, as a matter of fact, I realized not to surge this.

Gina appeared to be unwinding and taking my fingers effectively, so now I set them next to each other and allow her to have the entire length.

"Wow! That is so horrible large!"

"Will I stop?"

"NO! Try not to stop now! It's OK."

"Does it hurt?"

"Nooo . . . . a bit. Stings and I feel so extended. However, . . . it's abnormal. It nearly feels better - excellent. Try not to stop. Oooooooooooooo!" Harder, quicker, and more profound now before the last penetrate. At that point, I started to turn my fingers inside her to release her sphincter considerably more. "Jesus Christ! Goodness Fuckkkkkkk! Ooooooooooooh! Indeed!" Her body shivered.

"Gina, OK?"

"Gracious screw, yes. That was . . . clever! Unusual. Oohhhhh, continue to do . . . THAT!"

"Time, Gina, do you need my rooster in your arse?"

A winded, 'Yes," responded to me, "put your rooster in my arse!" Gripping my chicken firmly, I put the tip at her butt and pushed tenderly forward. This is a risky time, and I dare not peer down and see my chicken skewering her arse cheeks - I would either cum or drive somewhere inside in one stroke, and neither one of the options was great right now.

"Loosen up, Gina," I said delicately. 'give me access." I saw strain stream from her back, and my rooster slipped past the muscle just to be held firmly beneath the head where there is a characteristic misery from the circumcision.

"Goodness GOD!" she shouted energetically, "Screw Mike. Wow - that feels so wicked enormous!" Well, it was, truth be told - greater than the two fingers positively.

"Alright? Does it hurt?" I inquired.

Gina took a full breath. "Alright. Indeed. No. It's huge! A bit."

I wasn't exactly certain what she was saying. "Too enormous? Will I stop?"

"No - I don't think so. It feels amusing. Do some more - gradually, please." I drove another two crawls into her. My rooster is essentially a similar size as the head until simply over mostly down, so all Gina would feel present would be complete, no seriously extending. "Oooooooooo! It's so large. Full, so full." The last nearly to herself, at that point, "It doesn't do any harm - to an extreme! Goodness, god, you feel so huge, and I feel so full!" I pulled out then to facilitate the muscle and let her vibe me leaving. This brought another round of self-remark, yet she didn't advise me to stop. Practically out then back in gradually getting a charge out of the vibe of her sphincter sliding along my rooster and the hot elusive velvet hold of her lubed rectum. This is a radiant inclination improved all the for realizing I was the first there. What is it about that that makes it so exceptional for us folks? I don't have the foggiest idea, yet I do realize that it is uncommon. I pressed some more lube onto my cockerel and the rear-end.

I was screwing her arsehole now - just a large portion of my rooster sliding in and out - and it didn't appear to be excessively agonizing for Gina. I needed certainly nonetheless, so I inclined forward, still delicately stroking, and murmured, "Is that OK, Gina? Do you like it?"

She took a full breath. "I . . . I don't have the foggiest idea! Gracious God, it feels so enormous inside me. Oooooooooooh!" She was relaxing, and I had pushed recently somewhat more profound. I was practiced mostly now and starting to move slightly quicker. For me, the inclination is stunning. Hot: dangerous from the lube: and tight, quite close!

"Gracious dear! Good gracious! FUCK!" I was sliding only a smidgen more profound on each forward stroke, and now she was feeling the full width of my chicken, extending her rear-end and rectum. In any case, Gina appeared to have the option to adapt and wasn't advising me to stop. I raised my body back up and held her hips. I planned to fill her now - I was unable to keep down any longer. My cockerel felt like it would blast, held so firmly as it was in her radiant arse.

"I will screw your arse now, Gina," I said enthusiastically.

"Goodness, god! If it's not too much trouble! Gracious FUCK! Yesssssssssss!" Her answer was additionally winded. However, I was compensated with a slight reverse push as I drove into her. The main sign that, maybe, it was getting bravo. I had practically the entirety of my 7 crawls in her arsehole now and needed to control myself for I needed to cum so seriously, yet I hadn't actually screwed her arse, buggered her, right now.

"Here it comes, Gina, each of the 7 inches!" In this way, verbal play is so significant in sex, and now I gave her everything. My thighs met the cheeks of her arse as I pushed home and held her there.

"Gracious FUCK!" was her winded reaction. "Oooooowwww! So screwing BIG!!!!" she yelled at that point, "good god, it harms!"

Holding my hips exceptionally still, I inclined forward and nibbled the rear of her neck delicately and kissed her shoulders, holding her on my covered rooster. "Will I stop, pull out, Gina, love?"

I felt her take a full breath, then her body lose. "I need it!" she said delicately. "Please - simply move slowly. I need you to screw my arse!" After that, I required one minute to control and prepare for a more drawn-out screwing of her arsehole. More kisses on shoulder and neck at last finished when Gina turned her head and offered her lips. Mouths met in a furor of enthusiasm. I constrained my tongue into her mouth, screwing her with it as my hunger was cresting.

Pulling lips separated Gina, energy writ huge all over, said delicately, "That feels unusual at this point. It harms; however, it kind of doesn't!" I started to move my hips, sliding only a few crawls of the rooster in and out - welcoming her on. "Wow! That feels . . . Goodness screw I don't have a clue how it feels, however . . . . . ooooooooooh . . . try not to stop!" That was what I expected to hear!

This was her first butt-centric experience, so I realized that I could not pound her excessively hard - that may come later as she turned out to be more insightful. I reclined up, grasped every hip with a hand, and held her quick. Drawing my rooster practically that full distance, I gradually and tenderly drove right into her from the start. Gina shouted out, on the other hand, as I pulled out and drove back. Each push brought about a loud cry - apparently of joy, for she didn't advise me to stop. I was screwing her ravishing arsehole, buggering her, sodomizing her. I peered down at my cockerel skewering her cheeks, watched it slide into her arsehole, watched her sphincter vanish, then return as though sticking urgently to the meaty trespasser. It is more likely than not been OK for her because she inevitably started to meet my forward pushes with an opposition. I wasn't driving too hard, just gradually screwing her arse profoundly.

Utilizing my thumbs, I opened her cheeks, much really permitting the last millimeters of my rooster to enter her—another loud moan. "Goodness screwing damnation!" she cried in an outrageous Australian pronunciation that was what my ears were waiting to hear. At that point, "Goodness fuck however I like this MIKE! Do it! Do it!" Well, I was. Nevertheless, I didn't figure I could do it any longer. My balls were at blasting point, and my chicken felt like it planned to detonate inside the holding dividers of her rectum.

"I'm going to cum in your arse Gina," I said boisterously, "fill your arse with cum. You need that?"

"Goodness, screw yes! DO IT!" I am not very sure what I would have done had she said no, yet she hadn't, so now I removed the brakes for only a few pushes - that is all it took! The entire 7 creeps of my rooster sank into her arsehole as I pulled her on. Out of nowhere, it was there! My rooster expands in her rectum at that point, beat energy into her.

"YESSSSSSS! I can feeeeeeelllllll it! Good gracious!" Her entire body shook, and her rectum and butt crushed my rooster. It felt like she never needed to allow it to out as I beat a great many planes of semen into her entrails. Holding her firmly against my thighs, it was soon finished, in any case, after four in number heartbeats into her. I kept on freaking her arse through both our climaxes until my cockerel was too delicate to even consider making the return venture into her. We both fell onto the bed; Gina faces down me on my back. A couple of seconds to recuperate, then I inclined upon the one hand and peered down at her.

"Well?"

"Goodness god Mike! I don't have the foggiest idea. It hurt like blasts part of the way through at that point, unexpectedly, it felt . . . well not great however energizing."

Concerned, I reacted, "Gina, love, I'm heartbroken. I would not like to hurt you."

She grinned listlessly. "You didn't toward the end," she said, "toward the end, not long before you came, it was incredible! I never felt anything like that, and when I felt you cum in me. Wow! I could feel it, feel you cum inside me, hitting me inside. All warm." She snickered, "Made me cum once more!"

"Did you cum," I asked after a delicate kiss?

"Multiple times."

"Three?" I said distrustfully, for I thought it had harmed her.

"It's difficult to clarify," she reacted with a baffled look. "At any rate - you should know. You've done it enough!" She giggled, "In any event, that is the thing that you said!"

"I have Gina love, yet it's distinctive for every lady. When did you cum?" I was interested.

"You just need to know so you can do it once more," she snickered.

I twisted and kissed her cheek, "Gracious yes Gina, you holy messenger, I need to do that again and again yet just on the off chance that you need to."

She hushed up briefly, "I figure I do," she said happily. "Toward the end, it was fantastic!"

"Great! Presently advise me, three climaxes?"

"It's amusing," she reacted with a snicker. "You made me cum when you got directly in toward the start."

"I thought you said it hurt at that point - like the bursts?"

"It did, yet it made me cum. I was amusing - an interesting cum," she snickered. "Can't clarify it. At that point, after a short time of you screwing me . . ." I needed to take a full breath here. I adored how she wouldn't fret utilizing the right language. ". . . at that point the hurt disappeared. No," she said reluctantly, "didn't disappear, changed and got great! I began to need it in me more profound, so I pushed back, and I came when you got much more profound. At that point, your energy! Goodness. Also, you got greater!" She unexpectedly laughed. "Isn't this horrible. Discussing you screwing my arse like this?" I am certain it was a non-serious inquiry, yet I addressed it in any case.

"Actually, no, not in any way, Gina, love. It's acceptable to discuss it." I grinned lewdly, and she giggled.

"Just so you can do it again, you grimy elderly person!" The sting was removed from that by her incredible huge grin. "At any rate, I think I need you to," at that point, she added delicately and reluctantly, "yet . . . errm . . . I'm somewhat delicate."

Not irregular. That is the reason I had added some mitigating moisturizer to my buys. "I would not like to hurt you anything else than I needed to, Gina love, so I will put a portion of this on."

She appeared to be humiliated as she moved on her side to confront me. "I need to go . . . you know. Goodness hell! Turf it! Your cum's running out." Her open way was unquestionably tempting, and I chose to have some good times.

"Pleasant," I said cheerfully. "I like to see it running out."

"Don't," she gave a humiliating giggle, "you'll make me redden!"

"What's more, that will make you considerably more alluring," I reacted with an incredible huge grin. "Lay down." She did. I bowed up and peered down at her arse. So bleeding perfect, I was at that point starting to solidify thinking about the following time! I came to advance and separated her cheeks. Her rear-end was widened, not all that much, and extremely red. A minuscule spill of moxie and lube showed up as I watched. I suppose a few people with discover this somewhat off-putting. It's my moxie, and she was glad to allow me to see it running out.

I tapped her arse cheeks. "You proceed to tidy up Gina, love," I said delicately, adapting to kiss her. "Call me when you've done, and we can shower together."

She grinned another of her tired and sexy grins, "That will be decent - will not it?" she added provocatively.

I giggled, "You are an unquenchable minx," I reacted.

With that, she stood and strolled to the restroom halting at the entryway and thinking back behind her. "Indeed, do you like what you see?" she asked with a devilishly knowing grin.

I could see a slim path of my cum running from between the cheeks of her arse down her leg. Sexy undoubtedly! I snickered and grasped my cockerel, which had chosen to solidify again at her provocative conduct, "A lot of minxes!"

"Great." She vanished into the restroom. I laid there considering how this stunning young lady had, clearly out of nowhere, become very sexual. Is it safe to say that she was typically similar to that, or was it the impact of my affection making? I didn't have the foggiest idea yet. I speculated that a few evenings would have been energizing, to be sure! I hung tight for a couple of more minutes at that point, thumped on the restroom entryway.

~

8. Intermission - Dinner:

In which we manage the consequence of her first butt-centric and head out to have a great time:

~

"Alright," she called, and I entered to locate her in the shower. "I'm eager!" she said with a major grin, "so I figured a shower would be snappier. Don't have the foggiest idea what you have made arrangements for the shower - and I would prefer not to surge," she added playfully. I giggled and joined her in the shower - I was eager too, nor did I wish to hustle the 'shower' fun! The washing, stroking, and touching proceeded in the shower; however, it was fun instead of sexual. There was loads of soaping of rooster and balls on her part and much the equivalent of her tits and arse by me. She appeared quiet now, bare and in the shower - practically glad for her body and what she could mean for me with it. I just gloried some more in her smooth bends, her firm bosoms, the scope of her hips, her solid thighs, and her great arse.

"You truly like my arse, don't you," she grinned part of the way through the shower after I had gone through a few minutes soapily stroking her cheeks.

I grinned wanly, "Gina, Gina love, you have a magnificent arse and, for my transgressions, it has caught me!" I ran my hand over her hips and afterward her cheeks. "These bends are in this way, so erotic. You are so 'close' and here," I ran my finger along the joint between upper thigh and base, "so energetic. Look," I said, gesturing at my chicken, which was starting to see what my fingers were doing, "see!"

She giggled, satisfied at her force, I think. I don't know whether anybody had dealt with her like this previously. However, I was speculating she appreciated it! Her hand touched my chicken, "You need me there again, don't you?" she asked cheerfully.
"Indeed," I addressed truly, "yes I do - and, truth be told, as frequently as you would let me! You are thus, so exquisite there." I grinned, "That isn't to say that you are not beautiful wherever else," I added, moving my hand to her pussy at that point up to her sprightly bosoms.

"You," she said with a tremendous sulk that mellowed the words, "are a grimy elderly person!"

I chuckled, "For my transgressions, yes, I will admit to that! You, then again, are an exceptionally hot youngster." I kept on washing her, moving her hand from my chicken, "Who will, without a doubt, have your evil route with me later!" She chuckled. "Presently, be that as it may, I long for food. Food to help me manage the invite requests you will make of me sometime in the evening - well, I trust so in any event," I added, giggling.

She pulled my head down and kissed me, "Mmmm! positively am," she giggled, moving out of the shower.

We dried one another - more fun contacting and stroking. At the point when we were both dry and into the room, I went to Gina. "Facedown on the bed, Gina, love," I said cheerfully.

She looked shocked and uncertain. "Again - as of now?"

"No," I reacted. "I need to utilize this," and I showed her the cream I had purchased simultaneously as lube. "It will facilitate the irritation and bring any expanding down before long."

"So we can do it again, you sly man!" she said with a major grin.

"Just if you need to do it again, you hot woman?"

"I do," she said, laying face down on the bed with her legs marginally separated. Golly! Most likely since she knew precisely the thing she was doing. "It feels somewhat sore," she said, glancing back at me.

"I'm grieved," I said unobtrusively, "however it isn't uncommon. Keep in mind, just if YOU need to."

"I said, I do. It was interesting yet pleasant eventually." She snickered, "That is because that is the place where you were!"

"Minx," I chuckled, "presently lay still briefly while I put this on." So I tenderly facilitated her cheeks separated and applied the cream to her still close rear-end. I was red and marginally swollen. "I will put some inside," I said, 'simply unwind!"

"Mmmm," she groaned as I utilized my pointer to work a portion of the cream past her sphincter.

"Alright?"

"Mmm! A piece . . .OOOOOOOOhhhhh!"

"Sorry!"

"It's OK - truly. Very decent!"

I snickered. "Try not to disclose to me you are getting a preference for something in your base!'

She chuckled back. "Presently, wouldn't YOU like that," she reacted. "I don't have the foggiest idea," she added meditatively, "however I think I like it a considerable amount!"

I slipped more cream into her rear-end, tidied up with a hand towel, at that point planted a kiss on each cheek. I will be straightforward here and concede that I discovered it very troublesome not to press ahead and take her there once more. I don't figure she would have asserted, and my chicken was unquestionably available. Yet, I truly needed her to leave on Monday with a nice sentiment about her first encounters with butt-centric sex.

Time to prepare for supper. Gina wore an 'evening' dress that I had picked. Not unlike that which she was wearing when I saw her in the

Gallery. A dim, energetic, blue: still genuinely short of flaunting her dazzling legs, and slice tight - to flaunt her arse! As far as I might be concerned, she wore stockings with the hottest suspenders. It was not a 'fastener belt' but rather a lot more extensive, slight texture, which sat up around her midriff and had long suspender, also extremely dainty, which didn't show under the dress. She wouldn't allow me to see her put them on. "It's an astonishment for some other time," she said with a devilish smile. She additionally wore four-inch obeyed shoes, which made her nearly as tall as me - she looked fabulous. The dress was scaled low at the back and barely enough at the front to simply recommend her cleavage. In a word, she was sex on legs! It was phenomenal to realize that she was doing it, not just for herself [she said how great it felt to 'show herself off' like this] however for me. To have a young lady as lusciously alluring as Gina on my arm as we ate, meandered, and drank around the harbor was an incredible spirit sponsor.

I had chosen to take her to 'Aria' again, for I would not like to get excessively far from the lodging and there was so much going on around the Opera House. Frankly, I simply needed her to be seen - seen on MY arm! Goodness understands people's opinions, yet I couldn't have cared less and, after our conversation prior, Gina didn't mind by the same token.

It was a beautiful warm pre-fall evening. I just wore a shirt and slacks, not having any desire to be something besides the person on the arm of this lovely lady. It was occupied. Saturday night found the harbor and drama house region brimming with the two local people and sightseers getting a charge out of the sights, sounds, and vibe of this heart of Sydney. There were bunches of youthful folks about, sneaking looking for organization, and Gina stood out enough to be noticed.

The table was reserved [a need on Saturday evening] for 8 pm, so I recommended we fly into a bar for an aperitif before supper. There are various bars about, and we settled on a higher-class place.

"We should sit at the bar," Gina murmured. I caused a stir and grinned. "I feel provocative," she added, grinning back. So we did, and I requested punt e mes absent a lot of expectation. They didn't have it, so I requested two glasses of sweet Vermouth with ice, a large portion of a scramble of sharp flavoring, and a cut of orange - as near punt e me as I could get. I talked with the barkeep about the beverage and went to Gina as she got her glass. "Taste Gina love. Taste - at that point, swallow!" I had a major grin all over as I said this, and it was returned as she bowed forward and murmured, "Am I rehearsing for some other time?"

"Could be," I chuckled with a look at the barman who had heard the trade, "yet a little while ago, enjoy the beverage!"

"Mmm, OK," and she tasted the aperitif at that point, after gulping, "hell! That is severe!"

I snickered, "That is the reason I said taste! It improves!" It does, and we appreciated the beverage before deferring to the café for a lovely dinner. Leaving there, we strolled to the Opera House, where I was sufficiently fortunate to tie several passes to a show execution on Sunday night. That was significant, for I had purchased an extremely uncommon dress for Gina to wear. Very much like a dress worn in an image by Alberto Vargas in the Esquire Calendar of December 1946 - my top pick of numerous Vargas pictures. That dress is practically straightforward - Gina's was not, just hung the equivalent and flaunted her figure - once more, especially due to the four-inch heels she would wear with it.

~

9. The Evening

In which Gina postures and we have intercourse once more:

We halted at the Opera Bar for an espresso where Gina shone and was greatly respected. As we completed, she hungover and murmured, "How about we return!"

"It isn't so late," I reacted happily.

"I know," she said, grinning back, "additional time in bed!"

"Suits me!" We were rapidly once again at the inn and into the room. Right inside, after I shut the entryway, she transformed and dissolved into my arms.

"Contact me," she said before we kissed, "run your hands over my body." I truly didn't require a lot of convincing, for her forms are brilliant from her exposed shoulders, down her back, across the broad reach of her arse cheeks to her thighs. To and fro, all over, went my hands as we kissed. Moving into the room, I began to unfasten her dress. "No," she said, moving endlessly somewhat, "let me strip you, then you can watch." My shirt immediately vanished to the floor, followed quickly by my pants, socks, and undies. She remained there, running her hands over my body, appearing to appreciate the sensation of my hair through her fingers. One hand-measured my balls; the other tenderly jerked off my cockerel.

"Is that just for me?" she asked with a hesitant look.

"Obviously," I figured out how to answer croakily. She was so hot, so alluring - and hazardous a little while ago. Significantly more of this, and she would get a modest bunch of cum - not exactly where I needed to store it!

"Sit," she said, pushing me tenderly back onto the lounge chair, "and appreciate!" Well, I realized I would do that as she came behind and unfastened the dress. It tumbled to the floor, uncovering her clothing. The stockings appeared to protract her legs, and the hole between their top and the high suspender belt outlined her cunt and, when she turned, her arse. She was wearing scanty underwear under the suspenders, and she presently started to take them off. Remember, she had her four-inch heels on. Putting one foot on the end table, ensuring I could see her cunt, she fixed one side's suspenders, at that point the other, and slid her underwear off. At that point, dismissing showing her perfect arse, she did them up once more. A reasonable message that they ought to be left on - to be expected for I had revealed to her the amount I delighted in sex with clothing still on - and shoes end up like that. She looked so - words do bomb me her - attractive it was astounding. I imagine that numerous ladies don't understand that they are as alluring to wearing great underwear as they are exposed. She strolled here and there, her arse cheeks firm and pleased on her exquisite legs—postures highlighted by the heels. At last, she was stopping straightforwardly before me.

"Well!?" she said with the hottest grin.

"Turn," I said deeply - she did, and I was confronted with her extravagant arse. The substance-hued suspender belt sat high on her body, around her midsection; the suspender on each side is shaping an awesome edge for those exquisite cheeks.

I ran my hand from midriff - and the velvety material of the suspender belt - over her hips, at that point thighs, lastly, calves. Again and again, I touched her uncovered arse, my thumbs separating her under cheeks.

"You need my arse again, don't you?" she asked discreetly, thinking back behind her as she bowed her legs and pushed her arse towards me. "Indeed, Gina, I do: definitely." I could see, in any case, that she rear-end yet red and looked a triviality sore. "Not this evening, Gina. I would prefer not to hurt you - and put you off," I added happily. "Tomorrow?"

"Indeed," she said cheerfully. "I need to attempt once more!" At that, my chicken got significantly harder, and I just needed to get it inside her. That probably been in her psyche also, for she turned around to confront me and stooped at my feet, taking my erection close by.

"Mmm, time to taste!" Well, she would, for there was an extensive measure of pre-cum spilling out.

"Gina, love, be cautious - you may get a significant piece of cum!"

She investigated my eyes and said, eagerly, "I need it. I've felt you cum in my pussy and my arse, presently I need to feel it in my mouth," she grinned, "and, if you are up to it tomorrow, in my arse once more!" Well, that was excessive. I needed to grasp her hand off my cockerel.

"Simple Gina! Goodness fuck, yet you are some youngster! You need to go slowly, or it will be over too early - and I would like to screw you!"

"Indeed, please - however you cum in my mouth!" I came to advance and pulled her lips to mine - god, she was so stunning.

I slid forward on the love seat. My cockerel stood pleased and enthusiastic. I came up and held the cheeks of her arse and pulled her towards me. "Legs each side, Gina love, you will sit!"

"Mmm," she mumbled as she moved into place, "that sounds intriguing!" Her cunt was over my rooster now, and she tenderly brought down herself until her lips kissed the tip of my cockerel.

242

"Gracious YES!" she moaned as she pushed ahead and took three crawls inside her delicate, smooth vagina.

"Gracious screw Gina!" was pretty much everything I could oversee as she slid down the remainder of the way and my rooster held up completely inside her. I was confronted with a couple of brassiere-covered tits that I just needed to suck along these lines; as Gina settled herself down on my erection, I came to behind and fixed the catch and slipped it off. Her areolas were swollen and hard. I started kissing, licking, and gnawing delicately. Gina was murmuring and moving her body on my chicken, appearing to appreciate the contrasting impressions of my rooster covered somewhere down in her cunt. I zeroed in on her areolas - something she appeared to appreciate - and hauled my teeth along everyone. Gina solidified, shivered, and moaned my name as climax racked her body.

"Gracious my! That was fun," she mumbled as she inclined forward into my body. She was all the while skipping delicately on my chicken while moving her arse too and fro, yet, in this position, I couldn't get moving.

"How about we move Gina, love," I murmured. "I need to screw you!" She grinned a tempting grin.

"How?"

"Hard?"

"Indeed! Hard! Make me cum once more!"

"Over the arm of the couch, Gina," I said cheerfully.

She looked amazed however didn't challenge me as I assisted her with offing my chicken and into position. The arm was all around cushioned yet excessively high for her to stop, so her legs were loosened up, her head laying on the couch seat. This introduced her cunt and arsehole for the practically ideal situation to be screwed! I could not oppose bowing between her spread legs and devouring her wet cunt at that point, utilizing my tongue on her tight arsehole. She shivered when it contacted her butt and let out a noisy moan. I didn't test excessively hard there - to an extreme, and I question I might have controlled my mounting want to sodomize her again, and I would not like to do that presently: didn't have any desire to hurt her.

"Gracious Mike, Mike, please!?"

"If it's not too much trouble?"

"Gracious screw me - please!"

I shut her legs and stood straddling her beautiful thighs. Pointing my cockhead down, I ran it across her pussy lips then over her rear-end. Another murmur. "Good gracious! Right? Gracious God that feels so . . . great!" It appeared to be that Gina had made the most of her first butt-centric experience and was prepared for all the more yet not this evening. I moved my cockhead back to her cunt and slid two crawls into her.

"FUCK! Goodness yessss! Fuck meeeee!" I did! Driving my chicken into her velvet paradise, I began to screw her vigorously. This position has all the components of force. Crashing down into her body felt enormous. Gina was empowering, moaning my name, groaning, "Screw me!" again and again. With my hands on her arse, I drew the cheeks separated, seeing my rooster sliding all through her, watching her butt contract somewhat as I filled her the release as I pulled out. I was unable to oppose contacting that subsequent paradise along these lines, as in the past, I drew a portion of her fluid from the rear of her cunt with my thumb and hauled it over her arsehole.

"Gracious screwing damnation! Wow! Aaaaggghhhhh!" That, I thought happily, is a climax! Leaving my thumb covering her rear-end, I kept on freaking her hard and profound. Not near coming myself - I had guaranteed her a significant piece - I realized I could carry on for some time, and I was appreciating the hints of joy spilling from Gina's lips. I pushed more diligently on her rear-end with my thumb, having hauled some more fluid up. She was all the while making grateful commotions, so I pushed more earnestly until her sphincter opened and the tip of my thumb slipped inside.

"FUCKKKKKKKK!" she cried as her entire body shook. I held my rooster somewhere inside her at that point and began to, delicately, screw her arse with simply the finish of my thumb. A great many shivers shook her body as I worked her arsehole delicately at that point; as she appeared to quiet, I put one decisive advantage over the couch seat, pulled out my thumb, and got back to screwing her pussy hard and profound. I could see her butt currently, more open than previously, and I realized that I needed to take her there, in this position, tomorrow. These contemplations started to raise my temperature, and my climax was gradually drawing nearer.

Inclining forward with my cockerel covered inside her, I murmured, "Going to cum soon, Gina."

"I need it in my mouth," she reacted enthusiastically, "in my mouth!"

I pulled my chicken from her cunt as she moved to sit on the couch. She went after me and sucked my erection profound into her mouth, one hand measuring my balls, the other stroking the base. My hand grasped her head, and I started to screw her mouth - tenderly, I should say, for I didn't have the foggiest idea how she would respond to this. I didn't appear to bother her as she looked up at me and sucked.

It didn't take long, especially as I thought about her beautiful tight arsehole and of screwing it later. "Crap, Gina! Here . . . . . . aaagggggghhhhhh!' I groaned then started to expand and beat cum into her mouth. She coordinated her sucking great, figuring out how to pull energy from my rooster. I gave her four heartbeats before she pulled away and grinned up at me.

"Mmmm! 'ice!" she grinned then gulped. "Nice! You have decent tasting cum!" With that, her mouth covered my rooster again, and she kept sucking the remaining parts of my spirit from my now relaxing chicken.

"Screw Gina, that is acceptable however you - golly! No more - please!" My post cum cockerel was along these lines, so delicate. By all accounts, she was delighted to quit sucking yet at the same time washed the head with her tongue.

"Great?" she asked subsequently to gulping once more.

"Great!" I said with a grin. Then I lifted her, and we kissed, my tongue testing into her mouth and tasting the remaining parts of my cum on hers. "Fulfilled?" I asked happily.

"Indeed," she said unobtrusively. "I thought you were going to . . . you know . . . back there."

I grinned, "I needed to Gina love . . ."

"I needed you to," she interfered.

". . . yet, you probably won't have delighted in it. Tomorrow," I murmured with a grin, "as frequently as you need me to - and I can."

"Great," she grinned provocatively, "I think I will appreciate that!"

"I realize I will," I answered, chuckling and embracing her at that point, running my hands over her brilliant arse, added, "because you have a remarkable arse, Gina." She snickered provocatively. "You, minx, are a villain lady!"

"Mmm," she answered, "I've never truly felt like this. It's . . . I don't have a clue . . . you, this lodging, the circumstance. I feel like a vamp. You know," she giggled, "a trollop. I need to do everything, experience everything. I feel so . . . so sexual!"

"That is because you are," I grinned. "No limits?"

"No," she answered delicately, "no limits!" Well! I speculated that she wasn't mindful of what her answer could forfend in any case; in truth, I needed simply for her to appreciate me making the most of her body. In all likelihood, that would imply that tomorrow would see her arse well and genuinely screwed, however, just if she needed it.

"Will we shower or bed?" I asked cheerfully.

"Bed, I think," she answered, yawning, "I'm worn out!"

I chuckled, "You do require some rest to plan for later."

"Presently, for what reason would that be?" she chuckled back as I drove her into the room and to bed.

"Since, Gina, you minx, tomorrow will be loaded with incredible sex!"

"Mmm, I know," she said delicately, at that point, "thank you, Mike. Much obliged to you for this," she cleared her arm around the room, "and the garments, everything," she kissed me, "and for the sex!

I grinned, stroked her cheek, and kissed her back. "It's me who ought to thank you," I said delicately. "Taking off with an old codger like me!"

"You may be somewhat more established," she reacted, "yet I have never been dealt with like this," she laughed, "and I've unquestionably never been screwed so well!"

"Great! Presently cuddle up, and we should rest." So she did, and we did!

~

10. Sunday Morning:

In which Gina goes 'riding,' has her arse investigated, and has her arse filled once more:

~

I woke with the daybreak, the sun gushing in through the blinds that we had left open. It was too soon to rise notwithstanding, so I turned over and fell asleep back to the half-alert, half sleeping, the universe of the early morning. My psyche meandered over the earlier day, appreciating the recognition of Gina and her gorgeous body. That raised my morning erection, yet it was too soon to stir Gina, who was calmly resting. She looked so flawless, so guiltless, so alluring, laying there adjacent to me.

Time passed, and I have probably fallen into a shallow rest, for I longed for hands-on my rooster and balls. I wasn't longing, for course, for Gina had awoken and was at that point looking at my bundle!

"Mmm," she mumbled cheerfully, "do you generally awaken this way!" You know, ladies can be requested on occasion - decent, however!

I grinned back, "Quite often when a lovely young lady is stroking my rooster and balls," I reacted dryly.

She laughed - a brilliant sound that caused her to appear to be significantly more youthful. "I haven't seen many - cocks, I mean," she explained with a smile, "however I do like yours! How large is it?"

That was an unexpected inquiry. "Sufficiently large," I kidded as she jerked off me.

She snickered once more, "I realize that. How long, how wide?" She took a gander at me bashfully. "I'd prefer to realize how large a thing is going in my arse!" This caused a genuine jerk in my chicken. Her arse! Well, you can envision.

"You, Gina, are a minx! An Australian minx!"

"Is there something like this?" she snickered back, "at any rate, answer!"

"Alright," I reacted, "around 7 inches in length and 2 inches wide at the vastest. Don't have a clue how far round."

"Mmmm, it feels large, yet I haven't had many," she added with another hesitant look toward me. "Is it, you know, large?"

"You mean in correlation?" She gestured. "I don't have a clue," I snickered back, "I have been revealed to it's somewhat more and fatter than normal."

"I suspected as much," she mumbled thoughtfully, still inactively jerking off my strong erection and stroking my balls. "It's the greatest I've had! Would I be able to ride?" she proceeded out of nowhere.

I snickered, "Go right ahead, you sweet holy messenger. Hop ready and screw me!"

She took a gander at me suspiciously then grinned as she saw my smile. Twisting her head, she planted a kiss on the tip of my chicken at that point, moved to crouch my midsections. Gradually she dropped her body down onto me. I murmured as her under lips stroked my cockhead, then moaned as she sank and took me inside. A mischievous grin framed as she peered down at me and started to shake to and fro.

"Mmmm," she mumbled absently, "this is GOOD!"

I giggled, "Yes," I reacted, "generally excellent in fact!" She chuckled with me and began to bob all over, just as sliding to and fro. I could feel the tip of my rooster scouring inside her vagina, and I accepted that it probably been her 'G' spot since she started to murmur and moan. Her eyes shut, and she moved quicker and quicker, yelling a consistent, "Indeed, indeed, yes!" Finally, after several minutes of extraordinary activity, she tossed back her head, crushed her hands before her body, and shivered. Her climax probably continued for close to 60 seconds before her eyes opened, and she grinned. I grinned back, maneuvered her body down onto mine, and started to drive my cockerel into her. Eyes enlarging, she shivered over and over at this recharged tension on her 'G' spot. I screwed her hard for some time, directly during her climax, and afterward lifted her body.

"Kiss!' I said, grinning. It was an enthusiastic kiss with tongues meeting and weaving.

"I need to turn round," she murmured after a few kisses, "so you can see my arse!" she finished enthusiastically.

I caused a commotion, my rooster jerking at the possibility of her arse. "Why?" I asked delicately.

"I need you there once more," she answered, "so - check whether . . . you know! I don't feel sore," she added delicately.

Indeed, this was causing me a minor worry as my cockerel was as yet encased in the delicate velvet fasten of her vagina. Morning erections are consistently simpler to control at the same time, hell, I was covered balls somewhere down in a beautiful 22-year-old blonde, and she was looking at having her arse screwed! Taking a full breath and remaining still, I said delicately, "Gina, love, I need you there again as well. Turn at that point, however gradually," I added cheerfully, "I don't have any desire to cum a few seconds ago. Saving that for some other time!"

She snickered at that point, a chuckle that nearly sent me over the top; however, she was mindful of my concern for, rather than turning around on my chicken, she raised herself off, stood, and turned around. She wasn't to know that that was nearly as terrible, for I presently had the perspective on her gorgeous arse and, as she sat back, the spread of her cheeks and her little rear-end! I watched hypnotized as she brought down herself onto my cockerel, coming back as she did as such to direct it into her wet pussy. It was excessively! To see it vanish inside her cozy vagina with her little butt flexing marginally between her spread cheeks as she sat back made any control troublesome! I shut my eyes and attempted to consider anything rather than that great body sitting on my chicken. Fortunately, I oversaw as she was smashing my balls marginally and, being somewhat delicate there since the contamination after my vasectomy, that had the impact of turning me off! Still hard, however, yet no threat of losing it!

Then, Gina had settled directly down; however, she stayed still before thinking back behind her with an evil grin all over. "Like what you see?" Gone was the obvious ingénue, and in her place was a lady who understood what she needed, sure about her sexuality and her control over us helpless men.

"I like it definitely," I answered happily, "and just to show you the amount I will play!"

"Mmmm," she mumbled, then heaved as my thumb entered her vagina from behind my chicken. I had covered it with salivation and now hauled her juices up and across her tight minimal indirect access. No indication of the previous consideration remained, and the small star looked as new as in the past. I ran my thumb here and there over her sphincter, pushing marginally harder each time until, at last, the tip entered; she rear-ends prepared to take it.

"Gracious God!" she groaned, "goodness yes! Do that!" I would not like to go excessively far now, both for her and me, so I just pushed an inch of thumb into her up to the principal joint. At that point started to screw her arsehole gradually. I could feel her cunt grasping my rooster tighter and was appreciative of the tension on my balls. Gina started to moan, to moan, and to mumble unobtrusively, "Not too far off, yes!" again and again. She began to bob on my chicken and push back a little as though needing more in her arse, yet I adhered to simply an inch. On the off chance that she needed more in there today, it would be 7 crawls of the rooster! It didn't take well before I felt another shiver and a surge of her fluid over my chicken and balls. She descended from her high speedier this time, dialed her body down my rooster, and set down adjacent to me.

Her hand grasped my erection and gradually stroked. "I need this in my arse, you know," she murmured, "somewhere down in my arse!" She had adapted rapidly to how to turn me on!

I went after her wrist and halted her development. "You are a minx Gina, a radiant minx. I know, and I will screw your arse - long, hard, and profound, yet first, we need to eat, shower, and prepare you!"

She grin, "Mmmm, I am ravenous," she answered, then slid down and brought my cockerel into her mouth!

"Gina, Gina loves. Goodness poo! You're going to need to stop that!"

"I like it," she said, raising her head and grinning.

"I surmise, Gina. I do as well; however, I need your arse; you need it in your arse, so you need to give it a rest!' She moped.

"Gracious, okay!" she said with a hesitant grin at that point laughed. "Gracious Mike, this is entertaining!"

"I know," I answered, giggling with her. Also, it was. She stood and strolled to the washroom. My eyes followed her beautiful structure.

At the entryway, she turned, "I can feel your eyes from here."

I giggled, "I'll request breakfast. We can shower after we eat."

"I trust you will eat after we shower," she reacted with a splendid grin and slipped into the restroom. I stayed still for a couple of moments tuning in to the restroom's sounds at that point, called down for breakfast before going in and doing whatever I might feel like doing. I was astonished that Gina just remained there watching me as I stood prepared to pee.

"I haven't seen a man pee previously," she said cheerfully.

"Wanna hold it?" I asked, snickering as I helped myself remember the old joke about Adam and Eve in the Garden of Eden.

"Can I?" she reacted, snickering back. I gestured, and she went along with me. At that point, I took my rooster, delicate now, and pointed it at the bowl. "Alright, go now!" I chuckled and started. "Ooooh! That feels unusual!"

"Feels bleeding bizarre for me too," I snickered, "positively not used to this!"

"It's fun!" She moved my chicken marginally, watching the stream into the bowl. At the point when I had completed, she turned and kissed me. "I don't have the foggiest idea," she said discreetly, "it's so unique with you. No hang-ups. No standards. It's so natural to be with you."

I held her nearby. "There are 'rules' Gina love, yet they're really simple. Anything goes fundamentally. It should be fun, nonetheless, and both or anyway numerous there might concur. It's dreadful if somebody is compelled to participate in a movement they don't care for." I ran my hands over her gorgeous arse cheeks. "That is the reason it's up to you if my chicken goes in your arse!" I said cheerfully.

"Mmm, I know," she answered unobtrusively, grave briefly. "I feel that is it, you know, Mike. With you, I don't feel any strain to do anything I would prefer not to do," she laughed at that point, "and that appears to make me need to get things done!" There was a loud thump on the entryway. "Sounds like breakfast," I said and wore my housecoat. Gina followed me into the room; I went to the entryway and ate.

She came out dressed uniquely in the plainest pair of white underwear. The sight blew my mind because, for reasons unknown, I can't clarify [other than the way that she is gorgeous] she looked so fuckable it wasn't accurate. Her firm bosoms, uncovered this way, were exquisite and the white material, pulled tight across her pussy, showed the notorious 'camel toe.' At the point when she turned, the exquisite region of her arse was some way or another featured by the straightforward white cotton undies.

"Screw Gina," I said as she remained before me, "you are a grisly dream!" She grinned contemplatively, said nothing, and sat adjacent to me. At that point, she turned and kissed me.

"I know," she murmured discreetly, "I like being your fantasy. I'm eager!"

I chuckled, and we had breakfast together. All through the dinner, I was aware of her sitting close to me - practically stripped. My psyche ran over the thing was coming straightaway. What position would I acquaint her with? How hard would I take her arse? How long could I last? Would she have the option to adapt to a few episodes of arsefucking today? This consideration made me calm - and made my rooster jerk continually. Towards the finish of the supper, Gina went to me.

"It is safe to say that you are OK, Mike? That is no joke."

I turned towards her and grinned. "Simply pondering Gina's love, simply thinking about."

"Pondering what?" she asked bashfully, for I accept she knew!

"Examining you," I said with a wan grin, "your flawless body, your stunning face, and eyes . . ."

". . . what's more, my arse!" she contributed, chuckling.

I murmured in counterfeit reality. "Gotten out once more! Indeed Gina. Examining your arse, your awesome arse."

"What were you examining?" she asked, playing the game.

"You need me to be straightforward?"

"Indeed," she gestured, "I think you have been since Friday."

"Alright," I grinned, "I trust you're prepared for this! I was attempting to sort out which position for your second butt-centric experience." She caused a commotion with a hesitant grin.

"Have you sorted it out?"

I giggled, "Actually, no, not yet. We will discuss it."

"Mmm," she mumbled, "I'm anticipating it, you know." I grinned. "What else?"

I met her shimmering eyes. "I was considering how 'hard' I could screw you," I said delicately. "I would prefer not to hurt you - and I would prefer not to place you off having my rooster in your arse!" I added, chuckling.

"You were delicate yesterday. I need you to be delicate today, yet I need to encounter everything - I advised you!"

"I know,' I answered, "and I will be delicate - until you disclose to me in any case. As I said, the lone standard is that it ought to be enjoyable!"

"Alright," she chuckled, "it will be a good time for the two of us! What else?"

"You are a curious minx," I giggled.

"It's a characteristic of the Australian assortment," she snickered back.

"Weeeeellll," I answered reluctantly, "I was contemplating how frequently we would have the option to do that today and around evening time."
"Mmm, presently there's an idea!" She giggled, "It relies upon how well you please me! Furthermore, how often we can get this," her hand came down and snatched my chicken through my undies [all I was wearing].

"Valid," I giggled, "and the Cialis will be working off!" Gina looked disillusioned. "Try not to stress," I added, "I have Viagra too, and that does something amazing! It relies upon you too, you know. This is new to you, and you will be unable to manage a few 'interruptions' in your arse," I finished snickering.

"I need to," she said unobtrusively. "I need to definitely. It has been such a lot of fun being with you. Like nothing, I have at any point experienced, and I need to continue encountering it as regularly as possible."

I grinned and embraced her to me. Could there be considerably more? I set that idea to the back of my brain. "Also, I do, too," I said unobtrusively. "To be with a lady as excellent as you has been superb. I will cherish the recollections."

She grinned. "Great. Would we be able to shower now since I am getting outrageously horny!" she said playfully.

"You need me to wash you?" I said cheerfully.

"Obviously: what young lady wouldn't - particularly your 'unique' wash!" She said as she made for the restroom.

I chuckled and followed her. I washed her 'appropriately' the solitary contrast, being that this time she took two fingers in her arse - and appreciated it! The sensual experience of washing each other expanded my charisma and prepared me for the coming 'preliminaries'!

Dry, she went to me and said, "Shoo!" I caused a stir curiously. "I need to prepare - moron!" she said giggling, "except if you don't need my arse?"

I grinned, for I did! I went after her and pulled her nearby, my hands running down her back and across her cheeks. "Beyond what you can know, Gina. This is a fantasy for me! You are so flawless. It is stunning!"

She stroked my cheek. "I'm happy," she said, "because it has been similar to a fantasy for me also." She snickered, "I didn't feel that it would resemble this when I said yes at the Gallery," she said. "I thought, well, that you were soon after a fast in and out! Happy you weren't! Presently proceed to allow me to prepare for you. I do anticipate a couple of climaxes first," she said, grinning, "much the same as you said!"

"Mmm," I grinned. "Appears I make them investigate to do!" I stroked one finger along the wrinkle between the cheeks of her arse at that point, with the other hand, along her pussy. "Going to eat you out!" I murmured.

She reddened. "Go!" she said. I did and, shutting the washroom entryway, laid on the bed.
She was gone practically thirty minutes, and I was starting to puzzle over whether she had suffered from sudden anxiety 'cold feet' in any case, similarly. As I stroked my flabby chicken in assumption, the entryway opened, and she remained in the opening. I hadn't seen her taking anything in there yet. She was wearing simply 4inch high obeyed shoes. The splendid red ones we had got yesterday. She stood one arm on the door jamb and grinned.

"Well?" she said, pirouetting and pushing her arse out provocatively.

I took a full breath, for she was beautiful! "Words bomb me," I said and started to rise.

"No! Stay there." She grinned, "It would seem that you need a little assistance," she said, gesturing at my delicate chicken.

I giggled and held it up as it hardened. "Simply required a little poke," I said. "You were quite a while - is everything OK?"

She looked only somewhat humiliated at that point grinned provocatively as she crossed to the bed. "I needed to ensure that . . . presently you will make me redden!" I snickered, "No! Stop it! I needed to ensure that . . . well when you . . . you know, that it was acceptable because you said . . . you know, that you liked me a ton as such!"

I grinned as she stooped on the bed close to me. "You're jabbering."

"I know," she grinned back, "I figure I should focus on you for some time!"

"Suits me," I said as I gazed toward her. Her bosoms were amazing hillocks, areolas pleased [probably solidified by her enema], the slight vault of her stomach dipping down to the blonde fluff covering her mons. I made to contact her.

"No!" she said solidly, 'no contacting - yet in any case! My turn!" With that, she started to run her fingers through the hairs on my chest, getting them between her fingers. "I like your hair," she murmured nearly to herself, at that point to me, "the folks I've been with don't have a lot of hair. Yours tickles," she laughed. "I like it!" She proceeded, momentarily revolving around my areolas with her fingers before twisting her head and tenderly sucking everyone. At that point, her hands meandered over my stomach [no 'six pack' there tragically; however, she didn't appear to mind] and kept on prodding the hair around my chicken and balls. At long last, one hand orbited my chicken, and the other supported my balls.

She looked somewhat meditative as she gradually stroked off me and delicately crushed my balls. She twisted her head and started to lick around my chicken base, then down across my fixing balls to my perineum. She looked at that point and grinned before bowing again and running her tongue from under my balls right to the tip of my cockerel, licking the minuscule drop of pre-cum that had crawled out. She gulped and took a gander at me. "I like your chicken," she said cheerfully. "I haven't, well, you know, I haven't investigated one." She chuckled, "The young men I have been with the need to stick it in someplace rapidly. I like this: wrecking about!"

I giggled, "It's called 'foreplay' Gina love - and it is bleeding grand! You simply continue - don't stress over me!"

She looked contemplative again as her finger followed all around my balls. "It's decent when you, you know, put your finger in my arse," she said, "treat you so harshly as that?"

"A finger in my arse?" She gestured. "Indeed," I said, "feels better."

"Will I do that?"

"On the off chance that you need."

"I do!" She chuckled, "All things considered, you will place much more into my arse, so I guess I should!" She viewed my chicken as it jerked at the possibility of her arse. Her finger squeezed tenderly on my rear-end, then harder. I lose, and it slid inside. "Ooh, that feels entertaining," she said.

"Feels amusing for me," I snickered at that point, "FUCK!" as she started to tenderly screw my arsehole with her finger. "Poo! Gina love, not all that much!" She caused a commotion curiously. "I'll cum then you'll need to stand by!"

"Gracious! You like it at that point?" I gestured. "Great, I can do it some more later!" With that, she eliminated her finger at that point, twisted her head to kiss, and lick the tip of my chicken. "Your turn!" she giggled as she lay back on the bed.

I moved to my side, head on one arm, and peered down at her. Her undertakings with my rooster and balls had clearly 'warmed her up' for her areolas were standing hard and pleased. I followed a finger down her cheek, her jaw, her shoulder, and onto her bosom and orbited initial one areola than the other over and over. I squeezed a little and changed before bringing down my mouth onto her tits. I sucked; chomped tenderly, prodded, licked, and nipped her areolas for an age until at long last remunerated by a delicate, low groan and a shiver as she came. I lifted my head and grinned down at her. "Lick me," she murmured, "please!"

"I just did!" I prodded.

"Goodness," she said energetically, "don't prod! If it's not too much trouble! Lick me!"

I twisted and murmured, "obviously, you heavenly messenger!" She moaned and opened her legs in greeting. I moved between and put in no time flat looking down at her lovely body. "You have a lovely pussy," I said happily - for she did! She becomes flushed. I don't assume anybody had at any point said that to her previously! Bowing my head, I sucked her swollen labia on one side then the other before examining as profound as possible with my tongue and sucking her juices out. Gina groaned and pushed her midsections upwards into me. I tongue screwed her at that point, getting a charge out of the practically creature sounds that came from her as she cruised near climax. Sooner or later, I just went up and discovered her small swollen clit: sufficiently large for me to nip with my lips at that point bother the tip with my tongue. It was sufficient! Gina shouted at that point uproariously and pushed upwards considerably harder as her body shivered in the climax. I kept her clit caught as she rode the way of delight, drawing it out however much I could.

As she descended, I moved back to her vagina, licking somewhere inside again a couple of times before hauling my tongue down. Lifting her twisted legs at that point, my tongue discovered her tight butt and flicked at it. Gina moaned a delicate, "Gracious yes!"

I lifted my head, "Turn over, Gina," I said unobtrusively. She opened her shut eyes. "I need to lick your arse!" I said stupidly. She grinned a practically knowing grin at that point sluggishly moved face down as I moved out of her way. She quickly opened her legs again, and I moved back between. Here is the superb sight in the room - well, for an arse man like me at any rate. I could appreciate the delicate incline of her shoulders and flexible back down to the swell of her expansive hips underneath which sat the beautifully provocative cheeks of her heavenly arse. No air pocket butt her except for the scope of a developed lady's arse. Wide and disgusting with no overflow fat, simply that important to make the delicate bends. Like this, her cheeks were open, her little rosebud in plain view over the sexy wetness of her vagina - the two openings nearly asking to be filled.

I delighted in the sight for a brief timeframe before bowing my head to her vagina and licking up towards her rear-end. At that point, to the superb globes of her arse. I was stroking, touching, in some cases crushing. Kissing, licking, tenderly gnawing, bringing delicate groans of delight from Gina. At that point, her butt-centric parted. I ran my tongue all over, flicking her rosebud as I did as such, at that point concentrated there. My tongue tested at that point rimmed her arsehole at that point examined once more. Again and again, until I felt one more shiver from Gina and a low, winded, 'Yessssssss!" I pushed more earnestly, and the rosebud opened, and my tongue slipped inside. I could taste the enhanced lube I had got for her to utilize, the flavor of her squeezes that had run from her pussy, and the flavor of her. It's each of the amazing love potions! At long last, lifting my head, I supplanted my tongue with a finger and, surrounding a couple of times, pushed ineffectively to the principal joint. Coming to across the bed, I got the lube from the side table and pressed some onto my finger, pulled out somewhat, at that point back in. I did this a couple of times, pushing up to the subsequent joint and adding lube each time.

Gina glanced back at me, grinning. "You insidious man," she giggled, "you are preparing my arse . . . to fuck?"

I grinned, "You, young lady, are a vamp!"

"What's a 'vamp'?"

"An entitcingly alluring lady who eats men!"

She snickered and groaned delicately [I was screwing her arse gradually with 66% of my center finger after all!]. "I thought it was you who ate me!"

"Furthermore, decent it was as well," I snickered in those days stooped up, keeping my finger in her arsehole. "Is this acceptable?" I asked as yet chuckling.

The appropriate response was quite clear as she moaned and replied with a winded, "Yessssss!" I kept on fingering screw her arse until, at long last, it was inside; at that point, I added a subsequent finger, watching to see that she approved of the interruption. Her eyes were shut, and she gradually started to push back onto my fingers at that point, "I need you in my arse again, Michael," she said delicately, "please!" I descended adjacent to her and kissed her lips. "I need to see your face," she said delicately once more. "I need to see your eyes when you do it!"

"Mish is somewhat harder," I murmured.

"I couldn't care less," she reacted, "I need to see your eyes!" Anal in evident preacher can be something of a battle for the woman, particularly from the get-go in her butt-centric experience. "I need it all, you know, everything!" I took a full breath, for it was hard to hold off; however, I realized this was her post-climax want talking. As yet in her arse, my fingers were moving gradually to and fro, yet now I took them out and murmured.

"Turn over then, Gina, love." Again she did slowly as I cleared out. She opened her legs for me, yet I just stroked her cheek. "We need to raise your arse Gina if you need it like this?" It was an assertion and an inquiry. "Lift your bum!" She did, and I several firm cushions under her disgusting cheeks. This lifted her arse and would make the sections simpler for her.

"It feels weird!" she said happily; however, she settled down into the pads.

"Test your sanity back," I said as I lifted and separated her legs. She did and was currently totally open. Her pussy was drenching wet, her juices spilling down across her shimmering rear-end. I twisted my head and sucked her vaginal lips once more, delighting in the taste and scent of her excitement. Gina moaned noisily as I discovered her clit again and sucked it hard.

"Goodness god!' was all I heard as she shivered once more. I immediately stooped up and pushed my chicken delicately between the swollen lips of her vagina. "I thought . . .!"

"Indeed," I murmured, "goodness yes, Gina, however, this first - to welcome you on!" I filled her cunt then, in one crash profound into her body. Thighs conflicted over and over as I screwed her pussy long, hard and profound. It didn't take well before she was calling my name again and shivering in another peak. I screwed her through it at that point, pulling out my rooster and blessing it with plentiful measures of lube, acquainted the tip with her shaking arsehole.

"Good gracious!" she shouted as I pushed delicately into her. Her rear-end, that erotic rosebud, opened and acknowledged the top of my cockerel. Her eyes were open, centered around my face as the magnificent starting joy of her sphincter grasping me enrolled.

"Yessss!" she moaned delicately, "yessss!" I was all the while, watching her face for the response to my sporadic interruption. Gradually a grin crossed her highlights. "Go on, Mike - please! I need it!" I pushed forward, and two crawls of my chicken entered further into her tight arsehole. Her eyes enlarged significantly more, and her mouth shaped a practically wonderful 'O' of shock [although she is more likely than not recalled the inclination from the first time]. I peered down and saw my cockerel skewering her cheeks; her rear-end had vanished, driven in by my erection.

"More?" I asked unobtrusively.

"Goodness indeed, yes! More!" Another two inches - she had above and beyond a large portion of my chicken in her arse now, not long before I extended. She gasped, and I saw a glimmer of uneasiness cross her highlights, cleaning the grin away. I immediately pulled out. It's important to do this to facilitate the uneasiness of the sphincter muscle. I halted with simply the tip of my erection, breaking her rear-end. "Try not to stop Mike," she said, "please. It's OK now - truly. It just . . . for a piece. Please," she grinned up at me provocatively, "screw my arse." She knew!

I went after the lube and crushed some more onto my chicken at that point pushed once more into her arsehole. It was flawless! Tight, hot, and elusive. A velvet paradise that appeared to touch my rooster. I was before long moving gradually in and out, simply screwing her arse with 5 crawls of the rooster, saving the more extensive part and the rest until she was truly into taking my chicken in her arsehole.

Gina was grinning, her eyes presently shut and mumbling a delicate arrangement of "Yesss! Do that. Goodness, yessss!" It appeared to be that all the inconvenience had, for the occasion, lessened. Following a couple of moments of this, the time had come to give her every last bit of me, so I slide my full 7 creeps into her willing rectum. Her eyes opened, and a loud heave got away from her lips as my thighs met her cheeks.

"Gracious FUCK! Owwwwww! Enormous, so wicked large!" I was still hysterically attempting to clutch my longing to screw her firm. Clearly, in any case, this was harming her once more.

"Gina! Gina!" She appeared not to be hearing me, lost in the combination of sentiments exuding from her arsehole. "Gina - would you say you are OK?"

"Gracious God! Indeed, yes. It just . . . No doubt about it!"

"Not actually," I said delicately, "it simply feels that way!"

"I know. I know. Try not to stop now - please. I realize it will be OK." She grinned again, and I felt her rectum press my cockerel. She saw my appearance of shock. "See! Presently do what you did yesterday - make me cum! I need to feel it once more!"

I grinned down at her and started to move. Gradually from the outset. Long, profound strokes that nearly removed my chicken from her then back. All the time is watching her face as she became used to the attack of her rectum. This was moderate enchantment. I needed to keep going now, keep going for enough time to give her a great many climaxes. To let her vibe the joy of a chicken in her arse - to make her need it over and over. I changed my view to my chicken leaving at that point, entering her arsehole. I watched the tight ring of her sphincter appear to not need me to leave as I pulled out then vanish as I pushed back. I prodded her to rear-end with my cockhead, bringing low, delicate groans from Gina and a listless grin.

I started to accelerate as I noticed her climax drawing nearer, screwing her harder now, my thighs slapping hers. Out of nowhere, her entire body shivered. Her butt and rectum held my cockerel somewhere inside in an undulating handle.

"Gracious fuck - YES! Indeed! Indeed!" she cried as her eyes opened and looked into mine. "Goodness, YES! Screw me, Mike. If it's not too much trouble, screw me. I need it once more. Please!" I realized then that butt-centric sex was continually going to be something uncommon for Gina. I realized ladies like that. Ladies whose butt-centric climaxes were more exceptional than vaginal and a few ladies who favored their arses screwed.

I eased back once more, giving her future time down from her high, at that point twisted and kissed her lips. "Great?" I asked delicately.

Breathing vigorously, she murmured her answer. "Goodness indeed, yes. It was superior to yesterday. Oooooohhhhhhh - yes, do that!" I was moving my chicken in her arsehole gradually, tenderly, letting her vibe the entire length sliding over her butt and into her hot and tight rectum.

"Gina, Gina, your arse is paradise!" I murmured, my entire body responding to the smooth catch of her arsehole. "Once more?"

"Indeed, gracious yes - however, would we be able to do an alternate position?"

I grinned, "Anything specifically."

"Gracious dear! Goodness, keep dong that - please!" Now I was simply utilizing my cockhead to prod her to rear-end - a superb inclination that I truly couldn't see. Presumably something worth being thankful for

273

because I should concede that control was troublesome to some degree. "I don't have the foggiest idea - ooooooooo! No doubt about it!" I facilitated my rooster from the paradise of her arsehole, lay close to her, and murmured. "Spoon!" She grinned, then moved on her side.

The spoon is acceptable because you can stroke and kiss back and shoulder just as bosoms, yet you can't get very as profound. I moved near her and the rooster close by, squeezing the tip at her butt. She came to the back and lifted the cheek of her arse to ease the passage. "You've seen this previously," I asked with a chuckle.

"Mmmm," she mumbled, "it would seem that fun!" I started to tenderly screw her arse in this position, just a large portion of my rooster sliding across her rear-end and into her rectum. Gina groaned delicately, "Yessss! Goodness, that is GOOD. More!" I pushed further as she lifted her leg to encourage a much more profound section and screwed her hard. It was turning out to be a lot for me.

"I need you to face down," I murmured energetically, the creature near the surface. I needed to assault her arse. She glanced back at me, astounded.

"Facedown?" I needed her such a lot like that - my number one position - yet it was a battle for the beneficiary! I felt the contention inside - simply 'take' her with no idea for her or think of her as solace. "Gracious god - continue doing that. Aaaagggghhh!" The last won and my answer were to cum!

"You need my cum in your arse Gina? Advise me. Disclose to me the amount you need it!" Language is thus so significant, and I realized that it wouldn't take long if she started to talk this way. "I need to, Gina; I need to cum in your arse. Somewhere down in your body. Advise me!"

Gina groaned boisterously and turned her head back. "Screw me, Mike, screw me in the arse. Aaaaaaaggggghhhhh! Indeed, yes! Cum in me. Cum in my arse. Fill me! Goodness GOD!" It was sufficient. I crashed into the arsehole and held my chicken there. There, swollen in craving, it beat cum into her entrails. Her rear-end and rectum, appearing to respond to my climax, undulated and crushed, draining cum from my body. Gina shivered and shouted delicately. My entire body shivered as I felt Mr pith shoot along with my chicken and into her.

"Gina," I called noisily, "gracious fuck! Gina, Gina, Gina!" A beat of energy reflected each call of her name into her arse. It was extreme. I expected to kiss her shoulder, nibble even, claim the perfect young lady whose body was taking my cockerel and my spirit.

At long last, it was finished.

I held her nearby as she recuperated from what appeared to have been as extraordinary a climax as mine. My cockerel, mellowing gradually, was not quickly ousted from the velvet paradise of her rectum cuddled up near her as I was. I was glad to simply hold this exquisite young lady who had readily given such a large amount of herself to me. I was somewhat bothered with myself for nearly letting completely go and mishandling her trust, yet now I kissed her neck and shoulders, running my hand over the bends of her body, appreciating the smooth skin. Sooner or later, Gina moved away a laid on her back, gazing toward me.

"What is it?" she asked unobtrusively, obviously detecting something was upsetting me. "You didn't hurt me." She grinned, "It was acceptable, so acceptable. Far superior to yesterday."

I grinned wanly down at her. "I speculated," I said delicately. "It was fabulous, Gina love."

"What's going on at that point. You appear to be disturbed." I accept that legit is, in every case, best in the room, so I murmured and advised her.

"Gina love, that position . . . well it's effortlessly transformed into my top choice . . ."

"Your Favorite!" she interposed.

I grinned, ". . . indeed, my top pick. Facedown on the bed, legs together."

"Oooooooo!" she said with a devilish grin, "that sounds exceptionally fascinating!"

"It is," I giggled wryly, "be that as it may, Gina love, it is difficult - would not be simple - for you. It's a significant preliminary for the woman, and," I added with a bit of shame, "I do will, in general, move a piece diverted."

"For what reason isn't it simple?"

"Indeed, with legs shut, you would be tighter, and the point is extraordinary, down and in . . . hell," I chuckled, "this is weird - examining this with you>

"However, we can, we are - and that is acceptable because I need to do that for you!'

"Gina, Gina, love, you don't need to." I grinned, "You've given me such a lot of delight since we met, and I would prefer not to hurt you. Gina," I came to and held her, "I don't need you to leave tomorrow and feel . . . I don't have a clue . . . utilized, I assume. I need you to leave having appreciated all that we did. Leave and need to investigate considerably more."

She came up and pulled my lips to hers. "You have, you know. I have appreciated everything - and I need more. You are so kind and delicate that I'm not apprehensive. Regardless of whether you hurt me a bit," I shook my head. "No, no, regardless of whether you do, it doesn't make any difference since I realize you just do what you need to for me to appreciate it. So I need that - I need YOU to appreciate it, and I realize that, on the off chance that you do, I will also." She kissed me once more. "You have shown me such a lot of joy. Not to be modest in here," he arm cleared around the room, "and I realize that, when I leave tomorrow, I will have had the greatest few days of my life!" I should admit to an explosion of bitterness - she was leaving tomorrow!

"I think you have filled over the most recent few days?"

She moaned, "Yes, Mike sweetheart, I think I have," at that point, she snickered, "for the better, I think. I was a genuinely guiltless youthful thing on Friday - presently, I feel like a lady!"

I chuckled, "I don't think things happen that quick!"

"Gracious however they do, Mike. I've seen all that we've done - and a few things we will do," she added with a devilish grin, "at our 'young ladies DVD' evenings when we watch pornography. However, I did nothing other than straight sex and a little . . . you know sucks. No one could do that to me as you do - not my pussy or my arse. It's so glorious. What's more, my arse! I never knew, never acknowledged, how great it very well maybe. No Mike love," she finished gravely, "I feel 'grown up' presently."

"Well," I said happily, "you sure look it laying there with my spirit in your arse!"

"You are a horrible man!" she giggled, sitting up. "Presently, I need to proceed to tidy up." She stood and strolled to the washroom. I watched her perfect arse influence as she strolled and considered a stream of spunk as she did as such. She halted at the entryway and thought back behind her. Quiet with the circumstance, she grinned, "Similar to what you see?" and she squirmed her arse provocatively.

"Gracious god Gina," I snickered, "would that I was 40 years more youthful and I would screw you there again at present!"

"Mmmm, presently there's an idea," she reacted with an extraordinary enormous sulk, "however I guess I should stand by until this evening!" She snickered and vanished into the washroom.

~

11. A Short Interlude:

In which we lunch, visit the recreation center and the Conservatory

~:

I followed a couple of moments later, and we partook in a shower together - simply a shower this time even though it was consistently a joy to cleanse Gina's shapely body! In the wake of getting dry and wearing robes, we sat on the overhang sitting above the harbor drinking and visiting, attempting to choose how to manage the remainder of the day.

"I guess YOU need a rest," she asked tongue in cheek with a major grin.

I chuckled accordingly. "All things considered, yes, I presumably do. That is one of the issues us old folks face."

"Quality not amount," she chuckled accordingly.
"I like to think so; however, no one but you can pass judgment!"

"Anyway," she said with a shy articulation, "not exactly sure yet - we should perceive how things go!"

"Minx, I should tan your arse!"

"Mmm, that seems like fun, yet I figure I would prefer you screwed it," she added with an attractive smile.

"You make me wish I were 30 years more youthful," I chuckled.

"Be that as it may, at that point, we wouldn't have met, would we!?"

"Minx! Presently, how will we respond?"

"It's a particularly exquisite day," she replied, "for what reason don't we simply go to the recreation center and the Conservatory?" Well, they were both just a short leave, and I was certain that we would both appreciate the late-spring daylight.
"Smart thought!"

I dressed rapidly in pants and a golf shirt and trusted that Gina would prepare. I speculated that she would need to put her best self forward, so I wasn't shocked that she took some time; however, there was no rush. At the point when she at long last came out, my eyes almost jumped off of my mind.

"Screw Gina . . ."

"Expectation so!" she interposed.

"You can't go out that way - you'll cause an uproar!"

"Great," she giggled, "however, I wager I'm wearing significantly more than a large portion of the young ladies out there!" Well! She was 'wearing' a long-sleeved, bolero-type top of darkish pink chiffon, which left her waist, from bosom to belly, exposed. Her exquisite bosoms were just barely covered and, I accepted, upheld by a practically imperceptible bra. Her jeans, blue denim hot jeans with frayed shorts, sat low on her hips, nearly stressing the delicate vault of her uncovered stomach. Her open shoes had 6-inch heels with 2-inch stages. Her one piece of adornments was the dark choker I had gotten her with a little jewel pendant that sat just beneath. She looked STUNNING! I hadn't seen all that we had purchased together, and I realized that she had expected to amaze me with the greater part of the garments.

"Hell, Gina, you look wicked fantastic!" How might it feel, I thought at that point, meandering through the recreation center with this vision of perfection?

"I like looking great," she said. "Mama consistently said, 'on the off chance that you have it, parade it!' so I do when I can."

"Well, you surely do, and you are," I chuckled.

"You wouldn't fret?"

"Brain, how is it possible that I would perhaps mind. Each person in the recreation center will be puzzling over whether I have a huge chicken or a gigantic bank balance or both," I snickered.

"All things considered, I am certain you don't have either, and I am VERY content with what you do have!" She stood close and kissed me, her shoes bringing her up to my stature. I held her firmly, and we nearly didn't will go out as she squeezed into me.

"Devious!" she chuckled as she pulled away, "I thought we were going out!"

"Alright, OK, yes - we're going out!" I said with mock hesitance, "however when we get back . . .!" She caused a stir and grinned provocatively. ". . . at the point when we get back I will screw the arse off you!"

"Mmmmmm! Indeed please," she chuckled and drove the exit plan, her perfect arse, highlighted by the high heels and the hot jeans, influencing erotically. We strolled around the Opera House and sat watching the harbor and the scaffold featured by the late-spring sun. It was packed with local people and tourists - a beautiful ordinary Sunday. Inevitably we had some lunch at one of the restaurants around the harbor at that point meandered across to the recreation center. She was correct! She was wearing more than a considerable lot of the young ladies in plain view - and I utilize the word 'show' deliberately! However, I need to say that none contrasted with the exquisite lady I had on my arm! Also, she was on my arm.' She made it completely clear that she was 'with' me regardless of all the respecting looks that her sexy appearance induced. It's interesting, yet numerous ladies don't understand that dressed, they are hotter than exposed - and I mean ladies with incredible bodies. Gina stood apart because she was dressed - yet dressed provocatively.

In the wake of sashaying around the recreation center, we visited the Conservatory and saw the brilliant assortment of orchids that they have there. I truly missed my camera suddenly, for I might have some awesome pictures of Gina with them. I got some later, yet I didn't realize that at that point.

The evening passed before long, and we chose to have supper before getting back to the room. "We don't need to go out any longer at that point," Gina said with an underhanded smile, "and you can focus on me!"

I snickered, "I can't consider anything I would prefer to do!" So we ate, genuinely light truth be told, and were once again at the inn around 7. When we overcame the entryway, Gina turned, held me tight, and kissed me long and hard.

~

12. Back at the inn:

A semi-public fuck; some fun, and Gina gets arse-screwed face down:
"I need you!" she murmured discreetly, "I need you!" and she pushed her body against mine provocatively. I ran my hands down her back, chiffon first at that point uncovered skin: delicate, arousing exposed skin. At that point, over the swell of her arse cheeks and the tight material of her hot denim jeans. As far as I can tell, there is no doubt that this outfit was hot as hellfire since now my hands found the delicate skin of her thighs. Gina was pushing against me, her tongue meeting mine, practically devouring me.

I believed I expected to quiet her down a little - the hot jeans had been focusing on intriguing spots. "Overhang," I said cheerfully. She caused a commotion curiously. "You'll see. Simply a little test!" She grinned, turned, and sashayed to the overhang, her arse swinging provocatively. We were three stories up to peer down on the harbor, the scaffold, and the drama house without any problem. We could likewise see the groups underneath - I puzzled over whether they could see us up here!

She transformed and again liquefied into my arms. My chicken was remaining at complete consideration, having been enticed by her radiant arse and the positive chance of filling it later on: a reality which she saw as it squeezed into her belly. "Mmmm! I think I need that!" she murmured with an attractive grin.

My hands appreciated the delicate skin of her back and afterward meandered over the awesome bends of her base cheeks as I murmured consequently, "Turn, hang over the overhang and stick out your arse!"

Her eyes broadened in amazement. "Over here! Individuals will see!"

I giggled. "No. The boards are misty glass, so no one will want to see anything - yet you will want to see them! Intrigued?"

She snickered - and almost got screwed there and afterward with no artfulness! Her snicker has that impact on me! "It will be energizing," she said as she turned and inclined toward the midriff high balustrade - and she stuck her arse out. I nearly blew my mind as she appeared to normally plunge her back. I would not like to screw her arse a little while ago; she had not readied. However, it was an incredible allurement!

I came to adjust to her front, unfastening her hot jeans and moseying them down. She glanced back at me as I did as such, her eyes substantial with want, at that point lifted a leg so I could take them off. I just needed to stop and give recognition to her brilliant arse. I kissed the cheeks, licked and stroked them, at that point dug between. She had on the skimpiest of straps, which just measured her pussy with just a slim line of material between her cheeks. Moving it aside, I approached her lovely pussy. It resembled a bloom holding back to open - as of now marginally wet! Over the small opening of her butt, simply somewhat blushed by my past interruptions, yet close and unfathomably alluring. Gina heaved as my tongue discovered her vagina, sucking and licking, testing as profound as possible. Her wheezes and commotions of endorsement proceeded as I licked and sucked for some time at that point ran my tongue over-top her delicate butt. At that point, another heave, significantly stronger than previously, as she pushed her arse back into my face.

"Gracious god Mike! Lick my arse! Please!" It was certain that Gina had gotten touchy and had immediately figured out how to appreciate the consideration I paid to her tight butt. I wasn't going to pull away, needing her to be truly prepared for her arse to be screwed later. Not at present; presently, her pussy! As I licked and tested her tight sphincter, I came to down and fixed my pants, backing my erection out delicately. I stood and introduced the tip of my cockerel to her under their lips.

She thought back behind her, eyes substantial and with a mischievous grin. "Pussy?"

I grinned back, keeping still. "Mmmm! I'm saving your arse for some other time."

She grinned, then her eyes enlarged as I drove home. Gina bowed her legs marginally and pushed her base once more into me. We immediately got into a beat with the goal that I could get as profound as could be expected. She was making much more clamor than in the room, and I contemplated whether it was the enthusiasm of knowing there were individuals about [although three stories down]. With my hands on her shapely hips, I controlled the great standing fuck. I kept her still and screwed her hard and profound at that point, maneuvered her onto my rooster for a much harder beating. I think she came twice, and, I am certain, individuals underneath more likely than not heard her shout as the second huge climax hit. I was saving me, presumably last, cum conveyance for her arse, so I controlled my own emotions by guaranteeing that she delighted in every last bit of chicken.

As she, at last, descended from her high, she thought back behind her. "Goodness, you are a charlatan!" she grinned. I snickered; her Aussie intonation would never make that an insult.

"Valid," I chuckled, for it was, at that point, added, "And you are an attractive minx Gina. More?" I asked wickedly as I kept on freaking her pussy.

"Actually, no, not a little while ago!" she said with a snicker. "Try not to need you are wearing yourself, or that . . ." she gestured to her back, ". . . down. I need it in my arse once more. I don't have a clue why," she added meditatively, "it's simply that it felt so . . . great!"

"Also, you will get it there," I grinned, stroking her hips and arse. Pulling back from her pussy I laid the length of my rooster between her cheeks and started a screwing development, sliding the length across her delicate butt.

"Gracious, you bugger. Goodness indeed, do that. God, I need you there!" To be straightforward, the inclination was magnificent, and it was everything I could don't to bugger her absolutely and totally like this. Standing butt-centric is marvelous however she was not readied,

288

and, regardless of the amount, she seemed to appreciate a chicken in her arse; it was early days for her. I would not like to ruin her future satisfaction by pushing excessively hard from the beginning. I could stand by and, in any case, I planned to take her in my number one position [and trust that she appreciated it as much as I did].

I pulled away and turned her. We kissed: an energetic and long kiss that left my heart beating. I would not like to release this young lady! "Would you like to shower?" I murmured as we broke the kiss.

"Mmmm! I need to prepare for this exquisite thing . . ." she grasped my rooster, ". . . to go in my arse!" So we showered together, simply flushing the residue of the day away before drying one another. She followed me out of the restroom, grinning, and brought a transporter from the closet. "For you," she said with a mischievous smile as I loosened up in the room. "A shock!" and she vanished into the washroom.

I could hear her in there singing delicately to herself as she arranged for me. I took a full breath: for ME! Only one more night with her! My psyche was going over potential outcomes. Separated, I had no genuine ties back in the UK. My business, fundamentally worried about monetary managing in the City of London, could be overseen by those I left in control with observing me from a far distance. Did I realize that, as a guest, I could just remain in Australia for a half year and no more except for why not do that? If I did, would she stay with me? She was mature enough even though, at 22, she lived with her folks. There would be no specific protests should she choose to leave them for some time. Would the age contrast put her off?

I realized that I could lease a loft on a short rent [or a long one if I left Gina there] without a very remarkable issue. I threw the prospects around in my psyche. She was so stunning! To be with her for that timeframe! There could be no drawn-out responsibility; I realized that, yet for a brief timeframe, we could have loads of fun! I realized she would have a long break in the half-year time frame so we could travel - the prospects appeared to be interminable!

I settled on my choice; I would propose the topic with Gina and see what she said. The faint heart always lost reasonable woman! That would stand by, notwithstanding, until this night's diversion' had wrapped up. So now I just lay there and think about this magnificent young lady. I was in a dream when the restroom entryway opened. I turned my head to look and was struck idiotic, surprised, in shock!

She was wearing an undergarment, dull pink in shading with cuts at the front. Suspenders held up dark stockings. Her bosoms were free, areolas erect. Her light hair tumbled to her shoulders freely. 5-inch heels expanded her stature and flaunted her agile figure. She grinned and turned gradually, waving the pink strap in her grasp. Her arse was uncovered, outlined by the bodice's base, the suspenders, and the stocking tops. Goodness knows how she had bound up the back, yet she had! At that point, she was confronting me. I could see the delicate light hair of her sex between her legs. Her grin was wide and tempting. She didn't utter a word, just remained by the entryway.

"Wow!' I oversaw at last as I moved off the bed. "You are a fantasy, a holy messenger!" She grinned at that and turned once more, thinking back behind her. I needed to take a few full breaths to control my hustling beat. "Gina, Gina, loves. You are genuinely lovely!"

"It's for you, Mike, for you!" she said and grinned enticingly. "Take me!" she murmured and held open her arms.

I took another full breath, and she came to me, her delicate bends squeezing against my bare body. I could feel the sleek fabric of the bodice against my chest, the nylon of her stockings against my legs, and her hair brushing my face. We kissed. A delicate, delicate kiss turned more energetic as warmth filled both our bodies. My rooster squeezed into her and appeared to break to the sentiment of the circumstance. Her hands dug among us and caught my erection.

"Mmmmm!" she mumbled, then added, grinning, "Is this for ME?"

"Goodness FUCK Gina, yes. Each bleeding inch!"

"Great," she said delicately as she stroked me with one hand, the other measuring my previously fixing balls. Gradually she stooped before me and, eyes fixed on mine as I peered down at her, brought my cockerel into her mouth. Her tongue washed my rooster head as her lips framed an 'O' around its size. She appeared to delight in the flavor of me, for I was releasing plentiful measure of pre-cum into her mouth. For me? I was near paradise. A wonderful young lady bowing at my feet offering all - I would not tolerate maltreatment that offering! Gina was moving her head now, her lips sliding along my chicken. Her tongue kept on washing the entire length. I needed to stop her: much as I would have gotten a kick out of the chance to fill her mouth with cum again, I realized that I would not have the option to 'rise' once more. Viagra can't work supernatural occurrences!

"Gina, Gina, love. You should stop." Her eyes discovered mine again, and her eyebrows raised. "Christ Gina, your mouth is paradise . . . FUCK!" She sucked hard and licked, grinning around my rooster. "Gina! Stop, please! I need to screw you!"

She pulled her mouth from my cockerel and stood. "Mmm, I need you to - so I would do well to stop." She looked at me. "Have intercourse with me!"

"There isn't anything that I would prefer to do," I murmured as I drove her to the bed. "lay back!" Gina sluggishly fell back onto the bed at that point moved to the center.

"Have intercourse with me!" Her eyes were brimming with want as I moved to consent to her cravings. I bowed alongside her and kissed her lips, her cheeks, her eyes, her neck. Gina moaned delicately as I had intercourse with her brilliant body. Gradually I kissed down to her bosoms, licking and sucking her erect areolas.

"Goodness, god! Yes!" she cried as I sucked her areolas, and my hand discovered her sex. I stroked her pussy delicately, feeling the wetness previously leaking from her vagina. "If it's not too much trouble! If it's not too much trouble! I need you to such an extent!"

"Before long," I murmured as I dropped down her body. My mouth discovered her mount, sucking the delicate hide tenderly before tasting her sex. I opened her legs, stooped between, at that point, twisted my head to her cunt. My tongue discovered her clit, effectively swollen in her expanding energy. I licked her clit, sucked it inside my lips, utilized my tongue to prod it again and again as I heard her groaning in joy. A long, low moan got away from her lips as she shivered in enthusiasm; fluid streamed. I savored the flavor of her as my mouth dropped down to her cunt lips. Sucking them inside, I tested profoundly with my tongue: over and over, washing her under lips with my salivation, tasting the actual quintessence of her. She shivered again as my tongue dropped down further to her rear-end: her still close sphincter. I examined, licked, tasted her, and pushed against the muscle with the tip of my tongue. She opened it and took me inside.

"Goodness, please! I need to feel you inside me, Mike: somewhere inside me! Please!" I went up and took my strong erection close by, pointing the tip of my rooster at her vagina and sliding into her.

"Indeed!!! Gracious yes! Screw me, Mike, if it's not too much trouble, screw me!" I did, digging somewhere inside her, pushing an entire 7 crawls of rooster into her. She shivered as I screwed her hard and profound: full scale, all in. Our eyes met, and she grinned in her energy. "It's awesome! Do it, please. Try not to stop."

Moderate. Quick. Shallow. Profound. Notwithstanding the smooth paradise of her delicate wetness, I had nearly stopped my craving to cum, hanging on for the last demonstration somewhere down in her arse. Yet, I needed to keep going as far as might be feasible so she would recollect this keep going for quite a while. I forgot about time at that point, having intercourse with this stunning young lady. I watched her face, her eyes, as a great many climaxes shook her body. I gloried in this capacity to do this for and to her: to give her pleasure and show her the force of her body.

I sat back at long last, the tip of my chicken still in her pussy, and grinned down at her. A delicate sheen covered her bosoms. She licked her lips enticingly then grinned back. "Take my arse," she said delicately, "any way you need!"

I am accepting a full breath as my chicken jerked. "At that point, stoop, Gina love, bow at the edge of the bed." I moved back to permit her to move, which she did, slowly and bowed with her arse push back.

"Like this," her grin was brimming with demure mischievousness. "Take my arse," she said once more, "any way you would need!" A lady like this is difficult. It can draw out the monster in a man, and I was experiencing difficulty keeping down the devil that advised me to 'use' her without thought. I stroked my chicken, just crawls from her face, and she grinned up at me. "If it's not too much trouble! I need you to such an extent!"

This last appeared to quiet me, and I grinned back at her. "Indeed," I answered, "however just as you might want to." I moved off the bed and bowed, my face level with her arse. I revered her then, my tongue and mouth working over her wet pussy and tight arsehole. I could hear her delicate moans of delight as my tongue drove into her. Standing, I went after the lube and pressed a goodly sum onto her sphincter, utilizing my finger to work it inside. More lube and two fingers brought a noisy moan from Gina's lips: a sound which expanded as I pivoted my fingers in her arsehole.

I inclined forward. "Indeed? Gina love."

"Goodness, screw yes! Screw my arse, Mike. Screw my arse hard!" I covered my erection with lube then my chicken was at her tight ring. I pushed tenderly into her, breaking the contracting muscle. Gina heaved then loose. I took care of her a greater amount of my rooster, gradually, gracious so gradually, until she had 5 crawls inside her tight rectum. Hot: hot and satiny. Tight along the entire length of my rooster: her sphincter grasping. Out, at that point delicately back: to and fro. My hands discovered her hips, and I moved here with me. Gina didn't appear to mind: to be in any uneasiness. I push home inclination my thighs hit the cheeks of her arse.

"Good gracious, YES. It feels so amusing. Aaaggghhhh!" I was sliding in and out now, screwing her tight arsehole gradually. As in the past, I appreciated watching the tight muscle of her rear-end sliding along my cockerel. I was holding myself in charge, for this was just the start! I filled her at that point, holding her on my chicken, inclined forward.

"Do you need it, Gina? Need everything?" She bowed her head in reverse, and our lips met.

"Indeed," she said energetically, "yes! Everything! Fill my arse. Gracious God, this is so awesome! I never knew, never acknowledged, it very well maybe this way. Screw MY ARSE!" This was excessive. I almost lost it at that point and filled her insides with spirit, however, oversaw, by remaining still, to hang on.

"What?" she said, feeling me still and covered inside her arse.

I am accepting a full breath as the emergency passed. "Your arse is paradise Gina love, supreme paradise. I just needed to stop briefly. I need it to last!"

"I do as well," she reacted with a major grin. "It feels so huge. Enormous and interesting. Entertaining yet great." I started to pull out gradually. "Gracious God, yet that feels inconceivable. Kindly don't stop Mike. Have intercourse to my arse gradually." I did, pulling practically the entirety of my chicken from her gradually, watching her rear-end slide along with my cockerel. At that point, back, again and again, gradually and delicately.

"Goodness indeed, harder now, Mike loved. Harder." I went after the lube and included more of my rooster as it slid inside her at that point, hands on her hips; I started to screw her hard, quick and profound. It didn't take some time before she shouted delicately, and her body shivered. I push profound kept still as her rectum and butt held my chicken firmly through her climax. As she descended, I inclined forward once more.

"Prepared?" I murmured.

She turned her head, "Indeed, Yes, prepared! Do it, Mike, love, take me how you need!"

I pulled out of her great arsehole. "Forward Gina, in the bed, face down, legs together." She thought back behind her and grinned.

"Indeed, sir," she said with a chuckle.

"Minx! On the off chance that you truly need to play," I said as she lay face down, "you can reach back and hold yourself open!"

"Mmm, you are a grimy elderly person!!" she snickered; however, she came back and held the cheeks of her arse separated. "Like this?"

I stooped in position on the back of her shut legs. My rooster felt like an iron bar as I peered down at her lying there. I don't assume she understood the amount she had come to confide in me for; similar to this, she was totally at my leniency. Not that I needed to do something besides screw her arse like this. "Prepared?"

"Indeed! Indeed please."

I bowed my rooster down to her blushed arsehole and pushed tenderly forward. As far as I might be concerned, this position is the supreme. I could see the tip of my cockerel unmistakably breaking her still closed ring. She moaned as the head slipped inside the shouted out delicately as I two or three creeps down into her.

"Alright, Gina, love? Is it harming?"

She took a full breath. "I don't have a clue! It feels unique. Greater. I feel so full!"

"I can stop."

"No! No! I don't need you to. I need to do it like this. For you."

I moved my rooster to and fro delicately and gradually the crushed more lube onto my cockerel. Gina moaned delicately as I drove more into her arsehole. It was along these lines, so hard to keep down here. For me, this is as near flawlessness as one can get. The point is thus, so extraordinary and the inclination gigantic. I'm not under any condition prevailing in the room - I accept that sex is an organization - however, I should concede that there is something of the 'control' component about this position. As I took care of more rooster into her snugness, I inclined forward and took my weight on my arms, modifying the point of my cockerel in her arse: driving down instead of along.

"Good gracious!" she moaned delicately. "So enormous - it feels so large!"

"To an extreme?" I murmured delicately, then kissed her neck.

"No! No! Try not to stop. I like it - truly!"

I started to screw her arse now, practically the entirety of my cockerel in her rectum, even though it is unimaginable to expect to get very as profound like this. My thighs hadn't met her arse cheeks, yet I was pushing inside her. My energy was expanding now. "Hold yourself open, Gina, open your body to me!" Her hands had slipped aside. Gradually they climbed among us and pulled her cheeks separated. I covered her now, my body laying on hers and my hips pushing my chicken down into her. She was taking pretty much every inch, and I was losing it now in the energy existing apart from everything else, dismissing her pleasure. My entire being was centered around my rooster in her arse. So close, so hot around my erection: she was absolutely mine now, and I was utilizing her. Over and over, I drove my cockerel down into her. I could hear her groaning and murmuring; then, a monstrous shiver shook her body undermine. Her rectum grasped my cockerel. It was sufficient. I drove profound and held my chicken there as it beat and shot energy into her entrails. Over and over, swell, beat, swell, beat. Each fly appeared to raise Gina's climax to another level as her body shook.

At long last, it was finished. I was spent. I moved sideways off Gina and lay there, nearly lamenting my conduct. Thus, it is hard to consider the woman in that position, and I promptly lamented that I hadn't. Gina moved on her side and confronted me. She didn't appear to be bugged.

"Goodness screw Mike, that was . . . awesome! Better than anything previously." She connected and pulled my lips to hers. "Much obliged to you! Much obliged to you for showing me how great this can be. At the point when you . . . you know . . . came inside me maybe my entire body was ablaze: n fire with delight." She peered down at my spent cockerel. "I guess HE is past recuperation?"

I chuckled discreetly. "Gina love that was along these lines, so serious. Indeed. I'm. Unfortunately, I think I have shot my jolt - both in a real sense and allegorically!"

She snickered, "Mmm, and some jolt it was. I felt it. I can, in any case, feel it inside me. Ooooohhhhh!"

"What?"

"I'm spilling!" She immediately moved to the restroom two or after three minutes. She looked awesome, and I promptly lamented my age and powerlessness to proceed. Viagra can indeed do a limited amount of a lot. In truth, notwithstanding, I needed to hinder now and converse with Gina.

"Will we shower? I'm all damp with sweat."

She laughed, "I'm not astonished after that!"

"You are OK, Gina?" I asked delicately.

"Sore," she said delicately.

"Gracious crap! Gina, I'm grieved."

She grinned. "I wouldn't fret. I delighted in each second. I will not fail to remember this end of the week, Mike, for quite a while."

"I would not like to hurt you. I needed you to appreciate all that we did."

"I did, Mike, truly. It'll disappear, I know. I wouldn't have missed this for anything."

'Come here," I said delicately, "let me hold you."

She came into my arms, and we lay together on the bed. Time to perceive how she felt. "Gina love,"

"Mmm," she mumbled discreetly.

"I'm here for three weeks."

"Gracious, where are you remaining?"

"With my sibling. Well, I was."

She sat up, "You were?"

"That's right, I was." I turned towards her, fixing her eyes with mine, "yet after this end of the week, I'm considering remaining for a half year!"

"Why?" she asked bashfully, for I am certain she knew the appropriate response.

"Since I chanced upon you, Gina."

She snickered, "I figure you accomplished more than 'find' me!"

"Alright," I chuckled, "I surmise I did! Well . . ." I proceeded reluctantly, "I don't have a clue how to say this, Gina . . ."

She grinned delicately, "You haven't had that issue as of not long ago." Her eyes remained fixed on mine.

"If I did, would you stay with me?" It turned out in a surge, yet at any rate, it was out!

"Stay with you . . . Where? How?" Well, she didn't say no!

"I was simply thinking," I grinned, "and envisioning . . . I could lease a loft close to the school so . . ." I was peculiarly reluctant to think about what had occurred throughout the end of the week.

She thought for a couple of seconds. "I don't know, Mike. I don't know how mum and father would take it."

"It wouldn't be perpetual," I proceeded, "no responsibility." I giggled, "I'm too old for you, Gina, love. Only a half year of fun like we just had." She caused a stir curiously and grinned. "Alright! Alright! Maybe not exactly such a lot of sex; I need recuperation time! Genuinely, however, Gina . . . I would take as year rent and pay for it. You could remain on after. Allow you to be all alone."

She looked contemplative, then she grinned. "I like parcels a greater amount of this . . ." her arms depicted to bend of the bed, "I have had a ball to such an extent. I might want to consider it, Mike; however, I do like the thought."

"Great!" I said happily, "I can't look for additional. Will we shower now?"

"Indeed," she answered with a delicate grin, "I think I need a rest!"

I chuckled, "As do I! You proceed to clean up; call me when you are finished." I watched her arse influence enticingly as she strolled to the restroom.

At the entryway, she thought back behind her, "I figure I will, you know!" and she vanished inside. I followed when she called, and we showered and just showered. No play, for we were both a little gone through after the end of the week. After the shower, to bed. It felt extraordinary to rest with this wonderful young lady in my arms.

I woke with the sun again and went to see Gina resting. I moved and kissed her cheek. It more likely than not wake her, for she grinned, came up and pulled my lips to hers. I realized that I needed to get her to school by 10 am so I immediately checked it. Mmmm, 8.15. "Time to get up, Gina, love."

"Have intercourse with me once more," she murmured, "I couldn't care less about the time!'

Ever the man of honor, I started by kissing down her neck to her bosoms, losing the covers as I did as such. God, she is wonderful! My mouth meandered the firm hillocks and snacked at every areola, gnawing delicately as I ignored everyone at that point down across her stomach to the delicate hairs of her pubic hill. As I did so, I felt Gina's hands stroking my hard cockerel. I heard a delicate mumble of appreciation as she noticed my erection, then a moan as my mouth discovered her clitoris and sucked tenderly. I kept eating this perfect pussy for breakfast until I felt a delicate shiver rock her body. I moved then to between her legs and, bowing my head to her sex, sucked on her under lips. I pushed my tongue as profound as possible into her wet vagina and licked. At that point, down to her butt. Red and a little irritated, I thought from the exhaustive beating of the face down butt-centric of the past night. I attempted to soothe her there, washing the swollen muscle with my tongue until another delicate shiver shook her body.

After a couple of seconds, I raised my head and investigated her eyes. "Have intercourse with me. Please!" I grinned and moved my rooster to her sex and pushed tenderly inside.

"Gracious God, yes!" I pushed further. "Gracious indeed, indeed, yes. Suppose it's not too much trouble. Do that! Harder!" This proceeded as I screwed her more profound. Moderate from the outset yet profound, getting that superb inclination when my chicken reached as far down as possible inside her, thighs tight to hers. Our eyes bolted then as I held myself somewhere inside. "Screw me, Mike. Screw me hard." I did at that point, pulling back and driving profound again and again. It wasn't some time before she shivered once more; her legs held my midriff, and she moaned resoundingly. I kept on freaking her through her climax at that point as she descended, bowed forward, and murmured to her.

"Stoop Gina love. Pup!" I saw a look of misgiving cross her highlights, and I speculated that she was sore at the back. I had no goal of taking her there ill-equipped. I may do that later on - if she remained with me - when she was utilized to butt-centric sex. "Not there, Gina love: you need a rest from that."

She grinned. "I need it again, you know. I preferred it a great deal. I need you there." I took a full breath. Gina had made the most of their first experience with butt-centric sex. On the off chance that she remained, I was certain that loads of fun would be had in her secondary passage!

"What's more, I need you there once more," I said delicately, "again and again!" She grinned, clearly glad that she had caught me with her base! At that point, she moved face down, thought back, and grinned.

"Like this?"

I giggled, "Gina, you are a minx!"

"I know," she said, "yet I do realize you like minxes!" With that, she bowed up and pushed her base back. "It's all yours!" I speculated she was provocative, for she realized I wouldn't screw her arse ill-equipped. I climbed to her and took care of my erection into her vagina, and push home.

"FUCK!" she cried at that point, "yes - screw me!" as I screwed her: hard, quick, and profound for quite a while. I think she came twice before I, at last, filled her sex with my last cum store at the end of the week.

We both fell back fairly spent and lay together for a couple of moments. At that point, I was, at last, an ideal opportunity to end up at the end of the week. I requested breakfast, and we ate together, examining the end of the week constantly. Gina was loaded with what we had done, the amount she had fun, and with the things, I had brought for her. She chose not to take anything with her to her folks yet would get some garments from her companions after school. I would care for the wide range of various stuff.

"I get it will take some disclosing when I get to my brother's," I snickered.

"I assume so; however, I expect I will require it!" she said delicately. I took a full breath.

"Is that a 'yes,'" I asked, holding that breath.

"Indeed," she grinned, "it is a distinct yes!"

Get up to 10 eBooks Totally FREE?!

If you are a devourer of erotic books and would like to receive up to 10 books immediately and totally **FREE** of charge, all you have to do is register for my list!
See below for more details!

Benefits of registration:

As a member of the list, you will receive the following benefits:

- 2 FREE books upon registration

- After registration, you have the possibility to get 8 additional books totally free of charge.
- The chance to have access in a totally free way - FOREVER AND AT ANY TIME - to ALL THE BOOKS already published and all of those that will be later on!
- The chance to participate in the creation of future books that I will publish!

I always listen to the ideas and requests of my readers and I strive to bring new and intriguing stories for all tastes.

You will have the opportunity to let me know not only what you think of my books, but also to suggest particular ideas such as the topics, settings, or characteristics of the main characters in the stories!

Every month, I will choose a proposal from the list of subscribers and make it into an erotic story.

If your idea is chosen, ONLY IF YOU WANT IT, you can be mentioned as a special thank you in the story!

Go to the link below and register now!

http://bit.ly/Scarlett_Collins

I really hope you enjoyed the book!

As you know, Amazon and the community rely on people like yourself for feedback on products so that others can also be informed about what they are buying. A little of your time and a few brief words goes a long way!

If you feel like giving me a TON of help, please leave me a positive review on Amazon! It really helps and encourages me to write more and more and give it my all!